Also by Virginia

Malkins & Mages

Apprentice Cat
Journeyman Cat
Master Cat
Guardian Cat
*King's Cat*


War of the Malkin

Secrets of the Malkin
Huntress of the Malkin
Clash of the Malkin
Treasure of the Malkin
Blade of the Malkin
*Chalice of the Malkin*

# Master Cat

*Malkins & Mages*
*Book 3*

ISBN-13: 978-1502765857

ISBN-10: 1502765853

Cover design by Virginia Ripple
Photo image courtesy of Eric Isselée/Bigstock.com

To my fans,

Thanks for keeping my feet to the fire
and my nose to the grindstone.
May we have many more adventures to come.

# Chapter 1

He heard his own breath rattling in his chest, like the shaking of old bones. How much longer could he hold on to sanity? It already felt like a lifetime. Then again, perhaps it had been several lifetimes. He wasn't sure anymore. All he thought about now was the hope of final release, a hope his captor refused to allow him to achieve. The soft pad of paws made his ears swivel backward as a sigh escaped him.

"You sound terrible, old friend," echoed the tom's deep voice.

"Hazards of knowing you, I'm afraid," he answered. "Is it time to renew your magic already?" He opened his eyes a slit to see the black tom pacing gracefully toward his cage. The cat's whiskers splayed in a wide smile.

"I'm not here to exploit your power today. Perhaps another time."

His captor sat and pulled at his claw sheaths. Trying not to fidget, he considered all the possibilities his captor might have for venturing so far below his fortress. At last the black tom turned his piercing gaze back on him.

"How long has it been?" his captor asked.

"I've lost track."

The black tom chuckled and sat, curling his tail around his paws. "I suppose time has little meaning down here."

"It's not the place. It's the company. Time has little meaning when you have a resurrection spell."

"Ah, yes. That would make a difference. You know it took me a long time to perfect that one."

"It's still not perfect," he said, rolling onto his side and closing his eyes. His tail twitched, waiting for the usual growl from the tom. Baiting him would bring a short death, but it was a moment of peace for which he was willing to pay. The silence made his skin shiver. He opened his eyes and stared at the black cat. He was still smiling.

"I don't have time to play our little game today. You see, I only came to bring you some news before I'm due back at the council."

"What news?"

"It's your son."

"What about my son?" he said, flattening his ears and showing his fangs.

The black tom sat in silence, staring at him with his baleful green eyes and a wide-whiskered grin.

"Tell me what you've done to my son," he said as he rose shakily to his feet, his lashing tail making it difficult to keep his balance.

"Tsk, tsk," the black cat said, shaking his head. "Such manners. You've forgotten the magic word."

"Please," he growled between gritted fangs.

"That's more like it. Good to see that something still brings the fire out of you. I was beginning to think I broke you."

"If you've harmed one hair on his coat —"

"Hardly," replied the black tom, lifting a giant paw to his mouth. The rasp of the beast's tongue on his pads grated on his nerves.

"My son?"

"Hmm? Oh, yes," the tom said, raising his wide-eyed gaze. "I just came to tell you that he is becoming a most excellent student. A prodigy, even."

"You're lying."

"Not at all. You should have seen how he interrogated poor old Father Hanif. Your kit can be quite brutal when he sets his mind to it."

"Toby would never hurt someone."

"Tell that to the young girl wearing his claw marks on her back," the cat said, eyes narrowing.

He closed his eyes and thought of the tiny orange kit he'd left with his mother so long ago. He could still see them sitting on the curb as the coach door slid shut. If he'd known then that it was the last time he'd see either of them, he would have said something more. He would have told his mate how much he loved her instead of arguing with her, nuzzled the downy soft fur of his kit instead of lecturing him on the dangers of the cat killing spider the little tom had been stalking.

When he opened his eyes again, his captor's expression hadn't changed. He lowered his haunches back to the icy stone floor, dragging his tail around to cover his paws.

"You can't know any of this," he said.

"That would be true, if it weren't for your help."

"I haven't helped you."

"But you have," the tom said with a smile. "Thanks to your blood, I can watch the kit for as long as I need. And soon I'll have the means to complete my plans, thanks to the trusting nature of another feline much like your son. Kits seldom suspect the ones they care most about being the instrument of their defeat." The tom glared at him again. "I should know."

He shook his head, staring at the hostile glint in the black tom's eyes. "What happened to you, Adair?"

The beast pulled back as if he'd been stung by a rock and hissed. "That is not my name."

"You can call yourself whatever you please, but you'll still be the tom I met back at the orphanage. You'll always be Adele's brother to me."

Adair, growled. His fur fluffed to make him appear twice his massive size.

"That weakling died serving worthless humans. Only I remain, risen from the grave and prepared to do whatever it takes to save our kind." The black tom stood and lashed his tail once, then padded toward the door. As he waited for it to swing open, the tom turned back with a menacing glare.

"I am the Savior," he hissed. "I am K'Dash Shyam."

A twig snapped. Toby's eyes flew open. He searched the darkness beyond the tiny fire. It had been stupid to start one, but he was freezing and his mind was numb. He liked the numbness, but it was proving dangerous. Someone was watching him. He felt it in his fur, an itch almost as annoying as those times his ex-partner had tried to twist a third level spell during their first year at the King's Academy of Mages.

The night remained quiet beyond his cat-sized cave, save for the occasional slither and thump of melting snow falling from pine boughs. Toby shook his head until his ears popped. He glanced over at the leather-bound book the old yellow tom had given him.

"This will help you figure out what's the truth, what's important and what needs to be buried in the grave," he'd said when he'd given the book to him. "Keep it safe and it will guide you where you need to go."

Toby shifted, drawing his paws in closer under his chest and turning his gaze back on the fire. He'd reached to open the book several times over the last few weeks, yet every time he ended up pushing it away, unopened. Just looking at it made his fur crawl, as if skeletal fingers stroked his spine. He had so many questions and the old tom's words had promised answers, if he dared open that book.

At least he knew where he needed to go. The head temple cat had told him that much. What he needed was a map to Transformation Mountain, not an enigmatic book he couldn't stand to look at.

The flames danced and swayed, mesmerizing him until his eyes drifted close. The dream came again. His nose filled with the acrid smell of smoke as heat seared his fur. He twisted around, searching for a way out. A mound of tabby fur flew at him, raking him with needle-like claws and burying sharp fangs in his neck. A yowl escaped from his throat as skin and fur tore loose from his shoulder. He ripped free of the savage beast and ran through the burning corridors, flying around a corner into the child's room. The little girl's body was strapped to a chair, a strange contraption perched on her head, holding her eyes open. She turned her tear-streaked face toward him.

"Why didn't you save me?" she wailed.

"I couldn't. Please," he begged, "I wanted to, but I had

to put the mission first."

"Just like your father," another female voice said. "Always putting the mission ahead of your family."

Toby turned his head to see a black queen sitting on the other side of the room. The heat haze from the flaming walls made her fur shift and shimmer.

"Mother, I—"

"You can add abandonment to that list, as well," said a male voice behind him. He turned to watch his ex-partner step into the room, holding his bloody hand to his chest. Toby recognized the oozing slashes on the man's hand for his own handiwork.

"Lorn, I wanted to protect you."

"Protect me?" the man asked, waving his good hand toward the fire. "You call this protecting me?"

"You don't understand. It's that monster. He's making this happen."

"The only monster here is you," the little girl said.

"She's right, my son. You've become what you said you hated. How much longer until you are what you chase?"

Toby backed away from them. "I'm not a monster. I can prove it."

"All you'll prove is that you're less my son and more his puppet. Just like the children at the school," said a big black tom, padding forward out of the flames.

"Father, please. I am your son. I'm trying to save you."

"How can a puppet save anyone?"

He felt himself yanked into the air. He stared at his paws, seeing strings wrapped around them. They jerked him into a standing position, making him dance like a crazed toy. He turned to see what was making the strings gyrate his body and stared into a set of piercing green eyes.

"No," he screamed.

*Thunk!* Toby's eyes snapped open, focusing on an arrow embedded in the ground in front of him. A whistling sound made him jerk his gaze up while shouting the incantation for a solid mage bubble. A moment later several more arrows bounced off the shield. Toby calculated the direction the arrows came from.

"Ret URNto oRIGin ATE," he shouted, staring off into the darkness.

The arrows lifted into the air and, with the speed of thought, retraced their flight path. Toby's ears perked forward, waiting for any sign that one of them had found their intended target. Silence greeted him. He surreptitiously sniffed the air, knowing it was useless. The scent of pine covered any other smell. He might not have his super sniffer to count on, but he still had his feline hearing. He swiveled his ears back and forth, listening. A soft rustle to his left. Without looking that direction, he formed a fireball over his campfire. He listened for a moment more. Another soft rustle.

"Flah MAH ball," he said, jerking his gaze to the left.

The fireball zipped into the darkness, throwing light against the surrounding vegetation and sizzling past. There was a panicked squeak and then the ball burst into molten sparks as it hit its target. Toby rushed in, skidding to a halt with armored paw raised to shred his enemy. He stared at the dead squirrel.

He lowered his paw and searched the surrounding darkness for any sign of the archer. The night was still once more. He looked back at the deceased rodent and allowed his fur to flatten. With a growl, he batted the squirrel away and stalked back to his camp. He considered moving on, but decided against it. The sun wouldn't be up for several more hours. If he had to defend himself, he'd rather do it with the cave to his back than out in the open.

When he reached the fire, Toby shook himself head to tail. He wanted to indulge in a satisfying scratch. Instead he settled back onto his paws, tucking his tail around himself. He could still feel the watcher's eyes on him and it made him itch. Toby went back to staring beyond the fire, wondering who was staring back at him.

*Run.*

It was the only thought he allowed in his mind. Anything else and it would take over again. He couldn't let that happen. He wouldn't jeopardize his partner's life even if the orange tom didn't want him around anymore.

Altering that first arrow's path had taken more strength than he'd anticipated. He hadn't been able to do anything about the others after that one. If he'd had any choice, he would've allowed the fireball to end the struggle for domination. Instead he'd had to wait until it was occupied with watching the orange tom before ordering his body to run away.

That left him with just one option, to run as far in the other direction as he could before it took control once more. He hoped, if he ran far enough and fast enough, he'd be too winded to do more than lay on the ground panting. It might give his partner time to get away. Maybe...

12

## Master Cat

Young voices rang in the air, making Clarence O'dorn's visit to the run-down building feel surreal. A human child ran past, glancing over his shoulder and grinning. A scraggly yellow and gray tom skidded to a halt further away, his eyes searching the yard.

"You can't catch me, furball," yelled the boy. The tom's gaze jerked to the human.

"I'll make mouse meat out of you," he yowled.

The boy laughed and fled around the opposite corner, his nemesis close behind. Clarence looked at the ground behind them, seeing a set of yellow paw prints and a thin line of paint tracing their path. The old man smiled, thinking of another tom and his partner who had visited him when they were younger. A moment later the front door slammed open and a portly woman in a white dress, yellowed and stained, darted down the stairs a rag flapping in her hand.

"James! Darnell! You boys get back in here and clean up that mess!"

Two heads appeared around the edge of the building. The woman's gaze turned their direction. She placed her hands on her hips, the right hand clutching the rag in a white-knuckle grip, and glared at them. "Now, or there's no pie for dessert."

The boy and tom slouched toward the woman. "He started it," said the human.

"Did not," the tom said.

"I don't care who started it," she said, looking from

one to the other, "This here ain't the time nor the place to be feudin'. By the One, but you boys do try a soul. Now I don't 'spect you to dote on each other, but you *will* follow the rule."

The boys shuffled in front of her, eyes downcast. The woman lifted her chin a finger width. "You do remember it, don't you?"

They nodded.

"Mmm hmm. Let me hear ya say it, then."

The boys mumbled something Clarence couldn't here. The woman shook her head.

"Uh uh. Not good 'nuff. I wanna *hear* it."

The children straightened to attention, squaring their shoulders and raising their eyes to meet the woman's.

"You will love the One with all you are and love your neighbor as yourself."

"And what does that mean?"

"It means to have faith in the One," said the boy.

"And treat everyone else like you want to be treated," finished the tom.

"Good," the woman said, nodding and smiling. "Now, go on in there and clean up that mess. There's rags in the closet and paint cleaner in the shed. You do your best and I'll make sure Cook gets ya some pie when you're done."

"Yes, ma'am," they said together.

The two marched back into the building under the woman's watchful gaze. Clarence chuckled and walked up beside her.

"Seems you have your hands full," he said.

"They good boys," the woman said, turning a bright smile on him. "They jus' need a firm hand once in a while."

"Firm, but not crushing, am I right?"

"Yes, sir. The name's Maddie," she said, wiping her

hands on the rag and then holding one out to shake.

"William Carmichael," Clarence returned, taking her hand in his and bending over it. The woman grinned.

"Oh, ain't you a dandy? What brings you here Master Carmichael?"

"I'm doing research for a book I'm penning on the difficulties orphans have moving beyond their childhood memories to become upstanding citizens. I was given to understand the Head Mistress might be able to shed light on the subject."

A frown creased the woman's face. She darted a glance back at the building. Clarence looked at the orphanage, too, noting again its sad exterior where chinking had come loose in several spots. Several of the shutters swayed in the light breeze. He turned his attention back to Maddie.

"Is there something wrong, my dear?"

"Well," she said, biting her lower lip. She leaned closer, casting another glance at the building. "It ain't my place to say this, but I can tell you're a man who puts stock in the truth."

"Where would we be without it?"

"Amen, brother."

"Please, go on."

"Well, the thing is… Miss Opal… she don't care much 'bout these here orphans 'ceptin' in what they can bring her in money."

"Indeed?"

Maddie nodded her head and leaned back. "Yes, sir. This here buildin' would fall down, if it weren't for a couple kind neighbors and the repairs I have the young'uns do as penance for their pranks."

"I can imagine that makes it difficult to help the children and kits accept the Priceless Measure."

"Oh, yes, sir. You heard them say, "Treat everyone else like you want to be treated," but when they ain't bein' treated right, how can they believe it? My Papa, may he rest in peace, always said the best book a man could ever read was your life. And the best life a man could lead was one befittin' the One."

"Your Father was a wise man."

"Mmm hmm. That he was."

"So may I assume that Head Mistress Opal isn't the woman I thought I was going to interview for my research?"

"No, sir. I don't believe she would be much help."

Clarence stroked his gray beard and stared at the front door. He glanced at Maddie from the corner of his eye. "When did Head Mistress Opal take over?"

The woman squinted and stared at the ground for several moments before she said, "I believe it was just after the plague. Head Master Richard, may he rest in peace, died during the great sickness. Left us all wonderin' what would happen to the home. Then Miss Opal up and buys it. Said she was lookin' for a good… what did she call it?"

"Investment?" offered Clarence.

"That's right. Investment. I think she just wanted the money."

"From the looks of this place, I believe that is an apt assumption." The old mage shook his head and sighed. "It's unfortunate I already have an appointment with her. I hate to waste my precious time." He cast another sidelong glance at Maddie. "I don't suppose you know of someone else I might interview who may give me better fodder for my book."

The woman rested an index finger on her round little chin and stared at the ground. The front door banged open again, startling Maddie into looking up. A rail-thin girl came running out.

16

"Miss Maddie," she called as she trotted down the steps, "Miss Maddie. They're at it again."

"Who's at it?"

"James and Darnell. They're throwin' paint rags around the foyer. Miss Opal's about to have a fit. She's threatin' to take 'em out behind the shed and beat 'em herself."

"Those two are gonna be the death of me yet. I'm sorry, Master Carmichael, but I gotta go sort this out," she said.

"Think nothing of it."

The ample woman and the stick-like girl hustled back into the building, letting the door bang shut behind them. Clarence wondered for a moment how much longer the door would stay on its hinges. Shaking his head, he carefully placed his feet on the worn stairs, trusting that if they could hold Maddie's considerable weight that they would hold his as well.

He stepped across the threshold into chaos. A severe looking woman was holding in one hand the ear of the young boy Clarence had seen run past and in the other hand the paint splattered gray cat by the scruff of his neck. She glared first at one then the other.

"And why should I not horse whip both of them?"

"They just doing what boys do, ma'am," the portly woman said.

"Spare the rod and spoil the child, Maddie. These two have been at the bottom of more pranks and shenanigans than any of the other children, have they not?"

"Yes, ma'am, but —"

"Which brings me to my next question. Where were you when they decided to re-paint our pristine foyer this hideous yellow?"

The woman's glare could have melted glass, as she

glared at Maddie whose eyes were fixed on the floor, her work-worn hands wringing the rag in them. Clarence cleared his throat, gaining the beaky woman's attention and her glare. He straightened to his full height, then gave a deep bow.

"I'm afraid that is my fault, madam," he said, straightening again. "You see I distracted your housekeeper out in the yard as she was about to apply the rod to these two mischievous lads. She handled the situation admirably, I might add, and, had I not distracted the fine woman, I am sure she would have seen to it that they cleaned the entire foyer and beyond rather than allowing them to sink to such deviltry."

"And who are you?" snapped the severe looking woman.

"I am William Carmichael, master book smith and penner of tales most heroic."

The woman flashed him a bright smile and let go of the boy and the tom, who landed with a thud. Her hands fluttered to her hair, patting any stray strands back into place around her bun. Clarence glanced at the painted tom who was staring wide-eyed at the woman, his tail tucked between his legs. When he glanced at the boy, he saw him rubbing his reddened ear and looking to Maddie for instructions. Maddie was still staring at the floor like a broken slave. When he turned his attention back to their overseer, he found it difficult not to grimace at the flirtatious tilt of her head.

"May I assume you are the Head Mistress of this fine establishment?"

"Yes. My name is Opal Blakely," she said, offering her bony hand to him.

"The One must have gifted your parents with visions to see the flashing fire of your soul and bequeath you such a breathtaking name," Clarence said, bending to place a light kiss upon the skeletal fingers. The woman's high-pitched giggle grated in his ears. He straightened and gave her his most winning smile. "Mistress Opal, may we adjourn to your office to conduct our interview?"

"Of course. It's this way," she said, swinging her arm toward an adjoining hall.

"Lead on, my lady."

Opal giggled again, flashing her toothy smile at him, then sashayed away. Clarence touched Maddie's shoulder, bringing her gaze to him, then winked. She answered with a genuine grin and hustled the boys away as he followed Opal back to her office. The room he entered was befitting any noble woman's sitting area, from the needle-point cushions to the cherry wood secretary in the corner.

"Please," she said, motioning to an ornately carved chair, "have a seat. Would you care for some tea?"

"That sounds lovely."

The woman's skirts hissed as she sashayed to the other side of the room. She pulled a green velvet rope, then settled in the chair opposite Clarence, running her hands over her skirts to flatten any bumps and creases. She smiled coyly, staring up at him through her lashes.

"Your letter of introduction was very intriguing, Master Carmichael. I do so hope you will speak kindly of me in your new book."

"I shall endeavor to speak true of your guiding philosophy for these wretched souls and your," he said, waving a hand in the air indicating the room and the areas beyond, "beneficence toward your fellows."

The woman gave another sharp giggle, coquettishly covering her mouth with her hand. Clarence smiled. There was a knock at the door and Opal rose to answer it.

"Set it on the table, Maddie, and please be careful. Those are not the kitchen mugs you're used to handling."

"Yes, ma'am."

The ample housekeeper bustled in carrying a large silver tray set with a wild rose teapot and two matching cups with saucers. The old mage hid a frown with his hand. A tea set such as that would easily pay for new whitewashing and repairs on the building. He glanced at Maddie as she poured the amber liquid into each cup with great care, then straightened.

"Will there be anything else, ma'am?"

"That will be all. You may go back to your chores."

"Yes, ma'am," the woman said, making a quick bow. Clarence watched her leave until she pulled the door shut behind herself with a quiet click, then turned his attention back to Opal.

"Your housekeeper seems quite adept at handling many jobs."

"She manages as well as she is able," Opal replied, carefully handing a cup and saucer to him, then sighed. "Alas, it is trying at times. I must watch the help constantly lest they fall back on their idle ways."

"That would be trying indeed. Tell me, how many do you have on staff?"

"I have three who live here and oversee the day-to-day activities and five more who rotate through the week," she said, smiling with pride.

"That is quite a small staff for a place as large as this. However do you manage?"

"With efficiency, sir." The woman's cup clinked against its saucer as she put it on the coffee table.

"I believe that, madam. You have the air of efficiency about you. A noble trait, I might add," Clarence said with a smile. "I meant that such efficiency must be difficult to maintain."

"Not at all, though I do wish my staff were as determined as I to create the proper environment to care for these parent-less children."

"And kits?"

Opal waved her hand in dismissal and reached for her cup. "Of course the kits, too. It is my hope, however, that the High Council will soon pass a law of segregation."

"Why might that be?"

"Surely you know what happened," the woman said, looking at him with wide eyes. She took a sip of tea and gently placed her cup back in its saucer.

"I'm not sure I have. Please, tell me," Clarence said.

"I thought everyone knew by now. It seems there was a temple school in the Outer Reaches where cats abducted young humans and then experimented on them."

"Yes, I had heard of that. I take it you aren't among the ones suggesting all cats be rounded up and executed."

"Master Carmichael, I may not believe cats and humans can coexist peacefully, but I do not condone mass murder."

"That is good to hear. I do wonder, though, that you allow both humans and cats to live here."

"Unfortunately, when the original Head Mistress drew up our charter, she made it an iron clad rule that anyone without parents, be they human or cat, be welcomed here. Until the High Council makes it unlawful for humans and cats to coexist under the same roof, I am bound by that charter." She reached a bony hand to her temple and frowned. "It has caused me no end of headaches, you may be sure."

21

"That is lamentable." He took a sip of tea, watching the thin woman over the rim of his cup as she massaged her temple. "Whatever happened to the original Head Mistress?"

The woman curled her finger around the delicate handle of her teacup and lifted it to her mouth. She took a small sip, then replaced the cup on its saucer and glanced toward the door before placing both on the coffee table again. When she looked back at Clarence, her white skin had paled even more.

"I believe she inherited a large sum of money and moved away."

"How fortunate for her."

"Um, yes," Opal said. She stood and walked over to pull another of the green velvet ropes, then turned a wan smile on him. She clutched her hands together as she returned to the chairs. "I am sorry, Master Carmichael, but I'm beginning to feel out of sorts."

"Oh dear," Clarence said, placing his cup and saucer on the table. "I do hope it's nothing severe."

"Not at all," she replied, motioning him to rise and follow her to the door. "I'm sure it's nothing more than a migraine. Unpleasant, but not fatal."

The door opened and a young woman bowed to them. "You rang, mistress?"

"Eudora, please see Master Carmichael to the door."

"Perhaps we can continue our interview when you are feeling better," Clarence said, taking the Head Mistress's hand and giving it a gentle squeeze.

"Perhaps."

"This way, sir," Eudora said, holding her arm out in the direction they had come.

Clarence nodded and followed the young woman,

hearing the click of the office door behind him. He wondered what it was he'd said that had brought on the woman's sudden migraine. As he went out the front door, he smiled and thanked Eudora, then concentrated on making his way down the worn steps. He was so caught up in his own thoughts, he almost missed the hiss coming from the bushes near the orphanage's lane. The painted tom peered from beneath them.

"Don't look at me," he whispered. The old mage turned to inspect the building, using his hand to cover his mouth as he spoke.

"What do you need, friend?"

"Maddie sent me. She said you should talk to Head Mistress Florence Mann. She can tell you what you want to know."

There was a rustle and then silence. Clarence glanced toward the bushes, not at all surprised to see them empty of golden eyes. He smiled as he turned to leave. If Maddie thought Head Mistress Florence was worth talking to, then he best make an appointment soon.

David smiled at a passing council member, trying to seem as if he and his partner weren't on their way to crash the prince's birthday celebration despite their captain's orders. He glanced at the long-legged feline trotting along in front of him. More accurately, David was the one disobeying orders. His partner was just a coerced conspirator.

"This is not a good idea," the wildcat said over his shoulder, his Highland accent prominent, betraying his stress. His long-legged gait made it easy to keep up with his partner as they strode through the halls toward the prince's birthday celebration. "You're going to get yourself thrown out of the OKG if you keep pulling stunts like this."

"That's why you're here, my friend," David said. He smiled at a passing council member. "With your silver tongue, you can talk a squirrel from a tree and into your claws, if you want. Smoothing over my presence at one small party shouldn't be a problem."

"You're a right git, sometimes. You know that?"

"That's why you stick with me," he said with a grin.

The sounds of conversations and music filtered through the closed doors at the end of the hall. A line of nobles waited to enter, their hushed voices almost making their grumbles inaudible. Before anyone entered the great hall, two guardians standing to either side of the doors magically searched them.

David clenched his teeth as he considered what could be hiding beneath the skin of any person entering that room. So far nothing had turned up, at least no one had told him of any bomb threats nor had anyone officially told him about the other bombings that occurred around the kingdom. If it hadn't been for his partner, Aaron, he wouldn't have known there had been any.

When he'd found out about the prince's birthday celebration, he'd tried to talk the captain into allowing him to be a part of the security detail. What better opportunity, he surmised, would their mysterious terrorist have to throw the country into chaos than by blowing up the great hall when so many nobles, not to mention the royal family, were present. But Captain Gage wouldn't accept that, just as she hadn't wanted him to investigate any of the other recent terrorist threats. This time, though, he planned on being in on the situation if anything happened no matter whose authority he had to circumvent. He looked at his large feline companion. It would be up to him to get them past the guardians.

"Ready?"

"I should have my head examined," Aaron said.

"You pull this one off, buddy, and I'll pay for your therapy fees."

The tom sighed.

"Excuse me," he said, spreading his whiskers in a smile as he passed the nobles waiting in line, their impatience plain in their shifting postures and frowns. "My apologies, gentle folk, we're just here to see to your safety. Please don't mind us."

David hid his amusement as several of the older women bent to pat Aaron on the head. Some humans, it seemed, would always treat a cat as a brainless beast even when all evidence proved otherwise. At least Aaron was used to it. That was one of the things that made him popular in the Office of Kingdom Guardianship. No matter what the situation was, he was the utmost gentlemanly feline on the force and that made him in high demand in tense situations.

"Billy, m'lad," the wildcat called to the guardian on the right. "How goes the search?"

"Nothing, yet," said the young guardian, grinning at the cat. "What are you doing here?"

"Thought we might take a peek around. See what aid we might be."

Billy turned his gaze on David and frowned. "Not him. Captain's orders."

David bit the inside of his cheek. This was why he'd

asked Aaron to help him. He had to keep his mouth shut.

"Ah, now Billy, you know as well as I that the more eyes we have on the room, the safer all these good folks will be." A murmuring had begun behind them. David tried not to smile. He'd forgotten how easily his partner could work a crowd when he set his mind to it. "And that's what we all want, isn't it? To keep the realm safe from that felonious creature who would sooner kill ye as look at ye."

The young man shifted from foot to foot, glancing first at the line of nobles, then at the other guard. The other man shrugged and jerked his head toward the closed doors. Billy's shoulders slumped.

"Okay, fine," he said. He turned to glare at David. "But you go through the servant's doors."

"Billy, you're a fine lad," Aaron said.

The partners backtracked around the back halls and up the servant stairs from the kitchen. The single guardian at that door yawned and waved them past without a second glance. David considered giving the man a severe dressing down, but decided not to press his luck and went on through the narrow door.

Mage globes twinkled from the ceiling and reflected off the multitude of shiny mirrors. The women's bejeweled gowns and hair glistened in the fairy light. An array of food stood on tables awaiting hungry visitors. A white cake the size of a full-grown man sat sentinel over the entire buffet. Its purple streamers of fondant wrapped around each tier in a graceful spiral flowing from a spun sugar crown. David grimaced at the display of fortune.

"The money spent on this outlandish affair could have fed the Lower Districts for a year," he murmured.

"Aye, but we're not here to comment on the way they

spend their fortune, are we?"

David grunted and scanned the room. Two ways in or out. A mage search at each door. Guardians ringed the perimeter and King's Men, the kingdom's elite human and feline guards, lurked at the rear of the dais. Aside from the lax guardian at the servant's entrance, it didn't seem as if anyone would be able to sneak a bomb into the room.

Of course, they weren't looking for any ordinary bomber, either. Whoever it was might not even be aware that he or she was carrying an explosive inside them. According to what little information David had been able to find on the New Life Temple and School's experiments using children as weapons, the child wasn't aware that anything had happened to them. As far as what made them explode, it was still anyone's guess.

He scanned the room again, staring into the faces of young and old alike. It could be anyone. Just because the terrorist had used children before, didn't mean he wouldn't use an old man or woman this time.

"How are we supposed to find anything in this crowd?"

"That's a good question," Aaron said. He nodded toward the prince standing on the raised dais. "For all we know, it could be the bairn himself who has the bomb inside."

"Let's hope not."

"Maybe we should mingle."

"And then what? Ask everyone we meet if they have any unusual scars they don't remember getting?"

Aaron flattened his ears and narrowed his eyes at his partner. "This was your idea, remember?"

"I know," David said, pressing his fingers against his closed eyes. "I was just hoping it might be simpler once we got past the guardians."

He turned to watch a group of men and women circle in and out of an intricate dance. Simple would be nice for once, but that was too much to hope for this time. David continued to watch as the dancers twisted and turned. Step by step, their movements became increasingly complex until it became obvious who had performed this routine before and who was still learning. An idea filtered through his mind.

"What is the likelihood that the suspect has ever attended a gala affair like this?"

"The only bombers we've heard of were orphans, so the chances of it being someone from one of the Houses are slim," Aaron said.

"Exactly. I think we've spent more energy watching the nobles than we should have."

"I think I see where you're going. If you want to cause as much confusion as possible, you have to get your weapon as close to your target as you can before you trigger it. That means making it nearly invisible."

"And who at an affair like this, would be invisible?" David asked, raising an eyebrow.

"The servants. I'll go find a higher vantage point."

Aaron trotted away as David moved to get closer to the royal family, keeping an eye on any servants mingling among the crowd. He saw a serving girl taking a tray of food in the direction of the prince and moved to stop her. He grabbed her by the shoulder and spun her around, making her drop her tray. The sound carried across the great hall, bringing the music to a stuttering halt as all eyes turned toward the commotion. He bent to stare into her wide eyes. A hand fell on his shoulder. He turned to stare into the captain's dark glare.

"Just what do you think you're doing?" she demanded.

"I think this girl is carrying a bomb, sir. I needed to stop her before she could reach the prince."

The woman's brown eyes darted to the girl, then to the royal family standing on the dais. She turned and waved to a guardian near the main doors.

"On the off chance you're right," she said, scowling at David, "we'll scan this girl. But if you're wrong, you'll be stuck behind your desk until I retire. Is that understood?"

"Yes, sir."

A female guardian with a long metal wand stepped forward, glancing at the captain. She nodded and stepped back. The wand hummed as the guardian traced the girl's shape in the surrounding air. The woman looked at the wand in her hand, then up at the captain and shook her head. Captain Gage turned to glare at David. Her mouth opened to say something he was sure he didn't want to hear, when Aaron shouted an incantation from across the room.

A loud kerwhoom filled the ballroom, followed by a burst of light. Someone screamed. When he could see again, David peered around for his partner. The wildcat perched on the balcony over the dais. He pointed down with a paw to a maroon colored mage bubble five feet from the prince. David pushed his way through the crowd, the captain striding alongside. There wasn't much left of the body. He looked around at the gathered nobles, then at the young prince. The room was silent.

"Let's get these people back," ordered the captain, her voice carrying to the far reaches of the room. "And I want to know how this person got in here without being searched."

Aaron dropped to the floor beside them and paced toward the bubble. His whiskers clamped tight as he turned his gaze onto his superior guardian. "I almost didn't see the lad. Like everyone else, my attention was on the commotion when I saw movement out of the corner of my eye. When I looked toward him, he was moving fast toward the prince."

"Any idea who it was?"

"A page, sir. He was carrying one of the little letter trays."

"What made you think he was carrying the bomb?" David asked.

"His face. I haven't seen an expression that blank since I aided the rescuers at the New Life Temple. Add that to his lack of reaction to what was going on, it could only mean one thing." He looked back at the page's remains. "I hoped the bubble would be enough to keep it from being triggered, but…"

"You can't save everyone, guardian," the captain said, her voice filled with the echo of regret. She turned to pierce David with her steely gaze again. "I'll let you keep your post for now. You can thank your partner's quick thinking for that."

"Sir," David said, catching her attention again as she was turning to leave, "This page had to have come through the servant's entrance like we did. I didn't recognize the guardian at that door, but he was half-asleep when we came in."

"Or feigning it," Aaron added.

"Understood, guardians. I'll get someone on it. In the meantime, you two make yourself useful. Get this crowd under control and secure the doors. I don't want anyone getting in or out until we know what happened."

"Yes, sir," David said, clamping his teeth on the complaint of being assigned a rookie's job.

As the captain stalked away to coordinate other aspects of this new investigation, David glanced at his partner. Aaron sat staring at the remains. David knelt beside him and placed a hand on the wildcat's shoulder.

"Such a waste," the cat said. "He was just a wee lad." He turned a tight-whiskered look on David, his ears going flat against his head. "What kind of monster uses children to do his dirty work?"

# Chapter 2

The harsh scrape of a broom brought him out of his half-sleep. The young white cat was back to clean his cage and tidy the room again. Perhaps this time he could get the kit to talk to him.

"Hello, again," he said.

The tom glanced at him, but continued silently watching the broom swish dust and debris from the floor.

"You've done well keeping this place clean. I'm sure it's difficult, considering your master's penchant for experimenting." He looked around the room, glancing with raised eye whiskers at the blood spattered areas. "He certainly leaves a mess."

The white tom growled, but said nothing as he twitched his tail to speed the broom along.

"I hope you're being paid well. You deserve it."

"I don't deserve anything," hissed the tom. "And neither do you, traitor."

"Traitor?" he asked, forcing his whiskers together. He needed to keep him talking. "I'm not sure I know what you mean."

"Don't pretend you don't know what you did. It's because of you and that filthy human that my family's name is now a curse word in this kingdom. Master Shyam will change all that."

"Which "filthy human" do you think I worked with to slander your family name?"

"You know who. Master Ribaldy. He's the one that told the king our House couldn't be trusted and I bet you put the fake evidence in his hands to do it."

The broom shushed across the room, its bristles bending in half with the force of the white tom's anger.

"You're from Hielberg House, aren't you? Your father was set to be next in line on the High Council for your district, but then the king changed his mind."

"That traitorous fool changed it for him."

"I don't know what happened to make the king decide against allowing your father on the High Council, son," he said, shaking his head.

"Don't call me son. In fact," he growled, "don't talk to me."

He watched the white cat put the broom away, then sent a rag to wipe down the devices K'Dash used for his experiments. The tom's fur was matted in places, sticking out as if he seldom groomed himself. It was an odd look for a House feline, though he'd seen other nobles that had fallen on rough times that didn't look much better. He cocked his head to the side, watching the intent concentration play across the young cat's face. He had to be about the same age as his son. The thought made his chest constrict. Would he see his son again?

"What's your name?"

The tom glanced at him, then back at the rag.

"Did you go to the King's Academy of Mages?"

He continued to watch the rag do its job.

"I had a son your age. He was supposed to go there. I bet the two of you would've found the experience quite the adventure."

The young cat's fur rose along his spine and he heard the scrape of claws. He narrowed his eyes. He'd hit a nerve with the tom, but what was it that he'd said to bring on this reaction? He wondered if the head masters had chosen against partnering the kit with a human. Perhaps that was why he hated humans so much. But there was always the loner option. Unless, of course, the High Council had banned his family from ever practicing magic again? Surely that wasn't the case. He stifled a sigh. There were so many pieces of the puzzle he was missing.

"I sometimes wonder what happened to Toby. I like to think he's out there having grand adventures and solving mysteries. He was always clever when it came to those kinds of things," he said, scrutinizing the tom's reactions. The young cat's fur fluffed by claw lengths with each word and his lips curled over his fangs.

"I wonder what your father would say if he saw you now," he said, eyes narrowing.

The young cat hissed, twitching his tail and making the rag fly past. He turned and stalked away, stopping at the door.

"He wouldn't say anything," he growled, looking over his shoulder, "I'm a useless scrap of fur just like he was."

The white tom's tail jerked and he stalked out.

Wherever he was it was dark and someone was panting. "Hello?" he called. "Who's out there?"

Nothing answered. The panting continued. He listened closely, straining to hear any other sounds. Birds chirped in the distance, a muted, happy sound. *Okay. There's either birds in cages nearby or I'm outside. But if I'm outside, why can't I see anything?* He tried to move his head. It shifted a half a finger width, as if his head were laying against something that wouldn't allow more movement in that direction. When he tried to tilt his head the other direction, there was a sharp pain. He was certain he'd lain in the same position so long his muscles were protesting at the movement. How long did it take for muscles to lock up?

He'd figure that out later. He could move his head, but what about other body parts? *Eyes first.* He struggled to open them. They felt like iron doors rusted shut. *Heave!* He wasn't sure how long it had taken him, but he finally had them open a crack. Not that he could see much except snow-swept trees and brush. But one thing was clear, he was lying on the ground. That explained why he couldn't move his head very far in either direction.

*What about the rest of my body?* He concentrated on feeling his hands and arms. They tingled as if they'd fallen asleep. He moved on to his legs and feet, finding them tingling as well. It was familiar, for some reason, though alarming at the same time. He remembered falling asleep with his arms over his head before. The numbness made them feel thicker, like he was wearing someone else's arms on his body. He also remembered it took more concentration to make them move until the pins and needles wore off. Could he do that now?

He focused on the tingling sensation where his hands should be and willed them to lever his body into a sitting position. *It worked!* He stared at the numb appendages. They were his hands, but they didn't feel like his. As he sat there, wondering why his body was numb, he became aware that the panting was slowing. Where was it coming from? He concentrated on the sound, pin pointing its location. It was coming from him. *Why am I panting?*

The memories flooded back. Screaming in his own mind as his body aimed a barrage of arrows at his partner. Fighting to alter its aim just a fraction, enough to give the orange tom a warning shot instead of loosing a kill. Finding a way to take control of his body when Toby distracted whoever was driving it with a fireball. The run.

How far had he run before he'd collapsed from exhaustion? More to the point, how long did he have before his puppeteer took over again? Not long, he supposed. He had to do something, warn Toby somehow, before he lost control once more. He had to think. The buzz in his head was making it difficult. Maybe if he centered himself, then he could concentrate on a plan. It took several breaths and more counting than he wanted, but soon the buzz receded enough for him to think.

Whoever was taking over his body wanted Toby dead. That was obvious. As soon as it woke up, he'd be tracking his friend again, waiting for the right moment to plunge a dagger or something into his partner's furry body. If he wanted to warn Toby, he'd have to be close. At least he had that in common with his prison guard. Would it use arrows again?

He fumbled around for the bow and quiver, pulling them close with deadened fingers. The quiver was full. It was the most likely solution. Anyone finding Toby would assume he ran afoul of some native in the area who had gone hunting, though how anyone could mistake the tom's bright orange fur for game would be a mystery. Magic might be traced back to its originator. Arrows, however, were used by everyone.

*Magic.* An idea crept into his mind like a tendril of fog, and just as elusive. He allowed it to form on its own until it was complete in its stunning brilliance. He felt at his waist for a dagger, hoping his puppeteer had prepped him to appear like an ordinary hunter. When he found it, he wanted to shout for joy. Without wasting anymore time, he sliced open a finger and traced a double line down each of the arrows, thinking the tracking spell loudly in his mind. He placed each arrow carefully back into the quiver.

As he replaced the dagger in its belt holder, his body movements grew sluggish again. The master was trying to get its toy back. His heart leapt. He had one more thing to do. With agonizing slowness he crawled to a thorn bush and thrust his bleeding hand inside. His scream followed him back into darkness. Now all he could do was watch and hope he'd done enough.

She wondered again how long it had been since they'd started working on this puzzle. Sometimes it seemed like forever. She glanced at her human partner. Alie had her eyes glued to yet another document she'd pulled out of one of the boxes caked with dust at the very back of the filing room.

Dora shook her head. She licked her paw and rubbed it over her face, trying to get the cobwebs out of her whiskers.

She had to admit that Alie wasn't the only one who loved getting her claws into a good mystery. Tracking down this mysterious cat who had set the genocidal plague on everyone was as intoxicating as hunting the clever mice at the academy when they'd been apprentices.

She glanced at her partner again. The woman's dark curls looked gray with the dust that had accumulated in it. Dora turned to check the filing room door behind her, craning her neck to see around the rows of shelving and thankful that her night vision was better than any humans. The lighting in this room was dim enough to make her feel like they were spelunking instead of searching through old files.

"This is interesting," Alie said.

"What's that?" asked Dora, turning back to watch her friend run a finger down the page.

"Well, you remember that forged birth certificate we handed over to that guardian a few months ago?"

"Yes, what about it?"

"I found the original," the woman said, grinning at her. "Looks like whoever was trying to erase his existence stopped looking for all the copies of old documents not long after the council canceled the magitizing program."

"Seems you were right about government redundancies."

"A good thing, too, or we'd never have these little bits of information," she said, patting the air beside her on the table. It made a soft thumping sound.

"It's a good thing we learned how to hide things in plain sight, or we'd never be able to get these things to Toby. He's going to need this if he's going to bring this cat to justice."

"That's for sure."

"So do we have a name for this monster?" Dora asked.

Alie glanced back at the birth certificate again, then frowned. "Looks like it begins with an A, but I can't make out the rest. We'll need to clean it up before we can read it."

"We'll need to clean ourselves up, too. I hate going through these old files. They're fil— fil—." Dora sneezed, sending up another cloud of dust. She batted the air and squinted at Alie. "They're filthy and the dust tickles my nose."

"Yeah, but at least we're not too likely to run into anyone here."

"At least until Master Warrin comes looking for us."

Alie rolled her eyes and stuffed their latest find in their invisible box. Dora's whiskers splayed.

"That man is insufferable," Alie said. "We're the most efficient partners he has on staff, but the way he talks, you'd think we were dunderheads."

"He's not so hard to deal with, so long as you let him think what he wants. You just don't like letting him win an argument."

"Win? You can't win an argument if you have no clue what you're talking about."

"At least your superior intellect runs his mind in enough circles that he just lets it drop," Dora said.

"True, but how many times can he use a headache as an excuse before he admits he's dumber than a box of rocks?"

"Maybe it's thinking too hard that gives him a headache."

"Probably."

"He may be a pain in the arse, but it's better to have him as a supervisor than someone with more intelligence. Anyone else might have figured out what we're doing by now and handed us over to the enemy."

Alie shuddered at the thought. They encountered

enough rumors during their initial searching almost seven years ago to make them well aware of what their enemy was capable of. Since then, everything they'd turned up had done nothing to ease their fears of being discovered.

"We could always stop. Forget about everything we've found out," Alie said, rubbing her hands over her arms and staring at the space that hid their precious finds.

"Evil flourishes when good men do nothing – or in this case females."

"You ever wonder why we're the ones digging this stuff up instead of someone else?"

"Not really. I consider it logical. We've got the curiosity and keen senses needed to solve a mystery and we have access to the information needed to do it."

"Yeah, but we wouldn't have access if we hadn't applied to the office of clerks."

"And do you remember why we did that?"

Alie sighed. Dora didn't need to hear what she was thinking to know. Her partner had often accused her of being pedantic. Sometimes she wondered if they shouldn't have become teachers at the academy, but then they would miss the excitement of intrigues such as this case.

"Because," said Alie, "we wanted to help Toby find out who killed his mother."

"And what better way to figure out who that might be than to search through old files?"

The woman reached a hand up to scratch her head. When she looked at her hand afterward, she made a face of disgust.

"I need a bath."

"I know what you mean. I feel like I never get all the dust and gunk out of my fur."

They heard the creak of the door as it opened. Alie jumped up from her chair and flicked her wrist at the dusty box she'd been rifling through, sending it back to its shelf. Dora twitched her tail to float another box from a different shelf onto the table. It landed just as their supervisor rounded the corner. He wrinkled his beaky nose as he stared down at them from his lanky, too tall frame.

"I don't know why you insist on coming in here on your breaks," Director Warrin said.

"Someone needs to be sure the files are in order," Alie said, dusting her hands over her brown clerk's vest.

"Clearly, no one ever needs to come down here. These files are obsolete history."

"Those who do not learn from history are doomed to repeat it," she retorted.

"This isn't history. This is junk. The dust alone should tell you that," he said, waving an over-sized hand in front of his face, his thin fingers reminding Dora of a ladies' fan.

"But you just said it's "obsolete history." So which is it? History or junk? Because if it's junk why are we still storing it?"

"We aren't storing it. We're preserving it."

"You don't preserve junk. You preserve history. Ergo, your initial observation must be correct. This is history and if it's history, we should make sure it is readily available to anyone who might need it later."

The man raised his left hand to his forehead and massaged it with his fingers.

"Look," he said, "I don't care what you call it and, quite frankly, I don't care if you want to coat yourself in filth on your own time, but you're break is over."

"We were just putting this last box away," said Dora,

42

widening her whiskers in a cat smile. She glanced at her partner from the corner of her eye, seeing that she'd followed her lead and was picking up the box from the table.

"Whatever. Get back to work," he said with a glare. "And clean yourself up. You look like you wallowed in a pig sty."

Alie opened her mouth to make another retort, then closed it again. Dora exhaled softly as the man turned and left. They both glanced at the empty spot on the table and the indentation it left in the dust. Without another word, Alie put the container in her hands back on its shelf and Dora set the invisible box floating behind her as she leaped to the floor. Together they left, wondering how much longer it would take Warrin to figure out what they were up to.

The itch was back. It crawled through his fur, trying to distract him from the task at hand. He'd known the watcher would return to finish what he'd begun. This time, he wouldn't be caught with his tail up. He settled on his paws, keeping his eyes open a slit in hopes the watcher would assume he was asleep. A twig snapped in the distance. Toby's ear twitched. Whoever this enemy was, he wasn't worried about being found out. If he had been, then he would have taken care to watch for debris and undergrowth that would announce his presence.

A rustle to the left. He was circling the camp, looking

for the best shot. There were only two, thanks to the cliff-like drop behind him and the sheer loess slab to his right. His assailant was either foolhardy or had the ability to fly because if he continued to circle left, he would find himself dropping into the night. Toby almost hoped that would be the case. For a moment he considered what a body might look like at the end of a fall like that. He tried not to smile.

Another twig snapped further on as the would-be assassin continued to circle left. *That's it. Just keep going. Find that perfect spot to aim. Oh! And never mind that sudden drop.* Another rustle and then silence. Toby shifted in place, working hard not to swivel his ears and give himself away. The silence continued. *Not so foolish after all.* He readied his shield spell and shifted again. The soft sound of wood being drawn against wood, drifted to his ears. A moment later he heard the tell tale whoosh as the assailant released the arrow.

"SHY eeld boo BALL," he shouted, jumping to face the oncoming arrow and then racing toward the direction it came.

It bounced harmlessly off his mage bubble as he raced toward his enemy. He gathered his muscles and sprang, landing on the assailant. The human let out a satisfying "oof" and stumbled backward. Toby clung to the human's clothes, screeching and digging his claws into the cloth until he found soft flesh to puncture. The human raised an arm to protect his face and neck, continuing to stumble backwards.

Suddenly the ground dropped beneath them. Toby leapt free, scrambling at the loose vegetation at the cliff's edge. He turned his head to watch the human fall, expecting a bone crushing splat when the large body met the immovable stone ground. His eyes widened as the would-be assassin twisted in mid-air like a cat, landing on his feet and fleeing into the dark. *That's impossible.* He blinked. No human could do that.

His claws slipped a whisker-width, reminding him he was still in danger of falling. He pulled himself clear of the cliff edge and stood, looking into the night after the assailant. The itch was gone now. Likely it wouldn't return for some time. Toby shook himself from head to tail. Whoever this was, he was more than just human. His fur raised in a ridge along his back and his tail fluffed as he considered what kind of new weapon the feline monster he was going after might have created.

He closed his eyes and sniffed the air, hoping to get another clue as to who this strange human was. The faint scent of marigolds and wet metal tickled his nose. He sneezed. *Blood magic.* Of course it would be blood magic. It was the terrorist's stock in trade. He turned in a slow circle, gathering the smells around him and cataloging each. Mostly the normal woodland smells, then something familiar as his own nest caressed his sensitive nose. He opened his mouth to let the scent waft over his glands.

*Lorn?* It couldn't be. He'd left his ex-partner at the Office of Kingdom Guardianship, snuck out during the night so he couldn't follow. He drew the scent across his glands again. It was faint, but it was most definitely his human partner. He followed the scent trail, retracing his steps back to his camp. The scent led him to the arrow lying forgotten on the ground. Toby sniffed its shaft. It was Lorn's scent alright, but there was something more, a sharp smell as if a human had just come inside from playing in the snow. It made him wrinkle his nose.

He stared at the arrow, padding around it in a circle. When he looked at it with his mage sight, it looked ordinary enough, yet, when he bent with his chin on the earth and his nose a paw length away from it, it glowed a faint rust color.

*Odd.* He reached out and patted it, rolling it over. There was something painted on the shaft. He turned toward the small pile of twigs he'd gathered earlier for a fire and set them ablaze with a quick incantation. He turned back to study the arrow again and drew in a sharp breath. Whoever had loosed this arrow had painted two lines on the shaft and, unless he was hallucinating, the paint they used was blood.

"Rev EALTH t'SIG nah CHAR," he whispered.

The image of a twisted rope drifted from the blood into the air. All humans and cats had a magical signature, whether they used magic or not, and each one was unique to the owner. This one he knew as well as his own. It was his partner's. He turned to glare at the cliff, imagining the assailant running away. The monster had his best friend. He was taunting him, leaving Lorn's blood on the arrow that was supposed to kill him. Toby growled. The fire popped and flared in answer. Transformation Mountain would have to wait for a while longer. The prey was close and Toby was going to sharpen his claws on his fur.

# Chapter 3

David flipped through several pages of notes, thankful for Aaron's silver tongue once more. He'd been denied the opportunity to conduct any of the interviews, but his partner had managed to talk the clerk out of copies. So far, though, there was nothing leaping off the page at him. Whoever this mysterious terrorist was, he was superb at covering his tracks.

"The guy's a ghost," David muttered, closing the file he'd been looking through and pulling another one open. "There's just nothing here that suggests anyone at the party knew what was going to happen."

"Perhaps none of them did," Aaron said. He licked his large paw and swiped it over an ear.

"Maybe, but I'd think our foe would want to know if the job was done right. Remember when he ordered the plague to be distributed at the academy's spring festival over six years ago?"

"Aye, but if you recall, it wasn't our main guy that was overseeing the dump. It was one of his lackeys."

"Yeah, but we can't even find one of those in this group. It's like he's changed his whole MO."

"Or maybe he's feeling confident enough now that he doesn't see a need for anyone to keep watch for him."

"That's a terrifying thought," David said with a scowl. "If that's the case, then there's no telling what he has planned next."

He looked up at his partner, perched on the bookcase. Sometimes he wondered if the bookcase would topple over under the large wildcat's weight. Aaron stared at the pile of folders, his tail twitching.

"Dare we start another idea board?"

"I would, but I'm sure someone would confiscate it if we started getting too close to the truth. Same as they did when we were working on Adele's murder for Clarence."

"Ah, but what if we hide it?"

"You got an idea how we could do that without someone figuring out where it is?"

"I was thinking along the lines of plain sight."

"Wouldn't that be obvious?"

"Leave that to me," Aaron said, narrowing his eyes and splaying his whiskers. "First let's just get some ideas up."

"Okay. Where do you want to start?"

"Let's start at the end and walk it back."

"Sounds good. I'll start. It's a good bet that the intended target was the prince."

"Hmm. Maybe."

"The page was on his way to deliver a letter to him. Doesn't that make him the intended victim?"

"That may be what we're supposed to think. This wharf rat never comes at anything directly. There's always some kind of misdirection somewhere."

"Anything to keep us off balance," David said, tapping his chin. "Okay, so we concentrate on the facts and keep our assumptions out of it for the time being."

"Right."

"In that case, we know that the page was headed in the direction of the royal family."

Aaron twitched his tail and the image of a bee appeared in the air next to a crown. A moment later an image of an intricately carved door framed the two symbols.

"We know the page had to enter through the servants' door to get to the great hall."

"We also know that the guardian at the door was nearly asleep at his post."

"Tired or drugged?" asked Aaron.

"No way to know right now," David said, nodding toward the floating images. "I doubt the captain ordered any tests. What else?"

The partners spent the next hour detailing the facts of the case with Aaron setting floating images into an intricate pattern and David checking notes as they went. When they were finished, David smiled and nodded.

"Quite pretty for a murder investigation. You do good work."

Aaron's purr rumbled across the room. "I try."

"Now, where do you suggest we put these lovely images?"

"I thought, if you would be so kind as to transport your large navy rug here, we could set them into it and hang it on your empty wall. You could tell people you've taken up collecting tapestries."

"No one would believe that. Better to say you have."

Aaron shrugged and David smiled. Of the two of them, his partner was the more likely to invest his income on frivolous collections. With a flick of his wrist, the guardian moved the rug from his living quarters to his office and attached it magically to the wall. Aaron stared intently at the images until they floated backward and sunk into the rug. His whiskers widened in a cat grin.

"Now any casual observer will think those images are made from the finest gold thread."

David studied the makeshift tapestry, tilting his head to give it a better look. "Not bad. If you ever decide to leave the OKG, you might have a future in tapestry weaving."

"Thank you. However, unless you manage to get yourself tossed from the ranks, I plan on staying here until we can retire. In the meantime, we have some missing pieces we need to find."

"Like how the kid got by the sweep. Was it faulty gadgetry or was it sabotage?"

"Neither bodes well. If it's sabotage, that means our enemy is closer than we thought. If it's faulty equipment, we're back to square one."

David frowned at the pile of folders on his desk, then turned to look up at Aaron. "This calls for a visit to our favorite master artificer."

"Let's hope Master Sylvester has answers for us."

The scrape of the door opening roused him from his fitful sleep. He opened bleary eyes to watch the black tom pad toward him, whiskers splayed wide.

"Your son is very resourceful, Victor," K'Dash said. "I wonder if I should give the credit to you or your lovely mate."

"If Toby has thwarted your plans, the credit goes to him, not us."

"Perhaps, but he hasn't ruined anything for me. In fact, he has performed to my satisfaction. Before long, I look for him to join me in my vision."

"I very much doubt that, Adair," he said, tail twitching in annoyance.

The black beast's smile widened. "You cannot ruin my joy today, my friend."

"I can try."

K'Dash chuckled and strolled over to his tools. Victor swallowed, wondering if he would ever get beyond the fear those implements put in him. A brush of fur stroked his mind and calmed him. Without the overwhelming fear, his mind started working again.

"So I guess that means your plans are going off without a hitch? Your human puppet's working out the way you'd hoped?"

The black tom's fur rose in a ridge along his back. He twitched his tail, making a knife with a gleaming edge rise from the table. Victor clamped down on his surprise. It had been much longer since K'Dash had come to collect his blood magic abilities. He shouldn't have been able to open the door, let alone float an object. Victor tried not to think about what that could mean.

"No plan goes by without having to be tweaked," K'Dash said.

"Some missions go wrong no matter how much you plan. You of all cats should know that."

K'Dash glared over his shoulder at Victor, then turned his attention back to choosing an implement. He twitched his tail again, setting down the knife and floating a metal corkscrew rod, its serrated edges gleaming dully in the flickering torchlight. He turned his gaze back toward Victor, eyes narrowed and whiskers wide.

"Missions go awry when you depend on fools to do their jobs properly. However, when you expect them to fail, you can always be ahead of the game."

Victor's limbs grew weak as the black beast stalked toward him. He watched the wicked looking tool float behind the tom, his heart beating faster and his eyes widening. Victor hunched down and backed toward the rear of his cage. He was all too familiar with what this particular tool could do. What it could do in the paws of K'Dash, rather than one of his skilled underlings, was something he never considered finding out.

"Who turned you into this monster?" he whispered, more to himself than the malevolent smiling tom.

The black cat's ears laid flat against his head and he bared his fangs. "You did."

The whir of gadgets filled David's ears as he strode into the master artificer's workroom. He stood at the door, looking around to find Sylvester, expecting the dwarf-like bow-legged man to be perched against one of his enormous tables fiddling with one of his new inventions. The man wasn't anywhere in sight. He sighed and wandered over to a workbench on the far wall. Cogs and gears of various sizes filled the space next to a gadget that reminded him of a spy glass, except several times bigger.

"That's my newest baby," called a deep voice from above.

David turned to look up at Sylvester, who was leaning over the banister of his workroom stairs. "What's it for?"

"Don't know yet. I'll be down in a tick. Gotta finish up this flying critter and I'll be right with you."

David chuckled. The master artificer had a way about him that reminded him of the old saint who brought presents on Solstice Eve to all the good little girls and boys. He watched with fascination as the gadget in Sylvester's hands came to life, its little whirligig blades spinning so fast they were nothing but a blur. It rose into the air and hovered. David smiled at the old man's grin. In an eye blink, the thing-a-ma-jig zipped toward him. David threw himself to the floor, turning to watch it come around in the air for another attack.

"Shut it off," he yelled.

"Just a minute. I just gotta—"

There was a tick and click from the banister. The whirligig buzzed past David's head again, nipping a few strands out as it passed by. He rolled under a nearby table and scrambled onto his knees. He peered out from under, looking for the flying attacker. A high pitched buzz sounded behind him. He turned to see the gadget poised to attack again. He raised his hands to protect his face and heard a metallic clatter in front of him. As he slowly lowered his hands, he saw that the thing-a-ma-jig had dropped to the floor, and he sighed. Carefully, he reached out and plucked it up, then scooted out from under the table.

"Deadly little bugger," David said with a grin. He looked up to see Sylvester hobbling toward him on his crutches. "Planning an invasion with miniature flying contraptions?"

"Not exactly," the artificer said, "I'm hoping this little

beauty will be the start of being able to do remote location and surveillance."

"Brilliant." David handed the flying gizmo to his friend, then motioned toward the object he'd been looking at before being attacked by Sylvester's most recent invention. "What about this other spy glass thing? You don't know what it does yet or you're not sure what to use it for?"

"Oh I know what it does, I just don't know what good it'll be against our current enemy. I mean, it's not like we're at war in the traditional sense, is it?" He hobbled over to the work bench holding the giant spy glass.

"I wish we were," David said, following him. "A real war I understand. This phantom hit and run stuff is horse dung."

"My thoughts exactly."

David nodded at the spy glass contraption. "So what does it do?"

"Let me show you," Sylvester said with a grin. He reached over and grabbed a pair of goggles and handed one set to David. "Put these on."

David slid them on and squinted through the dark glass. "How am I supposed to see anything in these?"

"Just wait," Sylvester said, chuckling.

He heard the master artificer turn several gears and then a low pitch buzz. With a sizzle, a light popped on to the right of the spy glass object. The goggles made it appear dark purple. He watched in fascination as Sylvester positioned the light in front of the larger end of the contraption.

"Ready?" he asked, still grinning.

David nodded. With a flick of his wrist, Sylvester threw up a lever. The purple light streamed through glass at the large end and exited out the smaller end. David waited for something to happen. When nothing did, he looked over to his friend to ask what he was supposed to be seeing. Sylvester's attention was on a point far to their left. Confused, David turned his gaze in that direction. He didn't see anything more than a narrow beam of light striking the far wall.

He opened his mouth again to ask what they were waiting for when smoke drifted up from the wall where the gadget concentrated the beam of light. A moment later and the area burst into flames. David yanked his goggles off and thrust his hand at the flames.

"Ex TIN gwish flah MAH ball," he shouted. He turned to see the master artificer dancing a jig. "What was that?"

"That, my friend, was light at its most powerful best," said Sylvester.

David strode over to the wall and inspected the damage. In the middle of the burned out area was a small hole, deep enough he could have put his finger in up to his second knuckle. He turned wide eyes on the old man.

"You realize what could happen if this fell into the wrong hands?"

Sylvester sobered. "And what happens if we don't have any offensive weapons to use against this feline monster? Magic is all well and good, but it won't do anyone any good against simple machines."

"Machines?"

"That's what I'm calling them now," Sylvester said with a wave of his hand. "Shorter than contraptions. And you're changing the subject. You saw what my flying gizmo did. You were helpless against it."

"Only because I didn't want to destroy one of your toys."

"Pfft! Rat turds. It had you trapped under the table

before you knew what was happening."

David's lips thinned. Sylvester had a point. He might have been able to hit the whirligig before it could have finished targeting him, but that was provided he saw *it* before it found *him*.

"I didn't come here to argue about who would win in a fight, magic or machine. I want to know what happened with the sweeps we used during the prince's birthday celebration. Any ideas how that page managed to get through?"

"Well, I can tell you it wasn't because the sweeps were faulty. I checked them myself."

"How can you be sure?"

"I used an explosive planted in a dead mouse. When I waved the sweep over it, it gave a gawd-awful shriek make your ears bleed. No way you could miss that sound."

"Okay, so could someone have sabotaged them somehow?"

Sylvester frowned and stroked his straggly beard. "I don't see how. Not without causing visible damage to the thing."

"So you've seen them since they were used?"

"Of course. I checked them right after it happened. If they failed for some reason, I wanted to find out about it so I could get to work fixin' them. I even ran it over the corpse to be sure and it worked just like it was supposed to."

"So if they weren't faulty, and they weren't sabotaged, that means someone got to the guardian at the door."

"That's my guess. I wouldn't want to be in that boy's boots right now. Your captain took him into custody right after my demonstration in the Great Hall."

David stared at the spy glass for a moment, thinking about what they were up against. So far this terrorist had unleashed a genocidal plague, brain washed who knew how many children into believing humans were lower than dirt, and managed to place explosives inside humans and sneak them into the palace under the watchful eye of an entire contingent of guardians and King's Men. The terrifying thing was they were no closer to knowing who this maniac was or why he was so intent on destroying humankind. He shook his head and looked back at the master artificer.

"Thanks for your help, Sylvester. If I have of any more questions, I'll be sure to find you." He started to walk away, when another thought hit him. He turned back to the old man, nodding toward the spy glass. "You might want to lock that gadget of yours away. If this monster has infiltrated the OKG, then you can bet he'll find a way to steal it."

"I give you my word, guardian, that machine leaves over my dead body."

David grimaced at his choice of words. "Let's hope it doesn't come to that," he said and left.

Toby stared down through the pine needles into his most recent camp, ignoring the intermittent drip of snow melt on his head. He'd lit another tiny fire and constructed a doppelganger out of rocks and branches, casting an illusion spell over them before he swarmed up this nearby conifer.

From this distance, the illusionary orange tom looked remarkably lifelike. He hoped his assailant would come to the same conclusion from the ground view. He'd considered his plan of attack the entire time he'd spent tracking his prey. When he didn't find the archer, he had to reconsider his plans, choosing to make his enemy come to him. In the end, he thought it was more in line with what his father would have done anyway.

The thought of his father made his heart ache. The big black tom had been his idol. Now it was his turn to try to save him, but so far all he'd had were failures.

His first inkling that his father might still be alive came from the long-dead and unmourned feline Chivato, the monster that had not only created the genocidal plague, but had released it under the orders of his master. The gray tom had taunted Toby with the news that Victor was still alive and might even be cooperating with the maniac who ordered the deaths of countless humans. Unfortunately he had taken any other helpful information with him to the grave.

Toby clung to the branch and swallowed a growl as he considered his second failure to find his father and rescue him. He'd been so close. Death snatched answers from him once again, though, when the Head Temple Cat, Hanif, loosed his final breath beneath the blazing inferno of the New Life Temple and School. Toby's fur rose in a ridge as he remembered that night. *Riddles. That's all I ever get out of those fleabags.* Hanif's last words were what drove him toward Transformation Mountain in hopes of finding his father and putting an end to the mysterious feline's terror.

He stared into the tiny camp, swiveling his ears to catch any sound of his would-be assassin. *I'm getting more than riddles out of this guy. One way or another.* The thought of what that might mean drove his claws deep into the branch's rough bark, releasing a sodden pattering of snow. Toby took a deep breath and calmed himself. It wouldn't do to give himself away by dislodging snow at the wrong moment.

The sound of muted footsteps drifted up to his ears. His fur began to itch again, making his ear twitch as if a fly buzzed around it. Strange that he would still feel the itch when the human's eyes weren't on him. *Echo effect, that's all. Probably rebounding from the illusion spell.*

The ground beneath him was full of shadows. He slid forward, craning his neck for a better vantage point. He watched for one of the shadows to move. When it did, he gave a feral grin, spreading his whiskers wide and showing his fangs. He narrowed his eyes and calculated the distance. Casting a spell would have been more efficient, but not as satisfying as leaping on his prey and slicing through his soft skin with razor sharp claws.

He waited a moment more for the archer to take a step backward and to the left. The blood in his ears rang as he wriggled his haunches, ignoring the dangers of dislodging more snow as he prepared to drop on the man. A growl clawed its way out his throat, alerting the assassin. The man spun around, his head jerking up to stare at him. Toby let out a blood curdling screech and threw himself off his branch into the human's face.

The man's arms flew up, covering his head just in time as Toby's claws raked down the soft cloth. He felt a claw tear loose as it embedded itself in the fabric. It barely registered in his blood lust. The man flung his arms wide. Toby flew across the small clearing, impacting against another tree. He wobbled as he got to his feet, the image of the man swimming in front of him.

"Flah MAH ball," he growled.

A fireball launched itself at the human who dodged

aside. He rolled into a somersault, nocking an arrow as he righted himself. Toby threw up a shield as the assassin loosed his arrow. It bounced off the mage bubble. Using its new trajectory, he flung the arrow back at its owner.

"This is for Lorn."

The man threw himself to the ground and rolled. Toby launched more fireballs at him as he continued to roll away. It was working. The human turned his next roll into another somersault and stood. Toby threw another fireball at him, making the man take a step back — right into the invisible net Toby had constructed earlier. The ends of the net snapped around the human as he struggled to free himself, like an insect in a spider web. The more he struggled the tighter the glowing blue web became.

"What have you done with my friend?" The man jerked, then stilled. His head slumped against his chest.

"Answer me," he snarled.

No response. Rage filled Toby's mind. If this man was dead, he'd failed again. He wouldn't let that happen. Digging his claws into the soft pine needles, he launched himself toward the human and swarmed up his magical web until he was at eye level. He lifted an armored paw.

"Where is he?"

The man's head lolled backward, his eyes fluttering open for a moment. Toby gasped and dropped to the ground. It couldn't be. He shook his head until his ears popped, backing up several paces. Toby called up a mage light and stared back up at the man's face, the ragged beard and shaggy hair standing out against his pale skin and sunken cheeks. It couldn't be, but it was. His heart lurched as the man moaned. He took a tentative step forward.

"Lorn?"

# Chapter 4

Victor licked his parched lips. He would have sold his soul to the Demon King for a lap of water. His right haunch screamed in protest when he shifted his weight. He turned with care and gingerly licked the sutured wound on his leg. It was an odd sensation, feeling the slick bindings wrapped over lumpy flesh.

He tried to remember what had happened. All that came to mind was K'Dash's leering green gaze and searing pain, as if acid had been poured over his leg. After that was just the dark numbness of a blackout. He could smell the metallic tang of blood and the foul stench of urine.

The scrape of the door opening made him jerk his gaze around. He sucked in a breath and closed his eyes as pain stabbed through his leg again. When he opened his eyes a slit, he saw the white tom pad into the room, his cleaning equipment following dutifully behind him.

"I'm afraid you have a bigger mess to clean up this time," he said. "Your master was more enthusiastic than usual."

The white tom went straight to work, flicking his tail toward the rivulet of blood drying in its path toward a drain in the floor and sending a mop and bucket to wash it up.

"I've been thinking about our last conversation," he said, studying the tom. "You said something about fake evidence being given to the king and that's what kept your father off the High Council. I may know someone who can find out what that was and track the documents back to their source."

The cat's ears twitched. Victor forced his whiskers to stay neutral. The kit was interested, but how far would he go to clear his family name?

"I could contact him, see what he can dig up, but I can't do it in here."

The tom glanced at him and snarled. "Even if I was interested in your help, there's no way I could get you out, so why don't you just shut your filthy mouth."

Victor shrugged, then hissed as the sutures pulled. "Suit yourself, son. I just hate to see such a bright young kit as yourself wither away in this dungeon cleaning up my blood when you should be at the academy."

"I was at the academy," the white cat growled, whipping around to glare at him. "If it weren't for your son I'd still be there."

"Toby?" Victor's eyes widened as he lurched to the wire mesh and pushed his face against it, ignoring the scream in his leg. "What do you know about him?"

"He's a know-it-all mangefur," the tom spit. He narrowed his eyes and gave Victor a once over. "Just like his father, I'd say. He and his partner were in league with that Ribaldy traitor. My uncle told me as much."

"Who is your uncle?"

"Like I'd tell you."

Victor stared at him as he turned away with a flick of his tail to send his rags flying toward the torture tools. He ran through every name of the Hielberg House in his mind, trying to put this young tom's uncle in place. As he continued to watch the white cat, a name filtered through his fog.

"Chivato told you Toby was involved in some conspiracy, didn't he? He asked you to watch my son and tell him everything."

The cat's ears twitched again. He tried not to grin, as he considered what a terrible poker player this tom would be.

"But that wasn't enough, was it? What did he ask you to do?"

The tom kept his back to him, though his fur began to fluff again.

"It had to be something worse than spying. Did he want you to break Toby's legs, send a message to him because he was getting in the way somehow?"

The white cat growled. His tail thumped and swished against the floor.

"So bullying wasn't beneath you, so what was it then? What part of his plan did you serve?"

"It wasn't his plan," he said. "He was just a pawn like everyone else, a weakling like his brother—"

"Like you?"

The white cat hissed. His rags fell to the floor as his concentration failed. Victor wondered if he'd pushed him too far as the tom stalked toward the cage.

"If I'm so weak, why are you the one in a cage?"

He turned and walked away with a stiff-legged gait that reminded Victor of himself when he was younger.

"Cages come in all shapes," he said.

The tom left, slamming the door behind himself.

Toby had seen the pale brown stone temple hugging the cliffs early this morning. He'd believed he had enough energy to float his ex-partner to their doors and have plenty to spare, but now, as the sun set, his tail dragged the ground and his whiskers drooped. He glanced behind him, checking to see if the bound human was still floating or if he was being dragged along.

Seeing Lorn skimming the ground behind him reminded him of the last time he'd had to float his friend to safety. At least that time he was sure the man would awaken in a good mood. He checked the magical bindings again, glancing at the bulge on Lorn's chest to make sure the book was still safely tucked inside his shirt. If Lorn woke up before he was secured, Toby didn't know what would happen. He was sure the book would be lost, though he wasn't positive how he would feel about that.

He wobbled on his paws as he looked up the slanting drive leading to the temple doors. Taking a deep breath, he place one paw in front of the other, heading for the temple. Two steps was all he managed before collapsing. He stared at the temple entrance. It was less than a quarter mile up that road to gain safe haven, but it might as well have been on the other side of the world.

With the last of his energy reserves, he called up a mage light the size of a lightning bug and sent it to find whoever might be on the other side of those closed doors. His eyes closed and he floated into a half-sleep.

## Master Cat

The sound of running footsteps merged with the sound of his heartbeat in his ears. His mind attributed being lifted to floating into sleep and he allowed the voices to carry his thoughts away into dreams.

When he opened his eyes again, he was staring into the gentle blue eyes of a black and white she-cat. She splayed her whiskers in a warm smile.

"You're certainly someone I never expected this far into the Outer Reaches," she said. He tried to speak and she shook her head. "Just rest. You've drained yourself so low I had to boost your reserves with some of my own."

"Lorn?" he croaked.

"Your partner is fine, or, rather, he will be at some point."

Toby struggled to lever himself into a reclining position, but the she-cat laid a firm paw on his side.

"I meant it when I said rest. I know you want to get back to whatever mission you were on; however, now is not the time."

He laid his head back against the soft nest and sighed. He shut his eyes and floated in and out of dreams again. The next time he awoke, the she-cat wasn't there.

He rolled onto his side and gazed around the cell-like room. Besides his nest, there was a single narrow table that could be used as a nightstand or desk and an empty narrow cot on the other side of the room. *It's a Brother's cell.*

His skin shivered with the memory of being trapped in a room much like this with another Brother Cat named Bartholomew the night the students rioted and set the New Life Temple and School ablaze. His gaze darted toward the simple wooden door as his breathing quickened. He'd come for help. Had they locked him in instead?

He twitched his tail at the door. It didn't budge. The hair along his spine rose and a growl rumbled in his throat. He unsheathed his claws and slunk toward the door. He jumped when it opened, scrambling back to his nest and spinning around to see who had entered. The black and white she-cat blinked at him, the slow blink of friendship.

A memory floated to the surface of his mind. He reached out to grab it and it bobbed beneath the surface of consciousness again.

"I know you from somewhere," he said, cocking his head.

"I'm not surprised you don't remember. We met the one time. Didn't even have any classes together."

"You were at the academy?"

The she-cat nodded. "Do you remember orientation? The invisibility spell that went wrong?"

"That was you?"

"Yep." The she-cat padded further into the room, a tray floating behind her. "I brought you some food. I'm afraid it isn't fancy, but it's good."

Toby stared at the bowl of stew on the tray as it settled on the floor. Memories of slurping down food at a village pub where he met Lorn just before they made plans to rescue the children at the other temple rose unbidden, making his stomach clench. He looked up at the she-cat and ignored the stew.

"I don't remember you being Chosen."

"I wasn't. I was accepted into the loner-in-training program. Graduated with honors with a degree in social work."

"That's an odd degree for a cat."

"Not really. By the time I chose my degree, the plague

had decimated the human population and the relationship between cats and humans had deteriorated to the point that we felines were being treated as less than second-class citizens. Social work seemed the best choice to help both sides."

"Never thought about it that way."

The she-cat pushed the stew closer to him with a paw. He licked his ruff, then turned his gaze back to her.

"If you studied social work, what are you doing at a temple?"

"It's a long story."

"Give me the short version," he said with a smile.

"Well… sometime after the plague, I heard a story about this queen who had a special gift. She could heal the spirits of both humans and cats. I went looking for her. Had some wild adventures, then ended up here to finish my training in a somewhat different discipline."

"Okay, when I said give me the short version," he said, eyes widening, "I didn't mean you had to skimp on the details."

The she-cat grinned. "If I go into any details, then it wouldn't be a short story, now would it?"

"I guess not."

"So what about you? I know you ended up in the Office of Kingdom Guardianship, but what did you do after that? How did you end up here?"

"It's a long story," he said with a yawn. The she-cat smiled.

"In that case, perhaps we should swap longer stories after you've gained a bit more strength." She stood and padded toward the door, stopping to look back at him again. "I can see you're in pain, Toby. You're safe here. And Lorn can be, too… if you want."

He watched her walk into the hall and close the door behind herself with a quiet click. When he looked back at the stew, his stomach turned over. He pushed the bowl aside with his paw, then curled into a tight ball. Tail over nose, he closed his eyes and drifted back into what he hoped would be a dreamless sleep.

The crowd at the Cat's Tail Pub was sparse for dinner time. Of course, Clarence decided, that may have been because this was the pub where Master Natsumi's brutally murdered body had been discovered in the back alley. Despite the belief that the loner cat was somehow involved in his deceased partner's murder, he felt badly that the sleek gray tabby had met such a horrible end. There was no closure in it for anyone.

However, even though fewer cats and humans frequented the establishment, he knew they did a fair share of business during the week. Clarence was a little surprised at the lack of customers and not a little bit apprehensive at this secret meeting with his friend David. It had been David's suggestion to meet at the pub, saying it would be a good cover if they were seen together. Clarence wondered, with so few people or cats inside, if they shouldn't have gone somewhere else.

He found an empty booth near the back and ordered a pot of hot tea and a basket of cranberry scones. The server raised an eyebrow.

"Old men have odd tastes, my dear," Clarence said with a smile. "I suspect, though, my companions will wish to order dinner when they arrive."

The young woman smiled and went to put in his order. David and Aaron still hadn't arrived yet when the waitress came back with his scones and tea, so he busied himself pouring his tea into the heated cup. He took a sip of the hot amber liquid and sighed with contentment. Even if nothing came of this meeting at least he could enjoy a steaming cup of his favorite beverage.

He looked up as the bell over the door jingled its merry tune. David and Aaron stepped into the darkened pub, catching the server's attention. David leaned into speak to her. She turned and pointed in Clarence's direction. The guardian looked in the direction she pointed and Clarence waved. David strode past the girl without another glance, leaving Aaron to tell the woman thank you. He gave a short, inaudible laugh. It was typical David, leaving the social niceties to his partner. No wonder he wasn't welcome on more investigations within the OKG.

"Tea?" Clarence asked, motioning to the pot as his friends took the bench seat across from him.

"No thanks," David said. "I think I'll have something stronger."

The server returned and took their orders of ale, fish and chips for David and warmed, spiced milk and grilled salmon for Aaron. Clarence declined ordering anything else and the young woman left to put in their orders. She returned a moment later with the spiced warm milk and ale, then disappeared into the darkened recesses of the pub without so much as a smile. Clarence reached for another scone.

"You know," he said, "I imagine you'd be more welcome

at places if you would take a page from your partner's book."

"How's that?" asked David.

"He means you should remember to say "Please" and "Thank you" once in awhile. You were rather rude to that young lass at the door. I'm surprised she came back to take our order."

The guardian grunted and waved the subject aside, leaving Aaron to roll his eyes and shake his head. Clarence hid his smile behind his tea cup.

"So, what have you found out?" David asked. He placed his elbows on the table and leaned forward, clasping his hands together. The predatory look in his narrowed eyes reminded Clarence of Adele when she scented the answer to a problem they were having with one of their spells. He blinked and the moment was gone. Shaking his head, he placed his tea cup back on the table.

"Not a lot. Apparently the orphanage where Adele and her mysterious brother grew up has had three caretakers."

"That's interesting. What's their stories?"

"The current head mistress is in it for the money, which is quite obvious from the decor of her personal suite as compared to the state of the rest of the building."

"What about the other two?"

"The prior head master died during the plague and the original head mistress retired when she inherited a large sum of money."

"Hmm. I suppose those could all be natural coincidences, but my gut says our little fiend was involved in all of those replacements."

"It would make sense to remove the first caretaker, Miss Florence, if you wanted to erase all memory of your existence from the beginning," Clarence said, sitting back and stroking his gray beard. "A little odd, though, to give the woman a large sum of money and ask her to move away. It doesn't seem his style."

"No, it doesn't. But killing the other one with the plague, certainly does."

"Aye. And what of the current head mistress? If she's watchin' these wee bairns for no other reason than she gets some money, then she would be easy enough to control."

"She did seem rather reticent to speak about the previous caretakers. She even went so far as to claim she was getting a migraine."

"I'd say she's on our terrorist's payroll, then. Maybe she even supplied a few "students" for his New Life School experiment. How long has she been head of the orphanage?"

"She came on board just after the head master died. The housekeeper said they were worried about what would happen to the orphanage up until she took over, but now, I wonder if their worries haven't been compounded."

"I'm curious about this Miss Florence," Aaron said. "If our mystery cat likes to kill and control humans, why set one up in luxury?"

"I hope to find that out when I go visit her," Clarence said. He looked up, noticing the server headed their direction, and placed a surreptitious finger over his mouth. The young woman's smile seemed strained as she set the fish and chips before David.

"You needn't be nice to this curmudgeon, lassie," joked Aaron. "He's naught but a dung beetle anyway."

David glared at his partner. The server chuckled and grinned at the wildcat. "Will there be anything else?"

"No, thank you, miss," David said, turning a smile on the young woman. "I believe you've worked hard enough taking care of us for the time being."

The server blinked a couple times, her smile turning strained again, and then walked away. David turned to his grinning partner and scowled.

"Was that better?"

"Oh I'm sure she'll remember you now, though I'd bet it won't be with pleasant regards."

David shook his head and grabbed a fried potato string from his plate. "There's no pleasing people, so why bother, I say." He popped the chip into his mouth, then washed it down with a swig of his ale. "Anyway, we're here on business."

"So, what have you discovered?" asked Clarence.

"About as much as you have, I think."

"For starters, how much have you heard about the recent bombing attempt on the royal family?" Aaron asked.

Clarence's eyes widened as he put his cup down with a clink. "Good grief. Was anyone hurt?"

"Not for lack of trying," David said, tapping a potato on the edge of his plate. "If Aaron hadn't been there, I doubt the prince would be alive. Who knows how many others would have been caught in the blast."

"Did you manage to catch the person carrying the explosive before it went off?"

"Unfortunately, no. I managed to throw a shield over the lad, but it was just a moment before he exploded."

"Didn't Sylvester create some kind of gadget that was supposed to find the bombs?" David nodded and stuffed another chip into his mouth. Clarence sat back in the booth, frowning. "I'm assuming the captain had guardians with the contraptions at the entrances, so how did the child get through?"

"That's what we're trying to find out."

"As far as we can tell," Aaron said, "This terrorist was able to compromise the guardian at the servants' entrance."

"That seems likely. I do wonder, though, about the sweeps the guardians were using. Surely the one at the servant's entrance used his on everyone."

"Possibly. We just don't know," David said.

"Assuming he was drugged or half-asleep and he was at least trying to do his job, is it possible the gadget he was using was sabotaged?"

David shook his head. "I asked Sylvester myself. He said he tested the sweeps on explosives planted in dead mice before he gave them to us and then tested them again on the boy's remains. It worked just like it was supposed to."

"Well, we know our mysterious fiend has a lot of pull in the upper ranks of the government, it wouldn't be too much of a stretch of the imagination to think he has someone within the ranks of the guardians on his payroll."

"I think we both know who that might be."

"Toby's ex-supervisor? Do you think he would be able to pull something like this off?" asked Clarence.

"At this point I'd suspect my own mother," David answered with a frown. He downed another swallow of ale and pushed his half-eaten plate of fish and chips aside. "We've been going through the interviews and case notes, but so far all we have are more questions than answers."

"Just like Adele's case, isn't it?" Clarence's throat closed and he tried to swallow the lump. It had been months since her murder and it was still as raw as when he'd first found out. He took another sip of tea, forcing it down around the fist in his throat and avoiding the sympathetic looks he knew his friends were giving him. Aaron placed his paw on the table next to the plate of scones. Clarence looked up into the wildcat's narrowed gaze.

"We'll find this son-of-a-carrion-eater and make him pay for his crimes. You have our word on that."

He nodded and tried to smile. "Sometimes it's just difficult to accept she's gone."

"She was a unique and special queen."

"That she was," Clarence murmured, staring into his tea. He took a deep breath and exhaled, pushing his maudlin thoughts aside. "And she would be the first to tell us to get off our tails and go get some work done."

"A good work ethic." David smiled and jerked his head toward Aaron. "We're going to see what Gillespie knows about all this, find out if he has any connections to the guardian that was supposed to be guarding the servants' exit."

"Good luck with that," Clarence said, waving the server over to pay the bill. "I'll let you know what I find out with Miss Florence."

"Same here with Gillespie," David said. "If the One's as just as the priests say, maybe we'll catch a break soon and be able to plant ourselves a murderer in the ground with the spring flowers."

Clarence watched the guardian partners leave, then cradled his lukewarm teacup in his hands. He considered warming it up with a spell, then decided to do as his friend had done and down the cooling amber liquid. He handed the server some money for the meals and scones, then headed out the door.

## Master Cat

Toby padded through the ferns, his sensitive nose picking up the scent of nearby water. Picking up the pace, he trotted further on through the dense greenery. He was so thirsty. The scent of water drew him, faster and faster until he was racing, belly to the ground, yet it never seemed any closer. He skidded to a halt, lifting his nose to the air. Behind him. He'd passed it somehow. He whirled around and raced the other direction, only to stop and find it behind him once again. He opened his mouth to yowl, but nothing came out of his dry throat. He sunk to the ground and laid his nose on his paws, defeated.

Another scent, closer, more familiar. He lifted his chin, opening his mouth to let the scent caress his scent glands. Mother? She was near, but moving away. The ferns swished in front of him, disturbed by her movement. He trotted toward her scent, edging into a run, trying to catch up to her. Her scent never faded, never got any closer. Like the water he desired, she seemed forever out of reach.

He burst through a wall of ferns into a small clearing. There she sat next to a pool of clear water. He wanted to run to her, nuzzle her sleek black fur, but his paws wouldn't move. He looked at the cool water, a searing thirst drying his throat and mouth. He wanted to slurp the water in dizzying laps, but his paws refused to bring him closer to the pool's edge. He stared at his mother in desperation. She smiled at him.

"All is well, my son. He knows you are thirsty. Drink and be filled."

The young cat stretched his neck toward the water's edge, bumping his nose against an invisible wall. He looked back at his mother, still smiling and nodding at him. He turned back to the water, this time reaching a paw toward it and encountering the same invisible wall. He glanced back at the sleek black queen. She hadn't moved, nor had her expression changed. He stepped back a pace, then launched himself high into the air, thinking he could jump over the wall. He landed on thin air, sliding down the invisible bubble and landing in a heap at the water's edge. He looked at his mother.

"How am I supposed to drink if there's a mage bubble over the water?"

"There is no bubble. There is only you."

Toby lashed his tail, staring at the water and sensing the tug of magic around it. Why was his mother lying? A faint sound in the distance made him swivel his ears backward, but his thirst drove his attention back to the pool. His fur fluffed as he turned to unleash his rage upon the barrier. He came nose to nose with the black queen and jumped back. He stared into her piercing yellow eyes, the same stern expression he had grown up with as she tutored him in magic.

"You cannot obtain that which you desire most until you gain that which is strongest within you."

The orange tom shook his head and blinked. He peered past his mother at the water, his mouth feeling like it was stuffed with cotton. The sound came again, louder and closer this time. He looked behind, seeing nothing but ferns moving in the still air. His determination to quench his parched throat drew him back to the clearing. When he turned his attention back to the black queen she had disappeared. Startled, he whirled around, searching the clearing. She stood further away to his right.

"You must find the strength, Toby. You must—"

His nose filled with the acrid smell of smoke as heat seared his fur. He twisted around, searching for a way out even though he knew there wouldn't be one. The school was on fire and there was no escape. He knew what was coming. He searched the heat haze for the brown tabby. A yowl escaped from his throat as the tabby flew at him, skin and fur tearing loose from his shoulder.

He ripped free of the savage beast and ran through the burning corridors, flying around a corner into the child's room. The little girl was strapped to a chair, her glistening eyes staring wide at him. She opened her mouth. Toby flattened his ears and backed away, hoping he wouldn't hear her. The child's scream echoed through his skull.

"I had to put the mission first," he cried.

"The mission? The mission didn't keep us from dying, did it, Toby?" snarled his mother, stalking around the chair. The heat haze from the flaming walls made her fur shift and shimmer.

He turned to escape and collided with large human feet. Toby stared up at his ex-partner who was holding his bloody hand to his chest. Toby recognized the oozing slashes.

"We needed you and you left us," Lorn said, his face twisted in anger.

"You don't understand," he said, backing away from his accusers. "I wanted to protect you. All of you."

"Protect us?" the man asked, waving his good hand toward the fire. "You call this protecting us?"

Toby turned toward his mother. An arrow sprouted from her chest. He scrabbled back in horror as she flopped onto her side, her eyes cold and accusing.

"You killed your own mother," Lorn said, stepping

closer. "You're a monster,"

"I didn't—I couldn't—"

"Who else could have pulled the trigger?" the man asked.

Toby stared down at his paws. He perched on his mother's cat-sized crossbow, its line still vibrating. He leaped away, splashing into a viscous lake. The metallic scent of blood threatened to suffocate him as he paddled to keep his head above the thick liquid.

A big black tom padded on top of the fluid, stopping to stare down at him with narrowed eyes.

"Please, help me," Toby begged.

"Save yourself," the tom hissed, leaning closer, "if you can."

The beast's piercing green eyes grew until they filled Toby's entire field of vision. A hard paw touch his head, pushing downward as he struggled to keep his nose above the bloody lake.

"No," he screamed.

Toby jerked awake. He stared, wild-eyed around the room, trying to remember where he was and how he got here. He stood up and shook himself from head to tail, wishing the action would scatter the nightmare as well. It was becoming an unwanted friend twisting his dreams every night. Lashing his tail, he stared at the closed door. The she-cat hadn't offered to show him around, but she also hadn't given him any indication that he was a prisoner. He decided, if he were stopped by any guard types, he'd explain that he wanted to check on the man he'd brought with him.

He swept his tail right to left, concentrating on opening the door. It flew open, banging against the stone wall. He grimaced. If his mother were still alive and had seen that, she would have chided him on excessive emotion leaking into his magic again. The thought made his claws unsheathe. She wasn't alive. He had killed her. Just like he killed thousands of others.

Toby stalked out the door. He looked to the right, down a unadorned brown brick hallway, then turned to look down the opposite hall, also unadorned brown brick. His fur prickled with frustration. How was he supposed to find Lorn? His tail jerked as a memory burst upon him like a bubble on water. Use a finder incantation. He shook his head at his own idiocy. It was a basic level spell he'd learned even before he'd gone to the academy. He couldn't believe he'd forgotten about it until now.

"Fors AHK een," he murmured.

A bright green arrow materialized at paw level, hovering a whisker length above the floor. Toby followed it down the hall and around a corner. He held his breath as he slunk past a human Brother. This would be the test, he supposed, as to whether he was a guest or a prisoner. The monk continued on his way as Toby passed by. As he rounded another corner, he exhaled and shut his eyes. He'd almost forgotten what it was like to be in a temple run by real Followers of the One instead of one run by cats dedicated to the ways of the terrorist Father Hanif had called their savior.

"It's good to see you up and around," said a light female voice behind him.

Toby jumped and spun around, armored paw raised. The black and white she-cat smiled and gave him a slow, friendly blink. He lowered his paw and licked his ruff.

"You shouldn't sneak up on someone like that," he said, frowning at the she-cat. "I could have flayed you."

"But you didn't. You're stronger than you think."

He cocked his head at her. Admittedly his memory of her was fuzzy, but he was certain she hadn't been this self-assured back then. Add to that that he couldn't recall her name. He'd tried during the long hours last night between nightmares as a way to sweep the vivid dreams from his mind, but hadn't come up with anything. She continued to sit and smile at him. He chuckled and closed his eyes for a moment, dipping his head.

"You know, I've tried all night to remember your name," he said, looking back at her.

"I'm not surprised you don't remember. That was a long time ago. We've all been through a lot since school, so the names from our past aren't as important anymore."

"Some names are," he murmured, glancing behind himself at the green arrow still hovering where he stopped.

"I can show you to his room, if you like," the she-cat offered.

Toby considered going on alone for a moment. He studied the black and white feline, noting the tension in his shoulders ease.

"You might feel more welcome with a friend along," she said.

She stood and walked past him in the direction his arrow pointed. When he didn't follow, she turned and smiled at him. She nodded toward the hall, her tail crooked in a question mark. Toby took a deep breath, closed his eyes for a moment, then exhaled and followed.

"My name is Nadine, by the way."

They walked in silence for several minutes before Toby had worked up the courage to ask about what was bothering him.

"Why is it that I feel better when you're around?"

Nadine chuckled. "That's part of my gift."

"What gift?"

"Have you ever heard of the myth of the Barukh Sh'Toole?"

"Can't say as I have."

"How about the Great Exodus?"

"I heard about that one at the New Life Temple. Something about humans being exiled from the Garden of Light and Life because they fell to temptation and that's why the world is in such a dung heap now."

Nadine stopped and stared at him as if he were a mouse she were hunting, her blue eyes narrowed. It made his skin shiver. A moment later, she smiled and a warming sensation coursed through his body. He sighed as more tension left him. He couldn't help smiling back at her.

"I don't know how you do that, but thanks."

"You're welcome," she said, motioning him to continue following her. "As I said, it's part of my gift."

"So what's so important about the Great Exodus?"

"It explains a lot, though what you've been told is a somewhat incomplete version."

"What's missing?"

"Quite a bit, actually. For starters, we felines were originally called Malkins and we could all perform magic when we lived in the Garden of Light and Life."

"No kidding?" Nadine nodded as they continued walking down a set of stairs. Toby cocked his head to the side. "What happened? Why are there some cats who can talk, but not use magic and others who can't do either?"

"It all began after the great war with the Demon King and his minions. Somehow during the final battle, he was released into the human population. The humans didn't have the ability to see through his guile and charm and so they fell into temptation. The One had no choice but to exile them because purity cannot abide the presence of impurity."

Toby thought about Lorn's reaction when they'd been told that before by Hanif's personal aid. At the time, he thought his partner had been miffed at being called less than best, but now he was curious, too.

"If only the humans were exiled, then why are we here, too?" he asked, reiterating what Lorn had said and wondering if he would get an answer this time.

"That's a very astute question," Nadine said, turning to smile at him again. "We were given the choice to stay or go with them. Our kind chose to go with the humans and continue to be their companions until the day the Beloved returns."

"Okay, so that explains why we're here, but that doesn't explain why some of us can use magic and others can't."

"Like all things in this world, chaos and order are in constant fluctuation, always trying to balance each other. Over time, some Malkins lost the ability to do anything beyond what would be considered normal animal behavior. And, as with all things, there is a spectrum of loss from those who wield magic as easily as you to those who can think and talk as we do to those who are little better than a normal animal."

"I never realized that. I always thought we were just born different."

"We are, but just so much as is natural in the greater spectrum of life."

"I suppose that this spectrum also explains our much longer life spans?" Toby asked.

"Yes. Full Malkins like ourselves live as long, and often longer, than our human counterparts."

He mulled that over as they walked down another long hallway. What would that mean for him? Would he out live Lorn? He was still thinking about that when he bumped into Nadine's shoulder. He looked up to see a narrow door and turned a questioning glance on her.

"He's inside," she said, twitching her tail to open the door.

Toby stepped through into the windowless room. It was dark save for the torchlight filtering through the doorway, which illuminated a small patch of the stone floor under his feet. For a moment, he felt like he'd been thrown back in time to his first coach ride to the academy. The air was as thick as it had been then, as if he could slice through it with his claws. He heard a rustle of cloth and swiveled his ears to find the sound's location, almost expecting to hear Gravin Arturo's voice come from the darkened area. That human, however, was long dead, killed by the same plague he had helped develop with his twisted companion Chivato.

"You've done well," Lorn said, his voice taking on a cold edge Toby didn't recognize. "Although I am a little disappointed that you didn't carry through."

"What do you mean "carry through?" Carry through on what? Why have you been attacking me?"

"You have your father's penchant for ignorant questions."

"What about my father? What do you know about him?" Toby demanded. "What haven't you told me, Lorn?"

"Lorn?" The man's laugh rumbled through the room, raising the hair along Toby's spine. It was nothing like his partner's hearty chuckle. "How quaint. You are your father's son. That is for certain."

"Who are you? What have you done to Lorn?"

"Made him better," the puppeteer said using the human's voice, "like I plan to do with all humans."

"You won't get away with this," Toby snarled

"Come, now, Toby. That is so cliche, don't you think?"

"I'm coming for you. I know where you're planning to go and I will find a way to stop you."

"Tsk, tsk. I thought your mother would have taught you better than to announce your intentions to your enemy. The One knows you wouldn't have learned that at the academy. Those fools couldn't find a taper in a lighted room."

"Leave my mother out of this, you murderer."

A feline-like growl issued from his partner, making Toby's tail fluff.

"I did not kill your mother," Lorn snarled, then chuckled evilly. "I did, however, see to it that her true murderer was brought to swift justice."

In an instant, Toby realized who he was really talking to. It was the black tom from the cemetery, the beast who looked so much like the way he remembered his father. He was sure that, if he could see Lorn's face, he would see the piercing green eyes instead of his partner's warm brown gaze.

The tom had shown up at Adele's grave site just after the funeral service and promised to punish the one responsible for his mother's death. Toby still believed the beast was responsible, though it continued to confuse him why a killer would promise to catch himself. *Insanity. That has to be what it is.*

But how was he talking through his friend? The very idea that this piece of filth had access to Lorn's body made Toby's fur feel too thick. He burned to slash the black beast's nose.

"You don't need to hide behind Lorn anymore. I know

who you are."

"Do you? And who is it you think I am?"

"You're Councilman Damon's companion."

The beast chuckled again. "Is that all you've discovered? And here your father has been giving your intelligence high marks in solving puzzles. I must speak with him about his flights of fancy."

"What do you want with him? Is he just your play thing to torture? Is that what your kind enjoys, torturing good cats?"

"Your father is nothing of the kind," the black tom spit. The feline hiss coming from Lorn's voice was unnerving. "Perhaps before this is done, you'll see your father as he is, a traitor and a coward."

Toby unsheathed his claws and prepared to launch himself across the room at the taunting voice. A blast of cold seared through his mind, leaving him shivering on the floor. He stared around him, seeing nothing but a dark more dense than the blackest cave. He heard the thump of running paws, then felt warm breath on his cheek.

"Can't see," he whispered through chattering teeth.

"Stay still. I'll help you in a moment," Nadine said.

He felt her turn away. A moment later, there was a thump from the far corner and Lorn moaned. Toby's fur began to crawl, the itch working its way up his back and into his ears. For the thousandth time, he felt like he was back at the academy, ducking under their table to avoid one of Lorn's ill-formed spells.

"Where am I?" Lorn asked.

"Safe," Nadine said.

"Toby?"

"He's safe, too," she said, "Rest now. Save your

strength for the battle to come."

The man sighed. As suddenly as it had started, the itch disappeared. Toby sighed in relief. He squinted at the lighter shadow approaching him.

"Can you see anything yet?" Nadine asked, nosing his cheek.

"Just patches of light and dark," he replied. He blinked several times, trying to force his eyes to obey his desire to see more. "Lorn's never done that before."

"It wasn't Lorn."

"The beast did that through him?" A shiver ran down his spine. "How?"

"Remember when I asked if you knew about the Barukh Sh'Toole?"

"Yeah."

"The Barukh Sh'Toole is a feline with the special gift to heal spirits, both human and feline."

"Are you telling me you can see ghosts?"

Nadine laughed. "Not ghosts. Spirits. I can see the souls and emotions of every living thing around me as if I were living in a rainbow. It's quite pretty."

"What does that have to do with what just happened?"

Nadine sobered. "Everything."

Toby could feel her eyes boring into him, as if she were searching his heart for answers. Maybe she was. According to what she'd just said, it was possible she could see all his secrets. His skin shivered again, but it wasn't from the mind blast.

"I told you that I can see your pain. Do you remember that?"

He nodded, noting that he could see her blue eyes better.

86

"I know that your mother's death set you on a path you weren't ready for, but I can see what you may become, if..."

Her ears flattened to half-mast and her whiskers drooped.

"If what?"

"If you are willing to face your nightmares and embrace your fears so you can save your partner."

Toby glanced into the darkness where his friend lie sleeping. Images from his latest nightmare rose to mind, making his heartbeat speed up. Could he face the accusations again? And what about his fears? The way she said it, it wouldn't be about facing his fear of cooked vegetables. He swallowed and sat up, pulling his body to full attention.

"That doesn't sound too hard."

Nadine looked away toward the human. "It will be harder than you think," she said, "for both of you."

# Chapter 5

Clarence stood in the entryway, waiting for the housekeeper to show him into Miss Florence's receiving room. From what he could tell, the house was a modest affair, which seemed at odds with what Miss Maddie had told him about the head mistress moving away after inheriting a large sum of money. Still, his eyes did not deceive him. If he had to guess, he would say the entire home had no more rooms than Miss Opal's suite, save for a small kitchen and a room for the housekeeper.

"She's ready to see you now," announced the slim young maid.

She led him through the door into an open area consisting of a combination sitting and dining room. Miss Florence sat primly in a comfortable looking stuffed chair upholstered in dark brown material. The tiny woman looked like an antique doll nestled in an over-sized child's chair, her simple cotton dress pressed into precise pleats. Her chair was positioned so she could sit and stare out the window at the expansive view of farmland and the country road that ran between her yard and the farm.

Next to her chair was another, larger version of hers, with a squat rectangular table that doubled as storage space between them. Clarence glanced toward the dining area, noticing an unremarkable wooden table. The entire decor reminded him of his own cottage in the Middle Districts.

"Good day, Master Carmichael. Please, join me for a cup of tea," the older woman said, motioning to the larger chair with a frail, blue-veined hand. She turned and nodded to the young woman standing near the door, then turned her attention back to him. "Ayda tells me you're writing a book. That sounds terribly fascinating."

"It can be," Clarence said, taking the proffered seat. "Most of the time, however, it's tedious amounts of research and long hours alone with my pen and paper."

"I think I could handle that," she said with a smile. "I spend most of my time alone nowadays anyway, except for when Ayda takes a little time from her chores to sit with me. Perhaps I should take up writing to fill my time."

"I bet you have some wonderful stories to tell of your time running the orphanage."

"That I do, young man."

Ayda entered carrying a large tray made from woven twigs with a Brown Betty Teapot and two sturdy looking mugs. She set them down and poured a dark brew into the cups. The scent of lavender and bergamot oil drifted up from the steam, making Clarence's smile widened.

"Lavender Earl Grey, I presume?" he asked.

"What good is having money if you can't indulge in a few luxuries from time to time?" Miss Florence chuckled. She thanked Ayda and handed him one of the mugs. He took a sip of the fragrant tea, closing his eyes as it slid down his throat. He opened his eyes to see his hostess's eyes twinkling. "I see you're a man who enjoys the small things as well."

"Good tea, madam, is never a small thing," he said with a smile. "Although I am a little surprised to see such modest surroundings for one who obviously delights in the finer things."

Florence set her mug back on the tray and looked out her window. "After seeing so many go without, I cannot bring myself to throw away wealth on frivolous objects that'll remain here on earth when I die." She turned a fierce gaze back on him. "I live simply so others may simply live."

"Living out the Beloved's command to store your treasure where thieves and rust cannot destroy it?"

"Something like that. I met a man once, when I was much younger, who had studied the Books of the One and the life of the Beloved. He said he liked the way our Beloved lived and what He taught, but that those of us who claim to be Followers of the One more often use His words as a tool for division than for bringing more healing and love into the world. At the time, I thought he was a fool, but, now that I am old and have nothing but time on my hands to stare at this view, waiting for death, I wonder if I was not the fool."

"Youth is a time of great foolishness for us all. I would imagine you saw a lot of foolish things from your charges over the years."

The old woman smiled again and sighed. "Yes, they certainly kept life entertaining."

"I would imagine so. That is actually what I came to see you about."

"Oh, yes, your book. Tell me again what it's about."

"I'm writing about how certain individuals are able to overcome seemingly insurmountable obstacles to become highly acclaimed citizens later in life. I was given to understand that you might have a few stories about some of your charges that would be good material."

"Let me think," Florence said, sipping her tea and cradling her mug in her thin hands. "There was one kit who seemed to have unimaginable bad fortune in the beginnings of her life. I believe she graduated at the top of her class at the King's Academy of Mages and went on to live a life any mother would have been proud of."

"Could you tell me about her?" Clarence placed his mug back on the tray, then reached into an inner pocket and brought out a notebook and charcoal stub. The woman's eyebrows raised and he smiled sheepishly. "Do you mind if I take notes? In the heat of creation I sometimes forget the details and need to go back to refresh my memory."

"The memory is always the first to go," she said and winked. "I don't mind at all."

"Thank you. Please, go on."

Florence took another sip of tea, then glanced out the window again. "It was such a long time ago, but I remember that day as if it happened this morning. It was raining. Fitting, I suppose, for what had gone on the day before. We'd all heard about the terrible murder. Jealousy, they said. How a human could be jealous of his partner's mate, I don't think I'll ever understand, but there it was.

"Anyway, it was raining when the king's man, a skinny yellow tom, brought them to me. Two little black scraps of fur huddle together on my porch. He said they had no other relatives, their father was dead and their mother had abandoned them. It was a fairly typical story for my charges. I didn't think too much about it until I found out later that they had witnessed their father's murder. Poor dears." Florence shook her head and fell silent. Clarence waited a moment, then cleared his throat. She glanced at him and smiled wanly before taking another sip of tea and continuing.

"After that, I wasn't at all surprised at how fiercely the little tom watched over his sister. It got them both in plenty of scrapes and earned him enough chores to make a grown man weep, but he never complained about it. The two were inseparable.

"When the news came to us that their mother's partner was going to trial, they begged me to let them go. I was against it, but the little tom was so convincing. He said they needed closure to move on. Such a grown up thing to consider at such a tender age. How could I refuse them?" She frowned at the view.

"I should have kept them at the orphanage, but I didn't. As if seeing their own father killed wasn't enough carnage for their little minds to hold, seeing his killer torn apart by a mob certainly would be, I think. The poor little she-cat was still shaking when they were returned to us. After that day, they were different. I sometimes caught her looking at her brother as if he were some kind of monster, yet his protectiveness of her never waned. If anything it grew. But not for her. I lost count of the number of times they had to be separated when they fought."

"Did you ever find out what they fought about?"

"They wouldn't say. Whatever it was, it kept them together and pulled them apart at the same time."

"Fascinating. So what happened to them?"

"They grew up, like all kits and children do," she said with a shrug, placing her mug on the tray. "Just before they were old enough to leave the orphanage and find their own way in the world, the king's man came looking for them. He had another, larger black tom with him at the time, a scrapping young thing. I remember thinking at the time that this cat could have been my little one's twin brother—both black as midnight with the same piercing green eyes, except…" she said, frowning again and turning to look at Clarence. "There was a marked difference in those gazes. The bigger tom watched everything with intent interest, yes, but it was as if he were looking for an opportunity to help someone. My little one, on the other hand…" she continued, wrapping her arms around her thin body, "it was like feeling the heat of a blast furnace on your face while leaping into a frozen lake—if that makes any sense."

"Why do you think that was?"

"I always attributed it to all the things he'd seen. I doubt the other tom had experienced such atrocities in his young life." Florence reached for her mug again and brought it to her lips. For a moment she looked confused, then shook her head and smiled.

"It seems someone drank all my tea," she said and chuckled. "May I refill yours as well?"

Clarence glanced at his half-full mug and shook his head. He glanced over his notes as she filled her mug from the Brown Betty.

"Shall I continue, or have I bored you to death yet?" she asked, the twinkle back in her eye.

"Please do. This is fascinating."

"Morbid, more like."

"Only if it doesn't have a happy ending," Clarence chided with a wink. "And you said before you began that this young she-cat managed to overcome her unhappy beginnings."

"Indeed I did. Now, where did I leave off?"

"The king's cat had brought in a twin to the brother and was looking for the siblings."

"Oh, yes. They asked to talk to the young tom in private, so I offered them my little office. I remember peeking down the hall from time to time to check on the little she-cat.

94

Every time I looked, she was either pacing in front of the door or sitting, staring at it. It was almost as if she were trying to will it to open."

"What happened when it did?"

"The king's cat informed me that he was taking the young tom with him on the king's business and that was the end of discussion. I remember the little she-cat throwing herself at her brother, refusing to let him leave."

"That seems rather odd, considering how they fought."

"Not really, Master Carmichael. They might have fought and she might not have always looked at him kindly, but they were still family—the only family they had."

"I suppose you're right. Please, go on."

"Well, he pulled her aside and said something. I don't know what he said, but she let him go after that. I remember watching them with her as they pulled away in the coach. The look on her face was so sad, as if she knew what was going to happen."

"What did happen?"

"A few weeks later, the big black tom came back with an official letter for her. Her brother was dead, killed while serving the crown. I'll never forget that wail," Florence said, shuddering. "It carried all the way through the building."

They sat silently, looking at the bright sunlit day. Clarence tried to imagine what the she-cat must have been feeling and failed. He glanced at Florence from the corner of his eye.

"That must have been terrible for both of you," he said in a low voice. She darted a glance at him, then looked back out the window.

"It was the most terrible day in my life. I can't imagine what she must have felt. I couldn't blame her for locking herself in her room after that."

"How long did she stay in there?"

"Days? Weeks? I'm not sure. It seemed like forever. I feared for her life, but even though I had a key to her room, I wouldn't use it. We each deal with death in our own way. This was hers and I couldn't bring myself to deny her that."

"But she did finally come out."

"Yes. One day she came strolling in to dinner with the rest of the orphans. I remember watching her gulp her food. I was worried she'd make herself sick after fasting so long, but she didn't. I checked on her later, asked her if she would be okay. I don't think I'll ever forget what she said."

"What was that?"

"She said, "Living isn't for the weak. My brother taught me that." When I asked her what she planned to do now, she said, "I plan on living.""

"A wise young she-cat."

"She was."

"You said earlier she went to the King's Academy of Mages, is that right?"

"Yes. I believe she was partnered with an extraordinary young mage who went on to find a cure for the plague."

Clarence reached a hand up to cover his smile. He stared at his notes again, letting it all sink in. He had one more question he needed to ask before he left.

"If it's not too much to ask, may I have the names of the brother and sister?"

"I'm afraid that information is sealed, Master Carmichael. I'm not allowed to tell you their names."

He tried not to grimace. "I understand. Well, I thank you for this amazing story and the superbly brewed tea," he said, replacing his notebook and charcoal in his pocket, then levering himself up from the chair. He reached a hand out to her and bent over her fragile hand. "I believe your inheritance is in good hands, madam. May you enjoy it for many long years."

Florence chuckled and blushed. "Oh, it's in good hands, alright, but not mine. I have a trustee that takes care of all that. I just sit here and thank the One for Great Aunt Esther."

"And who might that be?"

"She's the one who blessed me with all that money when she died. The funny thing is that I don't remember ever having a great aunt named Esther." She shrugged a shoulder and smiled up at him. "Like I said, though, the memory is the first thing to go."

"Well, then," said Clarence, bowing again, "may the One bless your trustee and hold your Great Aunt Esther in his hand in paradise."

Ayda showed him to the door. As he mounted his horse, he couldn't help glancing over his shoulder toward the big picture window at the frail little woman. She might not have been allowed to give him the names of her orphans, but he was positive he knew who the she-cat was. For a moment he felt as if his departed partner was sitting on his shoulder again. He expected a lump to form in his throat, but it didn't. Instead, his mind turned to her mysterious dead brother. He suspected the tom wasn't dead at all. In fact, he feared the black cat was very much alive. The next question he needed to answer was who was pretending to be Great Aunt Esther and why?

The labyrinth stretched across the expanse of the temple gardens, each of the circuits illuminated by wrought iron lanterns. Toby didn't remember seeing anything so enchanting and yet haunting at the same time.

He traced the circuitous path with his eyes, noting that the lantern's were dimmer near the center of the labyrinth. A chill snaked down his spine. He knew what—or rather who—was at the center.

Wrapped in a blanket of darkness, his partner lay on the wood chip covered ground like a foul-looking caterpillar in a cocoon. Toby turned when he heard soft paw steps behind him.

"Ready?" asked Nadine.

"As I'll ever be," he said. "What do I need to do?"

She gave him a small smile and blinked slowly. "This labyrinth is unlike most. Instead of a single path into the center, there are two."

"Why two?"

"It symbolizes the path of life. We may at times feel like we are alone, but, in truth, we are never alone. Whether the One chooses to make Himself known through the fellow travelers in our lives or remain invisible, He is always by our side. You may choose either path to enter."

"What about you? Are you going in there with me?"

Nadine stared at her paws. When she looked up, he could see pain in the crinkle of her eyes.

"I cannot help you with this. By your choices during

this time, you and Lorn will live…" she said, then looked toward the center of the labyrinth, "or die."

"Wait. You didn't tell me we could both die if I do this. I can't make that choice for him."

"You make that choice for him whether you try to save him or not."

"What do you mean?"

"I've said more than I should already."

Toby stared at his friend, lying unconscious on the cold ground. The darkness around him seemed deeper now than it had been. His limbs went numb as he realized what Nadine was saying. His ears flattened to his head as he turned a narrowed gaze on the she-cat.

"You mean he'll die if I don't do anything. What kind of choice is that?"

"The same kind of choice we all have in life: do nothing and watch creation fall into chaos or do what we can and stand justified in the Havens."

His whiskers clamped tight and his ears flattened. "Is there anything helpful you can tell me about what's going to happen?"

"I wish I could, but this path is of your own making. What you face is going to be created for you alone to know."

Toby watched the lanterns near Lorn flicker and die. He shuddered as he imagined what might await him inside the darkness.

"You must go now. The longer you wait, the closer to death your partner comes."

He glanced at Nadine, then lifted his chin and strode toward the nearest entrance to the labyrinth. He wasn't sure what to expect at the beginning, perhaps some forcefield that would push him back or a lightning bolt he'd have to dodge.

The last thing he figured would happen was nothing.

The night was quiet, even for late winter. Toby continued walking the circuit, passing lantern after lantern. As he made the fifth turn, he realized it wasn't just quiet. It was silent. He stopped next to a guttering lantern, perking his ears forward. The flame flickered and danced as if it were in a windstorm, but not a sound came from it.

Toby's tail fluffed to twice its normal size as he searched the open air around him. To his right was the seething dark mass, its fog-like substance rolling outward a whisker width with each passing moment. To his left he could see Nadine, sitting with her eyes closed at the labyrinth's edge.

He swiveled his ears backward and forward, hoping to hear something, anything. The absolute silence made his skin tingle. Giving up, he began walking the path again, then stopped. He lifted a paw, unsheathing his claws and staring at them. Surely he would hear it if he scraped them across one of the stepping stones.

He narrowed his eyes and slashed at the flesh-colored stone beneath his paw. The silence held. He raised his paw to try again, then hesitated. Something dark was oozing out of the stone.

Toby stepped back and watched, eyes widening as the viscous fluid continued to flow out of the gashes he'd made. A wet metallic smell flooded his nose and he gagged.

Blood poured from the stone, forcing him back step by step. Toby mewled. He glanced behind him. The path was clear. He could retreat. A cry rose from the stream of red reaching for his paws, making the fur along his spine raise.

"You did this to me," it wailed. "I was enslaved and you treated me the same as my captors."

"No," Toby said, shaking his head and scooting away

from the oncoming flood. "I had no choice. I had to. My cover would have been blown."

"I was just a child. What did I do to deserve this from you?"

"Nothing," Toby cried.

He squeezed his eyes closed and sunk to the ground. The face of the young girl at the temple school he'd slashed across the back as she lay prone on the floor flashed into his mind. She'd been just one more puppet there to all the other cats. They thought nothing of punishing her as the criss-crossed scars across her back attested.

She expected to be punished, but his stomach still clenched when he remembered leaving his own five bloody marks on top of the others. It had been the choice between hurting her or risking discovery and probably death for both himself and Lorn. *It still doesn't make it right.*

"You deserved to be laughing and playing with other girls your age, not serving as some cat's whipping girl," he said.

He let the blood seep into his fur. He'd told her to go afterward, but that seemed hardly enough. He'd given Lorn a set of claw marks later, which had caused him to tear his shirt to use as a bandage. He'd been punished for that by the overseer, though it had been Toby's fault. He mewled again.

"I'm sorry," he whispered.

The smell of blood disappeared and the wailing ceased. Toby lifted his head and sniffed. The air was crisp and cold, not even the slightest trace of metal in it. He opened his eyes a slit and stared at the pale stepping stone. It shimmered in the lantern light. Toby stood and turned in a circle, looking for any clue as to what had happened. Everything looked just like it had when he had stopped at this turn in the labyrinth.

His tail jerked as a shiver ran down the length of his body.

That had been the least of his recent failings. What would happen when he came face to face with his darker nightmares? Would saying he was sorry be all it took to make them disappear? He doubted it.

David strode down the corridor on his way to see Gillespie, wishing he had Aaron's ability to sweet talk a hummingbird into standing still. He had no idea how he was going to find out if the guardian supervisor was somehow involved in placing the sleepy young man at the servants' entrance, let alone if he was involved in drugging him.Whatever happened, though, he had every intention of getting that information, even if it meant he had to beat it out of the little blob.

He rounded the corner to Gillespie's office and stepped back quickly. Councilman Damon had the man cornered against his closed door. David was sure they hadn't seen him. He glanced down the hall he'd just come from, making sure no one was going to question what he was doing, then leaned closer to the corner to eavesdrop.

"If this concerns our master, then this concerns you," Damon said.

"Pest control is not my job," Gillespie said.

"It is if he says it is."

"What do you expect me to do? I was barely able to

drug Perleski and have him assigned to the prince's birthday gala. I can't just go arrest some clerk because she's going through some old files. That's their job."

"We don't care how you do it, just get it done."

There was the sound of heavy footsteps coming his direction. David stepped back a couple paces to look like he was just on his way. There was the sound of a door opening and the footsteps paused.

"By the way," Damon said, "Master Shyam asks you to give his best to your wife."

David frowned. *Why would Damon's partner care about Gillespie's wife?* As far as he knew, they'd never had any dealings beyond typical High Council business that intersected with the Office of Kingdom Guardianship. For that matter, what was Damon talking about? Why arrest a clerk for going through old files? Was Master Shyam the one deleting Adele's brother's existence? If so, then why? More questions rolled through his mind as he tried to pull puzzle pieces together from the information they already had.

"Good day, Guardian," said the councilman as he rounded the corner. David looked up to see the man raise an eyebrow. "You look rather lost."

"Hmm?" David said, blinking his thoughts back to the present. "Oh. No. I was just on my way to see Guardian Gillespie about some assignment details I needed. Forgot my list of names, so I was trying to remember them before I got there."

"I can see where that might be distracting," Damon said.

David smiled and nodded, then moved to pass by. The councilman put out a hand to stop him. He looked at the doughy hand, then up into the man's pudgy face.

"I don't think Guardian Gillespie can see you right now. He seemed to be feeling rather ill when I left him. I think he was just on his way home."

"Oh. That's too bad." David shrugged and said, "I guess my matter can wait. Thanks for the tip."

"My pleasure."

Councilman Damon's smile didn't meet his eyes. They both stood for a moment longer. David wondered what the rotund man would do if he decided to try Gillespie's door anyway. Instead he turned back the way he'd come, feeling the councilman's gaze on his back until he rounded the corner for the stairs.

Toby's ears still felt numb from facing the little frozen girl and his tail burned from being singed in the temple school fire again. His paws dragged the ground as he approached the entrance to the center of the labyrinth. He stared into the darkness, waiting for the next nightmare to appear.

A lump the size of his partner's fist lodged itself in his throat as a sleek black feline strolled into view.

"My son," Adele spit.

She stared at him with narrowed yellow eyes. Her ears were swiveled back, her whiskers clamped tight. It was a look he'd received so many times growing up he wasn't certain his mother could look at him any other way. Even so, the sight tore at him.

"Mother, I—"

"I don't want to hear your excuses. You failed, Toby. You failed and you've tried to blame everyone but yourself for it."

"No, I—"

"What would your father say if he were here?"

Toby stared down at his paws. *If he were here…. I'd give anything to have either of you here right now.* He tried to swallow. She was right. He'd failed them both.

There was nothing he could say or do to make up for not being at the cottage to save her from Master Natsumi's cross bolt. He couldn't take back all the problems he'd caused by digging into his father's last mission. His mother's death and Lorn's captivity were both his fault. He'd come here to save his partner and he was about to fail again.

Whatever the black tom had done to Lorn might kill his best friend if he didn't get past this vision of his mother. He looked up at the black queen through blurry eyes.

"I have failed, mother. I didn't listen to your warnings and now you're dead and my best friend is lying in there dying," he said, nodding toward the darkness behind her. "I turned my back on family and friends trying to be someone I'm not."

"And who are you now?"

"No one I want to be," he whispered, looking back down at his paws. The silence stretched between them until he glanced back up at her.

"Well?" she asked.

He choked down a bitter laugh. Even in this nightmare form, his mother continued to teach him as if he were preparing for orientation week at the King's Academy of Mages. It made the hackles on his neck raise.

"I don't know who I am. Maybe I *am* just a failure who'll never live up to your ideals, but I know one thing, I need to save my friend and I won't let you stop me."

"Insolent, kit," Adele hissed.

She flew at him, batting his head between armored paws. Toby twisted to the side and raised onto his hind legs, claws unsheathed to return blows. He stared down at his mother, suddenly seeing the arrow sticking out of her chest, and froze. In an instant she toppled him, burying her fangs in his shoulder and pummeling his stomach with her hind claws, the arrow disappearing as if it had never been. With a wrench that tore his fur, he twisted away, putting a full cat length between them. He stared at the snarling black queen, remembering the fierce love she'd shown him since his father had disappeared, love he'd misinterpreted as disappointment in him. His heart clenched.

"I love you, Mother," he said, panting, "but I won't fight you."

"Then you deserve a beating. Only cowards back down."

Toby shook his head. "I'm not backing down. I've won. I'm putting all these nightmares behind me, including you. I know there was nothing I could do to stop what happened to you or any of the others."

"You didn't even try."

"I *am* trying. I'm going after the one responsible for everything."

"And who might that be? Just who do you think began this war you're going to fail to stop?"

The queen glared at him, her fur bristling. Toby flattened his ears to half-mast.

"You know who. It's that black beast who has my

partner trapped in there," he said, nodding at the dark fog creeping toward them.

"Do you know that for certain? Are you so sure you won't be meeting yourself in there?"

Toby hesitated, glancing behind the black queen. Shaking his head, he said, "No, I'm not sure who I'll meet in there, but I know I have to try to save Lorn."

Adele shifted back and forth, her tail lashing behind her. With each passing moment the dark fog crept closer, paw length by paw length. Toby moved to the right, attempting to move past his mother. She growled and leaped in front of him. He moved to the left only to have her block his escape again.

"Let me pass," he demanded.

She growled and lowered herself closer to the ground. "Never."

She leaped at him, fangs and claws bared. Toby caught her chest on his front paws and let her momentum carry her over him as he rolled onto his back. She disappeared before her paws touched the ground. He clamped a mewl behind his teeth. He knew it was only a nightmare copy of his real mother, but it made his heart ache with the loss again.

Toby closed his eyes, pushing the sorrow aside. He turned around, opening his eyes to stare into the wall of darkness. It looked as solid as obsidian. Taking a deep breath, he walked toward it, half-expecting to smack his nose against an impenetrable force.

Instead of a solid shield, he encountered something that felt more like thick mud. The darkness oozed over his fur, making him instinctively shake his paws as if he could dislodge the feeling from his pads. His ears flattened to his head and his lips lifted over his fangs in distaste. *What is this stuff?*

*It is the evil that lurks within your partner*, said a voice from the darkness.

Toby hunkered down, unsheathing his claws and staring around himself, wide-eyed.

"Who are you?"

A she-cat with glowing blue fur paced toward him. The edges of her image shifted and eddied like fog. Toby blinked.

"Forget that," he murmured, "What are you?"

*I am Barukh Sh'Toole, the healer of spirit and soul. I am the Huntress that stalks the night*, she said, *I am your friend.*

"Nadine? But you said you couldn't come in here with me."

*And that is so. I could not walk the labyrinth with you, nor can I be here with you except in spirit form.*

"I take it that's why you look so different."

The spirit cat rippled and Toby got the impression she chuckled.

*Not so different. If you had my gift you would see that we all look like this.*

Toby cocked his head, squinting at her bright blue form. Try as he might, he couldn't see the black and white she-cat in the blue feline. Yet it somehow felt like her. He wondered what he looked like to her.

*As much as I would like to show you,* she said, *We have more pressing matters to attend to.*

As she stepped aside, Toby saw his partner lying in a fetal position. Standing over him was a man in black leathers, his eyes glowing bright green. Toby squinted at the dark figure. The man had the same brown hair and beard as Lorn. His appearance was nearly identical right down to the man's slight build and average height. It was the same, at least, until he smiled. The feline grin was unmistakable.

"You," Toby snarled.

He launched himself at the dark man, going through his body as if he'd jumped through smoke. His claws scraped across the clearing, scattering woods chips until he smacked against a mage shield on the other side. An evil chuckle rolled through the air.

"You still have much to learn, kit."

Toby spun around and glared at the cat-man. "Stay solid for a moment and we'll see who learns something."

"You have your mother's spirit. I always admired her for her spunk."

"What do you know about my mother?"

"She never told you about me, did she?"

Toby stalked around the man, looking for an opening. From the corner of his eye he saw the blue she-cat watching them. His neck fur bristled. What was she waiting for? The man glanced at her then back at Toby.

"You'll get no help from that one."

"I don't need any help. I can take you down just fine by myself."

"And there is your father's blind arrogance. I never understood what your mother saw in him."

"I suppose you think she should have chosen you as her mate."

"Not at all, though someone like me would have been a better choice than the fool she chose."

Toby hissed and raced past the man, slashing at his leg with an armored paw. The blow was as effective as his first attack. He turned and snarled at Nadine.

"Why are you here if you're not going to do anything?"

"Tsk, tsk. I thought you said you didn't need her help."

"I don't."

Nadine's glowing spirit vanished. Toby whipped around, searching for her, his eyes going to the dark man's widening grin.

"It seems she took you at your word. She's abandoned you."

Toby's stomach clenched. He glanced down at his partner's helpless body. The man's chest rose and fell in shallow gasps.

"There won't be any help from there, either."

He looked back up at Dark Lorn, wishing he could slash the grin from the man's face.

"You see, there is nothing standing between you and your death now. It would be nothing to me to reach out and snuff your tiny spirit at this very moment."

"So what's stopping you?"

The man frowned and shrugged. "Curiosity? Hope? Call it what you will, but I'm willing to wait until I know the answer to my burning question."

"And what question is that?"

"Whose blood runs through your body?"

Toby's brow wrinkled in confusion. "You know who my parents are. What more do you want?"

Dark Lorn squatted down, piercing him with his glowing green eyes. Toby shivered at the fierce gaze. He felt as if he had jumped into a lake of burning ice.

"I want to know who you are," the man said.

He turned his piercing gaze onto Lorn and stretched out his hand. Lorn trembled and moaned. Toby moved to stop him, but Dark Lorn turned his freezing green eyes on him again.

"What is he to you?" he whispered. "He is the human who tried to kill you. He is the man who betrayed your mission to his own kind. It was his weakness that caused your failure to find your father at the temple school."

Toby glanced at his friend. The man's seizure was increasing in intensity. Toby's thoughts raced back to the riot at the school. Why would the human children have suddenly risen up against their masters unless they had been told about being used as experiments? Toby looked back at the sinister figure holding his hand over his doppelganger.

"Yes," Dark Lorn hissed, nodding.

"Why?"

"Why else? He is foolish and greedy. He only cared for the humans. He didn't want to save your father."

A choking gurgle brought Toby's wide-eyed gaze back to his partner. The man's face was paling, his eyes rolling back. He shut his eyes and swung his head away, his friend's struggles growing fainter with each moment. Memories rolled through his mind, times when the two of them had argued.

He remembered their first fight, clawing and cursing at each other in their room at the academy. It had been so much more honest than their last argument, hiding in a broom closet at the temple school. They'd left so much unsaid the last time. They both had their reasons for wanting the mission to end. Lorn wanted the children free. Toby wanted to find the monster holding his father captive. In the end, Lorn had gotten what he wanted, but Toby was still searching.

He could hear the blood pounding in his ears as he thought about the unfairness of it. Now he knew why Lorn had gotten his way. He'd told the students what they'd agreed they wouldn't. He'd given them the reason to revolt even though they both had agreed on a plan to overturn the temple cats' rule as quietly as possible.

Images of Lorn saying the incantation to fry him where he stood exploded in his mind. He could almost feel the blazing fire around him, searing his skin through his fur. Then the skinny old librarian cat was there, shouting a counter spell, and Lorn collapsed.

What was it the old cat had said later when he gave him the leather book? Toby squeezed his eyes tighter, trying to call the words to mind. It was just after Lorn had promised to help him keep looking for his father. He shook his head until his ears popped.

Another image burst into his mind of Master O'dorn, his mother's partner, coaching him on recalling important information. He'd been trying to remember what he'd smelled just before he batted the plague remedy away from his sick mother. Relax and let it come.

Toby drew in a deep breath and exhaled, thrusting the sound of Lorn's faint wheezing out of his mind.

*This will help you figure out what's the truth, what's important and what needs to be buried in the grave. Keep it safe and it will guide you where you need to go.*

He hadn't read the book, hadn't even opened it. What was in it that was so important? What did the old cat know about his parents? What did this diabolical feline know about them? And what about his partner? Was there anything in there that could have helped him figure out what to do now?

Not that it mattered. There was no time to go back and read it. His friend continued to struggle breathing, the fiend choking him just enough to torture him, but not enough to kill him.

Toby took another deep breath and exhaled. He focused on the last argument he'd had with Lorn. His friend wanted to reveal the experimentation to the children at the school and Toby had talked him out of it. The man's words floated back into his memory.

*"We'll do it your way," Lorn had said. "But if it were me being experimented on, I'd hope you'd have the guts to tell me."*

Lorn had been experimented on. That's what the headaches were about. That's why he had followed him and tried to kill him. They thought they'd broken the thing that held him mentally captive to the black beast, but he was still being controlled. That's what this was, a psychic link.

Toby opened his eyes and stared at Dark Lorn. The man in the black leathers leered at him, his toothy grin and narrowed eyes so unlike Toby's friend that it was hard for him to believe he had considered them identical. Memories flooded into his mind of Lorn volunteering to take the heat along with him when they began investigating Victor's disappearance and later when they stumbled on the information that Victor might still be held captive in the New Life Temple. This doppelganger was nothing like his friend.

**Do you understand now?** Nadine's voice floated through his mind.

He nodded, letting Dark Lorn think he was agreeing to Lorn's demise. Toby knew Nadine was standing just behind the man, but he didn't drop eye contact with the dark human. The man's evil grin widened as he turned his full attention back to killing Toby's partner. In a flash, Nadine's glowing blue claws slashed through Dark Lorn's outstretched hand.

**Hold tight to Lorn**, she yowled.

Toby leaped onto Lorn's shoulder and dug his claws into his cloak. Wind whipped around his ears, howling and spinning until he believed they'd all be ripped apart.

"Traitor," Dark Lorn screamed.

He squeezed his eyes shut and flattened his ears to his head, but the screaming echoed inside his mind. Pain shot through Toby's head, growing until it filled his entire body with a million knives. He heard the sound of cloth ripping and felt himself sliding down Lorn's body. He dug his claws in harder, determined to stay with his friend whether they came out of the storm alive or dead.

Victor's eyes fluttered open. Beyond the wire mesh, K'Dash paced, his tail lashing.

"Something bothering you?" Victor asked, whiskers inching apart in amusement.

K'Dash spun as if someone had stung his haunch with a stone, then licked his shoulder. When he looked back at Victor, he had recomposed his expression into smug satisfaction.

"Your son is very resourceful. It seems he's found an ally to help him save his human pet."

"Tossed you out, did he?"

K'Dash's tail jerked. He ducked his head to lick his ruff. His eyes were narrowed when he turned his attention back to Victor.

"Hardly," he said. "If it weren't for his little she-cat

friend I have no doubt your son would have happily let me end his pet's miserable life for him."

"Wishful thinking, Adair."

The black tom sighed and pulled at his claw sheaths. "Why do you insist on using that name? That tom no longer exists. The sooner you accept that, the sooner you can end this cycle of pain and resuscitation."

"You know why," Victor said, chuckling. "It nettles you."

"It serves as a reminder of how foolish I once was. That is all."

"We've all been foolish."

The two black toms stared at each other in silence. Victor found himself thinking about what Adair might have been like if he'd been able to extract him earlier in their mission. He shook his head. The black tom might not have become so familiar with the more subtle forms of torture, but he doubted his life would have been much different. *Water under the bridge.*

"Your thoughts are meandering again, my friend."

"Stay out of my thoughts, Adair."

K'Dash flicked his tail and yawned. "I don't need to rummage through your mind. You have a face a kit could read."

"That so? Then what am I thinking now?" Victor asked, glaring at the black tom. K'Dash chuckled.

"Do you know why I keep you around?"

"I have information you want."

"Oh I got all that I needed long ago. No, I keep you around because you amuse me," the massive tom said, swiping a large paw over an ear. He narrowed his eyes and smiled. "That and I believe you'll be useful very soon."

"You know I won't cooperate with whatever scheme you're planning."

"I never expected you to." K'Dash's smile widened. "By the way, how's your leg? I understand that stitches can be quite bothersome."

He turned to wash his shoulder. Victor looked down at the gash K'Dash's surgeon had sewn up. At least, he assumed someone other than the black tom had put him back together again. No one else had been around when K'Dash had done his work, but it wasn't the black tom's style to close up after "surgery." Regardless, he was glad the pain had eased, even if the healing itch had started.

"Your cat does good work. Doubt there'll even be a scar."

"That is good to hear. I would hate for our final appointment to be delayed because you're feeling unwell."

"What appointment might that be?"

"All in good time. First, I must send an invitation to our friend in the Department of Artificers."

"What friend?"

"Surely you remember your mate's partner has a new playmate?"

"I don't know what you're talking about."

"Oh that's right. You don't know who your old housemate's been playing with recently. I sometimes forget that you don't get out much these days," K'Dash said with widened eyes. He flattened his ears and narrowed his eyes to slits, his whiskers splaying as he leaned forward. "I have a special guest I plan to bring here to help me finish one of my toys. You see I need it to be functional by Resurrection Day so I can share it with the rest of the good little boys and girls of the world."

"Why would he help you?"

"Why because I'll make him an offer he can't refuse, of course. Besides," K'Dash said, ears perking up as he sat up straight, "he's already been working on a similar project. All I need him to do is tweak the contraption I already have."

"If he's like Master O'dorn, there's nothing you can offer him to make him do what you want."

The black tom stood and walked toward the door, his tail straight as a flag pole. He twitched his tail to open the door and looked back at Victor with a smile.

"We shall see."

# Chapter 6

"Are you sure you're up to this?" asked Toby, shifting from paw to paw as he watched his partner shake his limbs loose.

"Are you kidding me? I've been cooped up in my brain for weeks. I'm ready to get back into my body for a while. Besides, I need the practice."

"That's true enough. I could feel you trying to break through the link. Made my skin itch."

Lorn gave him a lopsided smile. "I never thought I'd need to know how to do that."

"Neither did I, but now we know better, so defend yourself."

Toby threw a fireball at Lorn, who cartwheeled out of the way.

"You're getting predictable," Lorn said, placing his inner wrists together and shooting a stream of water toward him.

Toby twitched his tail, forming a mage wall in front of himself just before the water hit. Sheets of liquid cascaded down, blurring the human's form. Toby concentrated on the edges of his shield pivoting his ears downward and forcing the wall to bend toward him until it almost formed a complete ball. He could feel the water buffeting the shield, trying to break his will by sheer volume. He smiled. Lorn would think the shield was weakening. When the shield was less than a whisker length from his nose, he snapped his ears up. The wall of water catapulted backward.

Lorn shouted. A mage bubble sprung up from the floor around him. Toby dropped his shield and grinned. His partner had trapped himself in his shield before he'd cut off his water flow. He now stood waist deep in freezing water.

"How's that for predictable?"

His partner shook the water from his hair and squinted at him through the bubble. He spun his hand in a circle, making the water spin around the shield and blocking Toby's view. He raised his eye whiskers in surprise. *Water vortex? That's rather simplistic.* A moment later the bubble burst open. Toby threw his wall up to deflect the expected spray. It splashed against his shield, continuing to make his partner no more than a blurry image.

He readied another spell. In the next moment his fur was soaked and clinging to him as a water whip came round behind him, dumping a bucket of liquid onto him. The sudden deluge shattered his concentration and his shield dropped. Lorn dropped his arm from where it was raised over his head, sweeping down to the floor and back up again. Toby's fur froze solid in the cold wind, sticking out at odd angles and making his teeth chatter. Lorn grinned.

"As I said, predictable. You always leave your rear unprotected. Someday I won't be there to watch your backside," his partner said, shaking more water from his hair.

Heat rose in Toby's skin. He narrowed his eyes and lashed his tail. Lorn hadn't been there while he traveled toward Transformation Mountain. In fact, it had been Lorn who had hunted him during his journey. And whose fault was that? Failures. Everything he padded through became a big stinking dung pile, but he wasn't the only one to blame. *Predictable?* A growl rumbled quietly in his chest. He might use the same spell more than once, but at least he had control over them. Lorn couldn't even be counted on for that. He needed a partner who could hold his own against magic. He thought back to finding Lorn facing off against Father Hanif. The head temple cat didn't even have magic, but Lorn's own inability to concentrate on complicated spells when he was under stress had made it impossible for the man to do anything more than lob fireballs at the cat. He'd needed Toby's help to even begin a net spell.

"LIHF ten THRO bawk," Toby growled. Lorn's feet were yanked out from under him by an invisible force and he was thrown toward the far wall.

"Cu SHIN," Lorn shouted. He slammed against a pillow of air and bounced off.

"Slee PAW coo WILL." Toby lashed his tail. Thin black quills shot from its tip, rushing with deadly force toward Lorn.

"Flo RAH."

The quills drifted to the ground, changed into white petals. Toby jumped, twisting in the air and kicking out with his hind feet as he shouted another spell. Spiked metal balls bounced off Lorn's hastily erected shield and embedded themselves into the wall. Toby followed with a volley of fireballs and energy shards. The shield hummed as the objects pummeled it.

"Enough," Lorn shouted.

Toby lashed his tail again, sending another volley of quills toward the human's mage bubble. Lorn's shield vibrated for a moment, then collapsed. The man slid to the floor, holding his hands up in warding. Toby rushed him, screeching a battle cry. He leaped, claws unsheathed—and slammed into an invisible wall. His ears rang and the world spun as tears welled up in his eyes. Lorn slowly put his hands down. He stared at his friend, panting and holding his side.

"What got into you?" he asked, "You've never taken battle practice that seriously before. You could have killed me."

Toby turned to nip at his flank, then glared at Lorn. "We need to be ready."

"I know that, but this was something more than getting ready to you. Was it something I said?"

"I just want to be prepared."

"Listen, Toby, I know you better than that. What's eating you?"

Toby growled and paced the floor. "I just—," he started. He sighed and turned to face his friend. "You almost died in that labyrinth. I almost let him kill you and when you said you might not be there to watch my back..."

Lorn scooted forward, placing a gentle hand on Toby's back. "Almost isn't the same as letting it happen. You've lost your way, buddy. You need some help, that's all."

"You can't help me."

"No, I can't," Lorn said, shaking his head, "but maybe Nadine can. She's a healer. Maybe she knows what to do."

Toby licked his ruff, then stared at his paws. When he looked into his friend's face, he saw the man's eyes crinkle at the edges and the deep furrows between his brows. Lorn was worried.

"Will it make you feel better if I talk to her?"

Lorn smiled and nodded. Toby cocked his head to the side and returned the smile. "You could talk a pheasant into the oven, you know that, don't you?"

122

"That's why we're partners. You find the trouble and I fix it."

"Sure," Toby said with a snort, "And pigeons don't poop on statues, either."

His partner gave him a friendly shove. Toby padded to the door, then turned to watch for a moment as Lorn began cleaning up their mess. The man's shadow fell across the far wall, reminding him of Nadine's words and he wondered. If Lorn had darkness within him, how much more darkness was there in himself?

Dora heard the window slide open at the front of the office. She perked her ears up, wondering who would be coming to the clerks department. They seldom had requests made in person. Director Warrin made sure of that with his rules of filling out forms in triplicate and then reviewing them himself.

"Guardian Gillespie, what can I do for you?" asked Warrin.

The man's lilting voice made Dora's fur crawl. He was never that polite to anyone. She peered around the shelves to see who he was talking to. The other man wore the black and gold robes of the OKG, which hung on him like a sheet on a skeleton, making her wonder how much weight he'd recently lost.

"I came to see if you had heard anything from our

friends on the High Council," Gillespie said.

"No, not recently. Is there something I need to be aware of?"

"One of them visited me the other day. Told me there's been some trouble with your staff and that I should look into it. You wouldn't know anything about that, would you?"

"My staff? What trouble?"

"Seems someone has been accessing records they shouldn't be."

"I've had no requests for *his* records."

"Well, *he* says someone is digging where they shouldn't and he's holding me responsible, which means," Gillespie said, leaning forward and pushing a finger into Warrin's chest, "I'm holding *you* responsible. Get my drift?"

"I assure you, everything here is under control."

"So there isn't anyone on your staff going through ancient history?"

"No, sir. I mean, yes, sir. I mean—"

"Well, which is it? Yes or no?"

Warrin glanced behind him. Dora ducked back behind the shelves, her ears swiveled to catch every word. The supervisor cleared his throat and continued in a higher pitched voice.

"I mean I had two clerks who were organizing the back shelves a while back, but I set them to rights as soon as I found them back there."

"That's good."

"You don't suppose he wants us to—you know?" Warrin asked.

"He didn't say so," Gillespie said. Warrin sighed.

"Best not to do anything yet," the guardian continued. "Remember what happened to Master Natsumi when she tried to anticipate his orders."

"You don't think he'd..." Dora heard the rustle of cloth and then Warrin whispered, "kill us, do you?"

"Just keep your mind on the business at hand and we won't have to worry about that."

"I pray you're right."

"Now, so it doesn't seem odd that I'm here, why don't you give me a stack of those request forms and..."

Dora stopped listening. She bellied toward the door to the back filing room, keeping her paw steps quiet as she fled. She swiveled her ears backward, listening for the men's voices, before twitching her tail to open the door just wide enough to squeeze through. It closed behind her with a quiet click.

She raced through toward the rear of the room, stirring up clouds of dust the further back she ran. Alie stood at a shelving unit, hand poised to shift a box back into place. She stared wide-eyed at Dora.

"What's wrong?"

"We've been discovered," Dora said.

Alie shoved the box back on the shelf and stooped down to look her in the eye.

"By whom?"

"Warrin was talking to a guardian named Gillespie. They're both in league with him."

"How do you know?"

"I overheard them talking. The guardian said that Warrin needs to keep better control of his staff or they'd both be held responsible and from the way he said it, I think he meant they'd be getting their walking papers, if you know what I mean."

"How much time do we have?"

"My guess would be just until they're done talking."

"That's not a lot of time. Any idea what he's supposed to do with us?"

"Gillespie said Warrin isn't supposed to kill us. In fact, he made sure he understood what might happen if he jumped ahead of his master's orders. Said they'd end up like Master Natsumi."

Alie bit her lower lip and looked toward the front of the room. "Good thing Warrin values his skin." She turned back to Dora. "We've got twelve boxes of stuff and no time to get it out. Any suggestions?"

"I say we play dumb. Come back tonight and grab what we have, then disappear."

"Good plan. We'll need someplace to go until we can contact Toby," Alie said. "Any ideas where he might be?"

"Last I heard he and Lorn were involved in that raid on the New Life Temple and School. He's gone off on his own since then."

Alie threw her hands up and let them fall, slapping against her thighs. "That's great. Well, there's no help for it now. We'll deal with that problem when we have more time. Where could we stay in the meantime?"

"Didn't Toby have a friend who left the academy to become a Brother?"

"Yes," Alie said, her eyes lighting up. "I remember seeing his records back here somewhere."

She rose and strode toward another shelf. The woman stared up at the numerous boxes, running a finger over their labels. She pulled one down and rifled through the files inside.

"Here it is," she said, lifting the file up and smiling. "Terence was originally under the sponsorship of Gravin Fedelis Arturo and his partner Chivato until the two were arrested for creating and releasing the plague. After that, he left the King's Academy of Mages Loner Program to become a Brother Cat at a small temple in the Outer Reaches. I have the address right here."

"Great. Is that in one of our boxes?"

Alie grinned and winked at Dora. "Not yet."

They looked up as they heard the door open. Alie stuffed the file back in the box and re-shelved it. Together they hurried toward the front of the filing room, using a side aisle.

"Alie, Dora, break's over. Get back to work," Warrin called.

Dora padded out from behind a shelving unit near the front of the room.

"We're already working, sir," she said.

"Was there something you needed us to do?" asked Alie, poking her head around another shelf further away. The supervisor spun around and glared at them.

"I have a stack of files that need to be copied and then taken to the Merchant Guild Liaison's office today. Follow me. They're in the front room."

Warrin strode past them to the door. Dora glanced at Alie, her ear twitching as she fought to keep her fur flat. Alie nodded and they followed the man back to the front filing room.

David made his way through the maze of halls into the

older section of the Hall of Records. He wondered how many
people were lost down here. By the time he got to the third
dead-end hallway, he was ready to give up. They needed that
mole, but finding their would-be informants down here was
seeming more impossible by the moment. He turned around
to retrace his steps and found a window tucked into the wall
behind him. The frosted glass was lit from the other side.

David frowned as he approached the window. He
lifted the tiny bell and shook it. The window slammed open,
and a skinny man with glasses perched on the edge of his
nose glared at him. He looked pointedly at the bell in David's
hand. David set it down on the window's edge.

He tried to imagine what Aaron would do in a
situation like this. The wildcat was a natural when dealing
with humans and cats, never seeming to have to think about
how to react in any awkward situation. He'd smile and say
something witty, which would make the other person laugh.
David tried smiling at the grumpy clerk. The clerk's brows
lowered further and he narrowed his eyes.

"Yes?" he said sharply.

"I need some information," David said, forgoing the
niceties he was sure Aaron would use.

The man looked him up and down, his nose wrinkling.
"You're a guardian."

"Yeah." *So what?*

The clerk lifted his nose and he harrumphed. "You
should know the protocols for information requisition from
the stacks."

David decided to give Aaron's way one more try. His
partner always said it was easier to catch flies with honey than
with vinegar. The One knew David was a vinegar type of guy
and look where it got him—virtually nowhere.

"Guess I never got around to reading the protocol manual, though I gotta say it makes a great door stop," he said, leaning on his elbow on the window ledge. The clerk glared at his elbow, then back up at David. He sighed inwardly as he removed his elbow from the ledge. He hoped he could get what he needed quickly, or he might get his chance to interview the young guardian in his cell from an adjoining one.

"So what do I need to do?"

The clerk disappeared from the window, slamming it shut. David stood and blinked at the closed frosted glass. He was reaching for the bell when the window banged open again. He wondered if the glass had to be replaced very often. The man dropped a stack of papers on the ledge with a thunk.

"Fill these out in triplicate, then message them down to this office. When we receive them, we'll review your request."

"What happens then?"

"The documents you requested will be messaged to your office, pending approval, of course."

"Of course," David murmured, grimacing at the large stack of papers. He looked back at the man's angular face and considered planting his fist in his frown. "How long does that usually take?"

"A week to ten days, depending on the amount of research required."

"And what if I just want to speak to one of your assistants?"

"That is against protocol."

The window slammed shut, forcing the stack of papers to flutter to the floor. *So much for finding the mole. I doubt it's that guy. He's a better gate keeper than anyone I've met save the captain.* He stared down at the pile of papers strewn across the floor and wondered what good it would do to fill them out.

He turned to walk back through the maze of corridors to his office, leaving the papers where they'd fallen, when an idea struck. He might not be able to get past the head clerk, but perhaps Aaron could. He looked back at the multitude of forms on the floor. If his partner came back with the paperwork, he might be able to find out more about who the other clerks were and who was most likely to be their future informant.

David stooped down and began picking up the pieces of paper, stacking them in his arms. He grimaced again at the thought of filling them out in triplicate. *I just hope it's worth it.*

"Master Sylvester," someone shouted from below. Sylvester lifted his closer-up eyes from his face and peered down from the top of the stairs. He groaned as he recognized the gaunt man rubbing his hands together. *Gillespie. What the devil does he want?*

"Be right down," he called.

He took his time putting his gadgetry and tools away, grinning to himself as he imagined the guardian's growing agitation. When everything was put into precise order, he grabbed his crutches and hobbled down the stairs placing first the crutches on the step, then his feet. Truth was, he could alternate crutches and feet as he descended, but where would the fun be in that?

"What can I do for you, Guardian Gillespie?"

Sylvester couldn't help wondering why the man's wife didn't bother taking in his robe since he'd lost the weight. Not that the skeletal look did much for Gillespie's appearance, let alone his irritating personality. Sylvester doubted hemming the man's robes would aid his looks at all. Gillespie glanced around the room, his eyes flitting over the light beam machine as he ran his fingers through his hair.

"I've been ordered to confiscate your light making contraption."

"On whose authority?" Slyvester demanded, glaring at the hollow-eyed man.

Gillespie reached into an inner pocket of his robe and handed him a piece of rolled parchment. He grabbed it, broke the seal and scanned the official looking document. His frown deepened when he read the signature at the bottom.

"How the blazes did you get the king to sign this drivel?"

"The king's a busy man," said a deep voice behind the guardian.

Sylvester peered around Gillespie, seeing a massive black tom pacing toward him. The paper in his hand shook as he met the tom's piercing green gaze. The hair on his neck rose.

"What are you doing here?"

"I've come to see that the king's interests are served."

"You mean your interests, don't you, Shyam?" he asked, hobbling back a step until his thighs rested against one of his work tables. He rested a hand on the table edge.

"You will soon see that they are one and the same," the tom said. When he glanced at Gillespie, Sylvester slid his hand closer to the whirl-i-gig remote. K'Dash turned his piercing gaze back on him.

"Be sure you handle the item with care," the tom said.

"Yes, sir."

As the guardian reached toward the gadget, Sylvester grabbed the remote and hit the attack button. The whirl-i-gig dove at Gillespie, then circled in the air and dove toward K'Dash, who scurried under a workbench. The guardian threw himself to his knees, aiming energy darts at the flying gadget. The darts exploded inches behind the machine, making Sylvester laugh.

"The controller, you idiot," snarled the black tom. "It's in his hands."

Gillespie turned to aim at him. Sylvester twisted a knob, sending the whirl-i-gig into the man's face. The guardian threw up his hands, trying desperately to fend off the flying menace. A black blur flew past Sylvester's eyes, knocking the remote from his hands and onto the floor. There was a screech of metal against stone as the flying machine crashed against the workroom wall.

Sylvester grabbed his crutches and darted toward the door. Something hard and heavy landed against his back, throwing him off balance. He toppled to the ground as his crutches clattered across the floor. Sylvester trembled as fear creeped over him with needle-like claws.

"That was very foolish," the tom's deep voice said in his ear.

# Chapter 7

Toby padded through the ferns, his hair prickling as he padded along the worn path. He knew what was coming. He could smell the water and his mouth felt drier than a wool cloak left in the summer sun. The scent of water drew him inexorably forward, his paws skimming the narrow, brown lane. On he ran even as his mind screamed that it was useless.

He skidded to a halt, lifting his nose to the air. Behind him. Just like every other time. There was no hope, it would always be out of reach. He sunk to the ground and laid his nose on his paws. *Why try? Nothing will ever change. I'll always fail.*

Another smell, closer, more familiar. He knew who it was. His mother was near, but moving away. The ferns swished in front of him, disturbed by her movement. He knew she would be like the water he desired, forever out of reach, yet his paws carried him toward her scent anyway.

When he entered the small clearing, she was exactly where he knew she would be, next to a pool of clear water. He stared at her for a moment, then turned to the pool. Light shimmered off its crystalline surface, reminding him of his searing thirst. His paws felt glued to the hard earth. He stared at his mother in desperation.

"Why do I keep having this dream?" he asked.

She smiled at him. "All is well, my son. He knows you

are thirsty. Drink and be filled."

Toby reached out a paw to touch the invisible barrier he knew would be there. He glanced back at the sleek black queen. She hadn't moved, nor had her expression changed.

"How am I supposed to drink if there's a mage bubble over the water?"

"There is no bubble. There is only you."

It was a lie, another riddle. His life was plagued with riddles.

"Only me? *Only me?*" Heat rose up his neck as his fur fluffed. "Then I should be able to take it down, shouldn't I?" he snarled.

He turned to unleash his rage upon the barrier and came nose to nose with the black queen. He stared into her piercing yellow eyes, half expecting to feel her claws fall upon his ear any moment.

"You cannot obtain that which you desire most until you gain that which is strongest within you," she said.

Toby growled and turned to looked behind, seeing nothing but ferns moving in the still air. He drew in a deep breath, shoving his anger deeper down. He'd faced his mother in the labyrinth. He could face her in this dream world. When he turned his attention back to the black queen she had disappeared. He turned his gaze to the right, knowing she would be back where she'd begun this dream.

The heat of anger continued to creep over his body, invading his thoughts despite his struggle to bury it. She was still expecting him to fail just like always.

"You must find the strength, Toby. You must—"

"No more," he yowled. Rage overwhelmed him and he leaped at her.

Toby jerked awake, panting and sweating. He'd faced

his nightmares in the labyrinth. Why had this one returned? He shook himself from head to tail, jumping when he heard Lorn moan in his sleep and roll over. He still wasn't used to sleeping in the same room with his partner again.

As quietly as he could, he untangled himself from his nest and headed for the door. He concentrated on opening it, moving his tail slowly from right to left so it wouldn't slam against the wall. Lorn might be dangerous when he attempted to use magic under duress, but Toby knew stress made his abilities just as unpredictable, though perhaps a little less likely to kill someone.

His whiskers clamped together as he remembered their battle practice that evening. He wasn't so sure his control was any better than Lorn's any more. He might not forget how to form a spell, but he had forgotten the purpose of the situation. Lorn wasn't ready for full-scale battle tactics after being under the iron psyche of the black tom. He was barely ready to face the normal life of a journeyman and what Toby had demanded of him was anything but normal.

He let his head droop. Maybe his partner was right. While Lorn had been the one in captivity, it was Toby that needed to talk to someone about what had happened. Nadine was the only one he thought would understand what was going on in his mind. *She's probably the only feline who could read my mind.* He shuddered. *Not sure I like that idea.*

He'd been thinking about what it meant to be the Barukh Sh'Toole and still didn't fully understand what she could do, let alone what she had done to break the link between the black beast and his partner. He turned another corner and paced down the darkened hallway. Seeing Brother Cats walking toward their unknown destinations on silent feet still made him uneasy. Thankfully, there were plenty of human Brothers in this temple as well.

As he rounded another corner, he stopped. He had no idea where he was going. He'd set off to find Nadine, but suddenly realized he hadn't the faintest idea where she would be at this time of night.

The faint scuff of sandals on stone drew his attention behind him. For a moment, he thought he was seeing a ghost. The man's round face and belly might have belonged to his friend, Brother Jason. Reality reasserted itself, though, when the Brother stopped and looked down at him.

"Are you lost little one?" the Brother asked, his voice deeper than Brother Jason's had been.

"I'm looking for Nadine."

"The Huntress? She is your friend?"

Toby frowned. Why would this human call Nadine a huntress? Unless he called all cats hunters. Certainly, they kept the temple clear of rodents, but the way he said it made Toby think it was more of a formal title than a descriptive term.

"Yes, we're friends. We met back at the academy. She said I could talk to her if I needed to."

"And what of your companion?" the man asked, looking around the hallway as if he expected to find Lorn hiding in an alcove. "Is he with you as well?"

"No. He's still asleep in our room."

"That is good," he said. His shoulders lowered slightly and he smiled, then nodded down the hall Toby had been walking. "The Huntress will be in the cloister by the reflecting pool. She spends a great deal of time there."

"Thanks," Toby said.

He glanced over his shoulder as he approached the cloister entrance, to see the Brother chewing his lower lip and clasping his prayer beads in a white-knuckle grip. The man started when he saw Toby watching him and spun around to shuffle quickly in the other direction. He watched the man disappear around a corner, then turned to open the door. Curiosity nipped at him.

He entered the cloister, admiring the arching colonnades surrounding the grassy square and its shallow reflecting pool. A breath of warm air caressed his whiskers as he passed through the mage bubble keeping the area in eternal spring. The black and white she-cat perched in the lower branches of the lone tree stretching over the calm water, her blue eyes almost glowing in the dim torchlight.

"I suspected you'd be ready to talk soon. I hope Brother Stephen didn't cause you alarm."

"Brother Stephen?"

She looked up at him and smiled. "The Brother you just met in the hallway. He's new here. I think I intimidate him a little," she said and chuckled.

"How did you know about me meeting him?" Toby asked, his tail fluffing. "Are you spying on me?"

"Not at all. It's part of my role here to keep watch over..." She paused and looked toward the door, her tail swishing under the branch. When she turned her attention back to him, her ears were flattened to half-mast. "I suppose you'd say I watch over the souls here."

"He called you the Huntress. I thought you were Barukh Sh'Toole."

"I'm both," Nadine said. She rose and stretched, then made her way back along the branch until she could drop onto the grassy knoll below.

"I don't understand."

The she-cat lowered herself into a ball, tucking her

paws beneath her chest. She stared at him for several moments, then sighed.

"Would you mind coming over here? I feel like I'm shouting across the cloister at you."

Toby shrugged and strolled over to sit beside her. "So, what's the deal?"

"Let me see if I can explain," Nadine said, staring off into the distance. "A while back, I went on an adventure to find a special feline with the rare ability to heal the spirits of both cat and human."

"Yeah, you mentioned that."

"Well, I found her," she said, cutting her eyes at him.

"You're kidding. Where is she?"

"Somewhere far away from here."

"Wait. You mean you found someone who could actually help end this war and you didn't bring her back with you?"

Nadine shook her head. "I tried, but by the time I found her her own spirit was so broken and tortured by something she'd done in her past that she refused to get involved."

"What do you mean she refused? How could anyone see what's going on and look the other way?"

"How can a partnered cat believe it is best to leave the one person who could make the difference between success and failure behind?" she asked, narrowing her eyes at him. Toby looked away, his fur feeling heavy and hot. The silence lengthened between them until he shifted from paw to paw. She was still watching him when he turned back.

"So what happened?" he asked.

"She helped me discover that I have the same gift. I can reach into a soul and knit the raw ends together again, but," she continued, lifting a paw to cut off his next question, "it's not an ability like I expected. I can heal spirits, but only if they are willing to be healed. Many cats and humans would rather continue to hurt than to begin the healing process."

"That's insane. Who wouldn't want to feel better?"

She cocked her head and stared at him again. He wished he could swallow the words, but they were already out. He stared down at his paws. He knew why someone would hang onto the hurt. It was easier than letting go. A memory of reading in the library at the New Life Temple flashed through his mind. The story of the Beloved's hanging still burned in his thoughts. *How could He forgive them? Why?* He shook his head until his ears popped, then looked back at Nadine.

"Okay, so that explains the Barukh Sh'Toole thing, but what about the other? Brother Stephen called you the Huntress."

The she-cat looked into the sky. Toby watched her, glancing up once to see the stars twinkle above the mage bubble. He cleared his throat. When she spoke, her voice was so quiet he had to lean close to hear her.

"When I was nearly finished with my healer training, my mentor was captured. I went to rescue him and met another cat," Nadine said, turning her blue eyes on him.

"She had a gift, one just as rare as mine, but very different. She could walk between the present and the future."

"That sounds amazing. I had no idea there were cats who could do those kinds of things. So what happened?"

Nadine blinked and stared silently at him. He felt as if he were being weighed against some unknown measure.

"Toby, do you understand that there is a war going on as we speak?"

"Of course," he said, wrinkling his brow. "That's why I'm going to Transformation Mountain, to stop that monster before he can kill anyone else."

She shook her head. "I'm not talking about that war."

Toby cocked his head and studied her, wondering if she was joking. When her gaze never wavered, he shrugged.

"I guess I don't understand, then."

Nadine turned to look at the pool again. "There is a war between good and evil going on that most cats and humans can't see."

"You're talking about demons and winged ones, aren't you."

She cut her eyes at him, then turned her attention back to the pool.

"You think it's a fairytale."

Toby shrugged. "I've never seen anything that would make me believe there are invisible beings fighting for our souls."

"Even after all the evil you've seen around you? All the terrible things that have been committed against humans and cats?"

Toby blinked and cocked his head to the side. "Those are things we've done. We can't blame demons for the wicked things a person or cat does. Those are choices we make, not things we're made to do."

"That's partially true, Toby. We do make those choices, but sometimes we're influenced by forces we can't see."

Toby licked his shoulder, then turned to nip his flank. When he looked back at Nadine, she was still giving him that soul-weighing stare that made his fur crawl. He shook himself from head to tail, then settled back onto the ground.

"Okay, so let's say that's true. What's that got to do with what Brother Stephen called you?"

Nadine blinked and turned back to stare at the pool.

140

"While I was trying to rescue my mentor, I stumbled into a battle between the Time Keeper and a man named Lucius. When it was all over, I discovered that I have a Calling beyond what I had expected—sometimes even more than I want."

When she turned her blue gaze on him again, he felt a warmth flood through him. He felt happier than he had since being accepted to the academy. All his doubts and fears disappeared in the warm light cascading through him.

*I am the demon stalker, the one who walks in the Light of the One*, Nadine said, her voice echoing in his mind. *I am the Huntress.*

Toby stared into her glowing blue eyes. He wanted to burst into songs of praise, to roll in the grass and purr, to leap and swarm up the tree. Nadine turned her gaze away and the euphoria began to fade. Toby panted and blinked rapidly.

"What was that?" he asked.

"That is what it means to be the Huntress."

"That's your gift?"

Toby wanted to twist and shout for joy. He'd found the weapon he needed to defeat the black beast. If Nadine could flood the foul creature with euphoria, it would give them a chance to finish him off before he could blink. He grinned at the she-cat.

"You have to come with us."

Nadine shook her head. "I can't."

"What do you mean? You could help us end this war."

"It doesn't work like that, Toby. I can dispel the darkness in your soul for a time, but, unless you're willing to give your all to the One, the light will fade." She turned her gaze back to him, her whiskers drooping. "I cannot make someone turn from their evil ways, just as I couldn't help you face your nightmares in the labyrinth."

"You don't have to change him. All we need is for you to distract him long enough so that we can knock him out or something, get him in a cage and on his way to prison."

Nadine sighed. "And then what, Toby? Am I to stay at the prison to make sure the beast isn't able to use his powers against anyone again?"

"Just until the execution," Toby said with a shrug. "I'm sure it won't take the judges long to process this case."

"Is that what you desire most, his death?"

"Of course. If he's dead he can't hurt anyone again. Isn't that for the best? The war would be over."

The she-cat stared through him again, making his fur twitch. "Your heart betrays you, my friend. What you say you want and what you truly seek are not the same. I cannot help you in this."

Toby lashed his tail and stood. "You mean you won't."

"We were given free will by the One and we are bound by our choices. You must find your own path to ending the black beast's reign of terror."

"What chance do I have if you won't help?" he snarled.

With another lash of his tail, he turned to leave. He glanced back at Nadine when he reached the door, remembering why he'd come here in the first place. A growl rolled up his throat. For all her sermonizing on defeating evil and defending good, she was the last cat he could count on. It had been a mistake coming here to ask her about his dreams.

"*Trust your dreams,*" he heard in his head. His fur rose along his spine. "*They will lead you.*"

Toby turned to the door and lashed his tail, not caring that it slammed against the stonework.

David slammed the office door behind him. *So much for professional courtesy.* He turned and stared at the tapestry of questions on his wall.

"I told you she wouldn't let you investigate Sylvester's kidnapping. You're too close to the victim," Aaron said from behind him.

He glanced back to see the large wildcat resting on his spot on the bookcase. He stretched a foreleg and yawned. David turned back to the tapestry.

"We should add that to our wall. Captain doesn't think it's related to the bombing at the party, but I think we both know it's part of a bigger plot."

A crafts guild symbol materialized in the air and floated toward the tapestry, sinking into the navy background.

"Did she give any indication of what else might have gone missing besides the good artificer?"

"No, but when I looked over her shoulder into the workshop I noticed his light machine was gone."

"That's not good."

David walked around and sat down at his desk, staring at the tapestry. "Blast it," he growled, slamming a fist on his desk. "We need a break in this. Now."

He heard the thump of Aaron's paws as the wildcat dropped to the floor. A moment later his partner jumped into the chair across from his desk, his yellow eyes narrowed and his whiskers splayed.

"I know that look. What canary did you swallow this

time?" David asked.

"I'm afraid it was a small one, but it was quite tasty," he said.

He drew a massive paw to his mouth and began washing it. The sound of his sandpaper tongue being drawn over fur filled the room. David drummed his fingers on his desk.

"So spit it out, already."

"It seems your information was correct. There is—or, rather, was—someone gathering information in the clerks' department."

"What do you mean "was?" What's happened?"

"Seems two of the department's clerks, an Alie Workman and her tortoiseshell partner Dora, didn't report to work this morning and several boxes of files have disappeared as well."

David leaned back in his chair and grinned. "So our mysterious fiend has more enemies than he knew about."

"Unless he was the one who took the files."

"That's possible, but that wouldn't explain the disappearing clerks."

"Eliminating witnesses, perhaps?"

David shook his head. "I don't think so. Councilman Damon was adamant that Gillespie take care of the problem, but why make it public knowledge that files are missing in the process? That's sloppy and our guy doesn't do sloppy."

"What about how Master Natsumi's murdered body was found in the alley behind the Cat's Tail or the guardian at the prince's birthday party?" asked Aaron.

"I think Natsumi's murder was a message to anyone wanting to go their own way instead of following orders," David said, shrugging. "As for Perleski, that seems to be

Gillespie's mess up, just like Chivato using a half-trained apprentice to try to infect the academy at the Spring Festival."

"So Gillespie was the one who planted the guardian at the servant's door?"

"Yeah. Overheard that little tidbit when Damon was giving Gillespie his new orders."

"So, we know who set Perleski up and we have two possible informants somewhere out there hiding." Aaron licked his lips and swiveled his ears outward. "We need to get to them first."

"The question is," David said, turning to look at a map next to his bookshelf, "where would they run to?"

He stared at the map. They could be anywhere. If it were him, he'd high tail it to the Outer Reaches somewhere. He glanced over his shoulder to his partner. "Do we know anything about these two?"

"I checked the work registry and asked around a bit. They came to work at the Hall of Records a few years ago after spending their journeyman time as liaisons to the merchant guild."

"Any reason they'd wind up as clerks?"

"None at all. In fact, that's what stuck out. Neither one of them fit the normal profile for someone wanting a job in records. They'd performed exemplary service to the guild and had several offers for work."

"Yet they ended up in a dead end job. Makes no sense," he said, turning to face his partner. "Did you talk to any of their friends?"

"They pretty much kept to themselves."

"What about past friendships? Anyone we know?"

The wildcat's whiskers widened. "Toby and his partner Lorn Ribaldy."

"Well, now," David said, smiling and turning back to the map. "That can't be a coincidence."

"And assuming they can't find Toby or Lorn any more than we can, I'd wager they'll go to ground with someone they know their friends would trust David stood up and searched the Outer Reaches. He placed his finger on a symbol for a small outlying temple and turned to Aaron.

"I'm feeling the need for a good old fashioned sermon. What say we go find ourselves a temple service to attend?"

Lorn shoved his extra shirt and breeches into the knapsack. He had to hurry. No telling when he'd left. He glanced at the empty nest on the other side of the monk's cell. *Not this time, buddy.* He threw the pack over his shoulder and yanked the door open. Toby jumped back, fur fluffed and teeth bared. Lorn stared down at his friend and blinked.

"I thought you left," he said.

Toby sat down, curling his bottle-brush tail around his toes. He shifted, looking at the knapsack on Lorn's shoulder, then ducked his head to lick his ruff. When he looked back up at Lorn, his fur had flattened.

"I went for a walk."

"You went to talk to Nadine," Lorn said.

"Are you checking up on me?"

He shook his head. "No. Just a guess."

"So what's with the pack?" Toby asked, thrusting his chin toward Lorn's shoulder. "Going back home?"

"Hardly. I was getting ready to follow you."

"You should go back home," Toby said, strolling past. Lorn turned to watch him knead his nest.

"I can't help you there."

"Who says I need any help?"

"You do," Lorn said, tossing his knapsack on the cot and shutting the door. "In every flick of your tail and twitch of your ears. You're a mess of nerves and unanswered questions."

"When did you become a mind doctor?"

"I'm not. I just know my partner," he said. He eased himself down on the cot and leaned his arms against his thighs. "Or at least I thought I did until you took off without me."

"It was for your own protection," Toby said, turning in a circle and lying down. The tom stared at the door.

"I didn't need your protection."

"Didn't you?" He cut his eyes at Lorn. "If it weren't for me, that monster never would have gotten his claws on you."

"If it weren't for you, I'd be leading a miserable life as a merchant. Instead, I've had the most fantastic adventures."

"You call being held captive in your own mind while some demon cat uses your body an adventure?" Toby asked, ears flattened to half mast and eyes narrowed.

Lorn shrugged. "Not my best moment, but I survived."

"Yeah. Thanks to Nadine."

"No. Thanks to *you* and Nadine."

"I almost let you die," Toby hissed. "How can you thank me for that?"

"I was there, remember. I know what happened. You stayed with me until the storm passed over."

Toby turned his head away. Lorn watched his tail tip

jerk and twitch.

"Wanna tell me what's really bothering you?"

"Nothing. I just think you should stay away from me so you don't get hurt. Next time I might not make the same choice."

"I don't believe that and I don't think that's what's eating you."

"Then what is it?" Toby snarled, glaring at him.

"I heard what that beast said about how I let you down back there at the school. We agreed not to tell those children what was happening to them and I went ahead and did it anyway. We've never talked about that. I know you stayed through the storm even though it could have killed you, but that's what partners do. It doesn't mean you're over it."

"You know what? You're right. That's it. This is all about how you betrayed me, so why don't you get out of my sight?"

The tom turned his back on Lorn, curling into a tight ball in his nest. Lorn frowned and leaned back on the cot. He watched Toby for several silent moments.

"You can stay angry with me if you want. I wouldn't blame you if you never forgave me for what I did, but you're not going out there alone again. We're partners whether you like it or not."

Toby remained silent. Lorn laid down on the cot and put his arms under his head. The silence lengthened. He glanced at his friend again, then turned his gaze back toward the ceiling. His gaze crossed a leather-bound book on the table between them. Lorn reached over and picked it up.

"This the book Harold gave you?"

Toby shifted position. "How do you know about that?"

"I tried to kill you, remember? I might not have had

access to my body, but I wasn't blind."The tom grunted and shifted position again.

"What's it say?" Lorn asked, thumbing through the pages.

"Put it down."

He looked at his friend. The tom was glaring at him again. Lorn put the book back on the table and turned onto his side, resting his head on his knuckles as he stared at Toby.

"You haven't read it yet."

"Not that it's any of your business, but no."

"Why not? Didn't Harold say it would answer your questions?"

"And you know that how?"

"Funny thing about being trapped in your own body by a power-hungry feline, you gain some of his abilities. I never realized how acute a cat's hearing is until then."

"Congratulations. You've learned the secret of being feline. We're all super spies who eavesdrop on private conversations."

"I wasn't eavesdropping," Lorn said. "Well, *I* wasn't eavesdropping. Can't say the same for the puppet master."

Toby rolled his eyes and curled back into a ball, tail over nose and eyes closed. Lorn sighed and rolled onto his back to stare at the ceiling again. He lay there tracing the cracks in the plaster with his eyes when an idea hit him. He rolled back over to look at his friend.

"What if we can use that link to our advantage?"

"What are you talking about?" groaned Toby.

"I mean, what if I can reach backward through that link to find out what our enemy is planning?"

Toby pulled his head up and stared at him. "Nadine broke the link, remember?"

"But what if it's not entirely gone? What if there's some little bit of psychic impression left? It could give us the edge we need."

"Are you sure you want to try that?"

"If it means catching the fiend who made me his puppet, I'd be willing to stand naked in the king's courtyard and dance a Highland jig," Lorn said, feeling a wicked smile curve his lips.

Toby sat up straight, his eyes narrowed and his tail thumped against the floor. "Then I think we need to talk to Nadine."

Sylvester jerked awake and tried to sit up, knowing he had to escape the black beast and his flunky. Leather straps held his body pinned to a hard metal table. He shifted as far as he could one way, then the other, but managed to move a finger width in any direction. He lifted his head, looking around at the crudely hewn cave walls and dim mage lights. When he turned his head to the left, he was staring into the malevolent green eyes of his captor. K'Dash smiled.

"I must apologize for the crudeness of your room," he said, waving his tail, "as well as the procedure you're about to undergo. We had a bit of a problem at our last facility and had to leave most of our equipment behind."

"I know what you left behind."

"Then you are aware of the extraordinary gift you are about to receive."

"Monsters can't give gifts."

K'Dash closed his eyes and lowered his chin. "A pity. I thought you of all people would find our advancements in the study of humans and gadgetry noteworthy."

"So you plan on putting a bomb in me, too?"

"Perish the thought," the tom said, his tail sweeping around to cover his paws. "I would sooner cut off the hands of a master painter. No, I have need of your services."

"You're crazy."

"I've been called worse."

"I'll never help you."

"You have no choice in the matter. Either you do as I ask of your own free will, or..." K'Dash shrugged.

"Do your worst."

Sylvester laid his head back on the table and stared at the ceiling. The tom shifted.

"Are you sure you wish to go through with the procedure, then? I can be merciful, Master Sylvester. All you have to do is say you will perfect this one tiny project of mine, and I will release you."

Sylvester pressed his lips together, gritting his teeth against the insults he wanted to spew. Movement from the corner of his eye caught his attention and he glanced toward it. The black tom leaped onto his chest.

"I can tell you that I will enjoy the procedure much more than you," he said, his whiskers widening into a feral grin.

The tom's eyes seemed to grow with each breath, his pupils widening until there was nothing but a sliver of green around them. Sylvester felt his heart beat faster as he fell into the black abyss.

# Chapter 8

Clarence watched the small office from the alley, his breath steaming past his eyes. He pulled his scarf tighter around his neck and adjusted his cloak a little higher. The number of clients coming and going from the trustee's office dwindled the closer it got to the mid-day meal time. He wondered if the little man he'd seen entering early this morning would go out to lunch or if he would send his assistant to bring something in. He hoped it was the former.

The bells of the nearby temple chimed and the little man popped out of the building. *Punctual.* Clarence had to smile. If he weren't in need of the information in this man's office, he would have laughed. As it were, the man's precise movements and punctual nature gave him a short amount of time to get in, get the information he needed and get out again.

He counted to one hundred before strolling toward the business door, rehearsing his scam as he walked. It had been decades since he'd even thought about the cons he and Adele had perpetrated in the name of the king. This time she wouldn't be there to back him up. Placing his hand on the doorknob, he took a deep breath, then plunged into the small inner office.

"Good day," he said in a cheery voice. "How are you my fine fellow?"

"Fine, sir. How can I help you?" asked the young clerk behind the counter.

"I'm here to see Master Porter about an inquiry I need to make for Aunt Florence."

"I'm sorry. Master Porter has just left for lunch. I don't expect him back for an hour."

"Oh, dear," Clarence said, glancing at the clock on the wall. "He said I could drop by on my way out to Auntie's house for lunch, make sure everything was in order for the next year's stipends."

"I'm terribly sorry, sir. I wish I could help you."

"It's not your fault, young man," he said, waving a hand in dismissal. He glanced out the window and adjusted his cloak again, then turned his attention back to the clerk. "It's just that I promised Aunt Florence I'd check on her account before I dropped by. The poor dear worries so about having everything in order, just in case, you know."

"Certainly. It's always a good idea to have our affairs in order. One never knows what could happen."

"Precisely, and Master Porter said the same thing. He said he'd have those ready for me, so I could look them over and put Autie's worries to rest. I guess he must have forgotten." Clarence looked at the clock again and back out the window, wrinkling his nose. "I suppose I could wait, but I'm afraid Auntie will think something terrible has happened to me," he said, turning back to the clerk.

The clerk glanced at the clock, then at the door.

"She does worry so," Clarence added.

The young man looked toward the filing system in the back of the small office, then turned to smile at Clarence.

"Perhaps I can check the files for you," he said.

"Would you? That would be so kind of you."

The clerk's smile widened and he stepped toward the files. "What did you say her name was?"

"Florence Mann."

The man quickly searched through the files, pulling a fat folder from the drawer. He opened it and flipped through the pages as he brought it to the counter.

"It looks like all the files are in order. Was there something specific you needed to know?"

"Well, Auntie said she wasn't sure how it was all set up, whether there was a stipulation on how her funds should be distributed."

The clerk flipped through the papers again. "I don't see one. It looks as if the principle funds have been invested and your aunt is currently receiving payments based on the interest accrued. Anything she doesn't spend from her stipend is reinvested."

"Is there anything in there about giving to others, specifically if she were to pass away?"

"No," he said, shaking his head as he searched the documents. He looked up at Clarence with raised eyebrows. "Was there something in particular about that you were looking for?"

"Well, Great Aunt Esther was a bit peculiar in her ways, didn't much care for my brothers and I, so Auntie wanted to be sure she hadn't put in something that said she couldn't leave her fortune to one of us if she decided to. Seems she has some misguided notion that she needs to pay me back for all the errands I've run for her," he said with a smile.

"That would be very generous of her." The man's smile grew strained.

"More than generous," Clarence agreed. "I'd say bordering on foolish, especially when it comes to my brothers.

So, I want to make certain her money goes to a charity rather than to any individual. I'm hoping Great Aunt Esther put a clause in there about such a thing."

The clerk's smile widened again and he nodded. "A shame when families have such strained relationships," he said and perused the file again. His brow furrowed as he came to the bottom of one of the documents. "I'm sorry. Who did you say originated this trust?"

A flash of fear raced through Clarence's mind. What was the name he and Adele had used for their other information gathering cons? He reached back in his memory and smiled when it slipped to his tongue with ease.

"My great aunt, Esther Sibbet."

"That's odd," he said, shaking his head. "Did your great aunt go by another name?"

"I didn't think so, but, then, we didn't know her very well. It's possible Esther was her middle name."

"Do you know if Sibbet is her maiden name?"

"Why, yes, why do you ask?"

"Ah, then I know precisely why these documents don't match with the name you gave. You see, your great aunt used her proper first name, middle initial, maiden initial, and married name. See here?" he said, turning the file around so Clarence could see the signature at the bottom.

"Indeed she did," Clarence said, hiding his delight behind a serious face.

"And it looks as if your great aunt did put in a restriction about who the money would be transferred to upon Ms. Mann's passing. It is to be given, with the same stipulations of investitures, to the Little Angels Orphanage," the clerk said. He looked up and smiled at Clarence as he said, "It seems your great aunt was a very generous woman. Not many people leave their earthly wealth to an orphange that cares for both humans and cats these days."

"Yes. I believe you're quite right," Clarence said, smiling warmly. "Thank you so much for all your help, young man. I can tell Auntie that her finances are in good hands."

He shook the clerk's hand and left, whistling a jaunty tune. The cold breeze sneaking under his scarf was a minor annoyance now, easily ignored as his mind turned over the name at the bottom of the page: Adele E. S. O'dorn.

The temple was quiet, save for the echoing notes of the choir practicing in the chapel. David shifted in the straight-back chair, sliding his feet to the chair legs. He glanced at his partner curled languidly into a C-shape on his chair, a foreleg dangling on one side and his tail on the other. The wildcat was the epitome of relaxed diligence. How his partner kept so calm was a mystery. For all they knew, this Brother Terence was helping their informants disappear while they were forced to sit in this tiny room. Every moment they were kept waiting rubbed against David like sand in his under-breeches.

The sound of sandals scuffing against the floor brought his attention back to the small entryway. David looked expectantly at the human monk.

"Brother Terence apologizes for the delay, but he is in a counseling session, which may take a while longer. He asked that I see to your needs."

David opened his mouth to speak, but Aaron interrupted him.

"Thank you, Brother. We were wondering if there was a more comfortable place to wait, a library perhaps?"

"Of course. Please, follow me."

Aaron flowed to the floor as David stood. He cast a questioning glance at the wildcat. Aaron twitched his ears and licked his lips, their silent signal that they needed a quiet place to speak. David wondered if this temple's library was as well-used as the ones closer to King's City. If that were the case, even their whispers would be overheard. He studied the halls as casually as he could on their way, noting more empty rooms than people.

"You have a lovely temple, Brother," he said. "It seems very well taken care of."

"We do our best. It's challenging at times as our numbers have continued to dwindle."

"I would guess that the fiasco at New Life didn't help bring in new initiates."

The Brother shook his head. "No it didn't. Many don't understand that what one group does is not indicative of the entire people."

"Bet that makes you glad those buggers won't be let out of prison anytime soon."

The monk glanced at him with a sad smile and shook his head again. "The One brings rain on the just and the unjust together. It's not our place to decide who is deserving of the One's love and who is not."

David grunted. They entered a larger room with a dozen book shelves on one end and a cozy sitting area on the other, a fire burning low in the fireplace. Between the two sides of the room stood two long wooden tables with benches.

"Here we are," the Brother said, leading them to the sitting area.

He retrieved a poker from the stand near the fireplace and jabbed at the burning logs. They shifted and popped, sending bright sparks floating up the flue and catching the unburnt portions ablaze. The new warmth flowed from the fire, though it didn't help David relax any.

"Can I get you anything else?"

"No, thank you," said Aaron, leaping onto the chair closest to the hearth.

The monk bowed and left, his sandals shushing across the room. David shook his head, watching the man go.

"I don't know how anyone can spend his entire life in such ignorance."

"He didn't seem ignorant to me," Aaron said, stretching out a paw and yawning. "An idealist, yes, but not ignorant."

David grunted again, pacing toward the bookshelves and looking up toward their labels. His gaze darted down each aisle as he strolled past, then walked to the sitting area. Aaron's tail waved lazily in front of the chair. David faced the fire, putting his palms toward the cheery blaze.

"Eyes?" the wildcat asked.

"Nope. Ears?"

Aaron shook his head and curled his tail around his body. David turned to warm his back side and watch the room.

"Good. So what do you make of this?"

"Could go either way. If I read these Brothers right, then they're basically honest believers and want to do what's right."

"Yeah, but you heard that monk. Right and wrong are subjects best left up to some invisible deity."

"Not exactly," Aaron said. "I think it's a case of them not judging anyone's character or whether their souls will go to the Havens or the Pits. I think when it comes to standing in the way of an action that could cause more harm than good, they'll do the right thing."

"I hope you're right, because if this Terence is going to hide our possible informants from us, we could find ourselves dead in the water."

"He's Toby's friend, right?"

"Sure, but he was sponsored by Chivato while he was at the academy."

"True, but he left the academy after Chivato was arrested for releasing the plague and came here."

"Given what we know about our master fiend's plans now, coming to a temple could mean he's on their team. How do we know he's not being groomed to be another Father Hanif?"

"I think we can trust him to make the right decision," Aaron said, ears flattening.

David closed his mouth on what he was going to say as a gray and white patched tabby entered the room. The little tom looked around the room, then smiled at them as he padded their way.

"Hi," he said, leaping to the other unoccupied chair. "I was told you're lookin' for me."

"Brother Terence?" David asked. The patched tabby tom nodded, his whiskers splayed and his eyes wide with obvious curiosity. "I'm Guardian David and this is my partner Aaron."

"Nice to meet ya. What can I do for you?"

"Are you familiar with a woman named Alie Workman and her tortie partner Dora?"

160

"The name sounds familiar, why do you ask?"

"They were friends with your classmate, Toby. Do you remember him?"

"Of course. We're still friends. Haven't seen 'im or his partner since their mission at the New Life Temple, but that's not real surprising."

"Why's that?"

"From what I heard, Toby took it real hard when that Father Hanif died without giving them any useful information on how to find his father. Even split ways with Lorn and left the OKG."

"How did you find that out if you haven't heard from either of them?" asked David.

"Master O'dorn told me."

"So you're friends with Toby's former house mate, too?"

"'Course," Terence said. He looked from David to Aaron and back, his eyes narrowing. "Listen. Why don't we cut through the who knows who questions and get to the point? You already know who I'm friends with or you wouldn't be here. So, what is it about this Alie and Dora that you wanna know?"

Aaron's whiskers twitched, betraying his desire to smile. David had to admit, the little tom had moxie.

"We think they have valuable information on the terrorist we've been hunting, but they've disappeared," Aaron said. "We were hoping you might know where they went."

Terence closed his eyes and shook his head. "I'm afraid I can't help you, fellas."

"You can't or you won't?" David asked.

The little tom cocked his head and stared silently at him, looking as if he were listening to someone David couldn't hear. The patched tabby blinked and turned to Aaron.

"I'm sure, when the time is right, the One will guide you to the answers you seek, but for now, you'll just have to go on faith that I'm telling you the truth."

He looked back at David and gave a slow blink, then dropped to the floor and left. David stared after him, heat rising up his neck. Moxie wasn't the right word.

There was a scratch at the door. Dora perked her ears and listened. The rhythmic scratch came again. She nodded at Alie. Her friend stretched out a finger and traced the pattern on the door. It opened just wide enough for the patched tabby tom to enter. He waited until it closed before igniting a mage light.

"They're gone."

They let out a sigh. Dora's whiskers drooped with exhaustion and she yawned until her jaw creaked.

"I always thought being on the run sounded so exciting. I never would have guessed that it would be so exhausting," she said.

"Agreed," Alie said with an echoing yawn. "I don't suppose they'll stay gone."

"I doubt it," Terence said. "They remind me of Toby and Lorn. Maybe 'cause they're guardians, too, but I think it's more'n that. I think you could trust 'em."

Alie shook her head. "No. This cat's got his claws in

deep in every department from the OKG to the clerks and who knows how far spread out. We can't trust anyone."

"You trusted me."

"That's because we know you've been friends with Toby for a long time. You helped him take down the New Life group."

"So what are you going to do now? I have no idea where Toby is."

"We don't know," Dora said, shaking her head and staring up at her partner. "You were our best hope."

"What about Master O'dorn? You could see if he could help you," Terence said.

"We thought about that," Alie said, "but we don't know how to set up a meeting with him without alerting this Adair cat."

Terence squinted at them for several moments, then his eyes widened.

"Leave that to me," he said, his whiskers wide. "It might take a few days, but I think I can set something up. Meanwhile, you can rest here at the temple."

Alie yawned again. "Think we can get a bigger room? Maybe one with a bed?"

"I can't give you a big, soft feather bed, but I think we can manage a room with a cot," he said with a chuckle. He opened the door and led them out.

"Thanks, Terence," Dora said, trotting out behind him. He turned and looked at her, his whiskers clamping together.

"Don't thank me yet. We still have to contact Master O'dorn and there's still the chance that our message will be intercepted. If that happens, then you'll need to be ready to run as far and as fast as you can."

He stared at her for a long moment, then motioned

them to follow. Dora looked up at her partner, seeing the woman hugging herself. When she turned back to follow the tabby tom, his words echoed through her mind again and a shiver ran down her back.

"This has to be the worst idea I've ever heard," Nadine said, looking from Toby to his human partner. "Do you realize the danger you'd be putting yourself in?"

Toby forced his fur to lie flat. He stared at the black and white she-cat standing between the cloister's lone tree and the reflecting pool. He wished he had her ability to influence others with her gift, so they could dispense with the arguing and get to the job at hand. Lorn dropped onto his heels and held his hands out in supplication.

"So he tries to kill me again. That's why you're here, to keep that from happening."

"And what if I can't?"

"Look, all you need to do is keep me alive long enough to relay what I find out, after that..." Lorn shrugged.

"There's more to it than that. Once I reconnect you, he'll have access to everything you know. Any plans you've made so far will be compromised."

"Good thing we haven't made any plans, then," Toby said.

Nadine glared at him. "And you're willing to sacrifice your friend just to find a faster way to your enemy?"

"It's not his choice," Lorn said.

"And what about you? Are you willing to risk Toby's life for this? Because that's what you're doing. You know this feline has had your partner in his cross hairs since before we were at the academy."

"I'm willing to risk it," Toby said.

Nadine lashed her tail. "Boneheads. The both of you."

"Does that mean you'll do it?" Toby asked, flexing his claws and digging into the grass.

"I can see there's no changing your minds," she said and sighed. Her gaze jerked to him, her glare making him glad all she was doing was looking at him. "And for the record, I would never use my gift to change someone's mind like that."

Toby glanced at his partner, embarrassed heat climbing up his shoulders at the man's raised eyebrow. He cleared his throat and looked back at Nadine.

"What do we need to do?"

"We don't do anything," she said, settling herself on the ground and tucking her paws under her chest.

"What do you mean "we don't do anything?" I thought you were the one who had to reconnect the link," Lorn said, sitting on the ground next to Toby.

Nadine shook her head. "Once the link is created, it will always be there. What happened when Toby and I rescued you was to force the one who created it to abandon its use and then to bury it so deep you could only access it if it was something you desired."

"You mean he could take control of me again any time he wants?"

"Possibly, but I doubt he'd want to."

"Why's that?" Toby asked.

"Because, thanks to Lorn's deep desire to keep that

165

from happening, he's created enough internal booby traps to make the process a lot less appealing to his former captor."

Toby stared at his friend. Lorn's eyes widened.

"I didn't know I could do that."

"It's something we can all do. That's one way we move beyond some of the most painful memories in our minds. We seal them in a box and then set traps around it that remind us just how much pain we'd have to endure if we ever open that box again. After a few times, either the pain becomes preferable to the life we are living or we abandon the memory in preference to creating happier moments in our lives."

"So how does he access that box?"

Nadine looked from one to the other again. "Are you sure this is what you want to do?"

Toby stared at his partner and cocked his head. Did Lorn want this mangefur as badly as he did? Lorn closed his eyes and took a deep breath. Toby wondered if he was going to back out. His claws dug at the grass as he kneaded the ground. What would he do if his partner did change his mind?

"I'll do it," Lorn said, opening his eyes. He turned a fierce gaze on him. "I'll do it for Adele and Victor."

*After everything I've done to him, he's still willing to throw himself in front of a cross bolt for me.* Toby's throat closed and his eyes grew hot. *I don't deserve a friend like this.* He blinked and turned to nod at Nadine. The black and white she-cat shook her head and sighed, but said nothing.

"In that case, let us begin."

Nadine instructed Lorn in how to concentrate on his breathing and then turn inward to look for the buried memory link. Toby waited, staying as silent as he could, while his friend traced the path back to their enemy. He alternately watched Lorn and Nadine. Both looked as if they were asleep.

His tail thumped an impatient rhythm on the ground, until Nadine's eyes opened a slit and she glared at him. Taking the hint, he stood and sauntered over to the reflecting pool. He stared into the deep, clear water at his bright orange fur and spring green eyes.

For most of his life he'd felt cursed by the orange fur caused by a magical accident that had happened while his mother was pregnant with him. It not only made him stand out, it made it impossible to see a resemblance between himself and his parents. Black cats just didn't have orange offspring. He wondered for the millionth time if he would ever get to see his father again.

A brush of fur crossed his thoughts, feeling like the soft warmth a kitten enjoys when its mother returns to the nest. Toby smiled, glancing at Nadine. He was sure she had used her gift on him again, though she looked as if she was deep in meditation at the moment. His ears swiveled back, wondering if she did this sort of thing as effortlessly as breathing and didn't even know she'd done it.

Suddenly, Lorn's eyes flew open. Toby raced across the short space between them and studied his partner's empty expression. He glanced at Nadine, who sat up and watched the human with narrowed eyes.

"What do you see?" she asked.

"It's dark," he said.

"Open your eyes," Nadine said.

Toby stared at her, then turned to his partner. How could he open his eyes any wider without his eyeballs falling out? He looked back at the she-cat, opening his mouth to ask that question, when Lorn spoke again.

"I see a blank wall."

"Turn your head. What else do you see?"

"Everything's cockeyed."

"You're laying on your side. Sit up."

Lorn's breathing accelerated for a moment, then returned to normal.

"There's a wire mesh cage. It's glowing with energy."

"Who is in the cage?"

"A big black tom."

Nadine glanced at Toby, raising her eye whiskers. She jutted her chin at Lorn. Toby took a step forward, studying the man's eyes. They were a piercing green instead of the normal soft brown of his partner.

"Who is the tom in the cage?"

The green eyes lowered and focused on Toby, a feral grin spreading across Lorn's face.

"Clever kit. I knew you had it in you to sacrifice this puny human."

"I'm not sacrificing anything," Toby said, placing his paws on Lorn's chest and stretching up to be face to face with him. "Who is in the cage?"

"I don't think I need to tell you what you already know."

Toby raised an armored paw and Lorn narrowed his eyes.

"Tsk. Tsk. Are you so angry you would injure your pet and end our conversation so soon?"

Toby growled and lowered his paw. "Why have you kept him so long? Why not end his life by now? Surely you have all the information you could ever need. What are you planning that you still need my father?"

"Strategy, dear kit. Your father is the first and last piece of my game."

"What game? This war you've started with the humans?"

"Oh it's much more than that. I have great plans for this world."

"You know we're going to find you and stop you."

"Perhaps," the tomcat said through Lorn, "but even if you manage to find me before I make the final move, you cannot end the cataclysm I've begun."

"What cataclysm?"

Lorn gasped, his eyes widening. Toby dug his claws into his friend's shirt, searching Lorn's face for any link to his partner. He turned to Nadine. Her whiskers were clamped together.

"What's happening?" Toby demanded.

"He's losing his hold on the link. Your enemy is reasserting control. There's not much time."

He looked back at his friend. The man's expression flashed between wicked delight and extreme pain.

"Lorn," he shouted, "grab what you can and let go."

The man's expression changed again, an evil smile spreading across his lips, his eyes narrowing as he focused on Toby.

"There's no letting go now. Your friend is mine."

Lorn's body jerked and fell backward, bringing Toby crashing down on top. He dug his claws in further, piercing the man's skin as he held on. Lorn shivered and flopped as if he were a fish pulled from the gazing pool. Toby's hair raised in a ridge along his spine.

"Get out of there!"

His friend jerked again, then his eyes rolled up and he was still. Toby grabbed his face between his paws. Drool slid down the man's cheek and pooled in his fur. Toby stared in horror. He turned his wide-eyed stare on Nadine. She shook her head. Toby collapsed on his friend's chest, a yowl dying behind the lump in his throat.

# Chapter 9

Victor watched in fascination as K'Dash flopped to the ground like a felled tree. The black tom lay there, not moving for several moments. Victor began to wonder if he had died of heart failure.

"It's dark," the black tom said.

Victor glanced toward the torches flickering on the wall. It wasn't any darker than it had been a moment ago. He looked back at the cat lying on his side facing away from him and wondered if he'd had a brain seizure.

"I see a blank wall."

The tom's voice sounded different, almost human. Victor perked his ears forward.

"Everything's cockeyed."

*Cockeyed?* That was a word K'Dash would never use. The black tom rolled over, his paws waving in the air for a moment. Victor stared at the cat's eyes. Gone was the piercing green gaze he'd become so familiar with. In its place was a compassionate, yet curious, brown stare. He blinked, thinking maybe he was the one who was having a seizure. It had certainly been a long enough time of prison and torture. He was bound to crack eventually. *Surprised it didn't happen sooner, though.* K'Dash sat up, wobbling a bit at first, then steadying.

"There's a wire mesh cage. It's glowing with energy."

There was a pause as if he were listening to someone ask him a question. "A big black tom."

The tom's eyes flashed green. His whiskers widened and his eyes narrowed, though his gaze still seemed focused on something far away.

"Clever kit," he said with a purr.

*Toby?* Was Toby trying to communicate with him through K'Dash? *That's insane. Surely he knows Adair can kill him with a thought.* Then he remembered. No one but Adele and he knew what the black tom was capable of and they'd agreed never to tell their kit any of what had happened.

"Toby," he called, hoping something would get through. K'Dash was already reasserting his control. "Son, you have to get out of his mind. You have no idea what he's capable of."

"I knew you had it in you to sacrifice this puny human," K'Dash said.

It wasn't his son, then, that was linked to the black cat. *His partner? But how? Why?* He had to stop them somehow. He glared at the mage shielded cage, wishing he knew how to unravel the spell on it. Victor turned his heated gaze back on his captor.

"Leave them alone, Adair. Just cut the link."

The tom ignored him, listening again to his silent conversation partner.

"I don't think I need to tell you what you already know."

What did Toby know? Victor ran through the side of the conversation he had overheard. The human linked to K'Dash had said "a big black tom." Did that mean Toby was now asking about him? It would make sense to find out all he could about who was being held in the cage. And if Toby wanted to know specifics about who was in the cage, then it stood to reason that he already had a good idea who it was.

He blinked overheated eyes. His son was still looking for him. After all these years, Toby still believed he was alive. Pride and sorrow overwhelmed him. His son was as noble and strong as his mother, but it would be the death of him, just as it had been for her. K'Dash shook his head and grinned.

"Tsk. Tsk. Are you so angry you would injure your pet and end our conversation so quickly?"

Victor tried to imagine his son baring his fangs and preparing to slash at the offending voice, but the image dissolved. Instead he saw the sweet orange furball he'd left standing on the walkway as he entered a coach that would take him on the mission that would end with his capture. A shiver ran down his back as he thought about what the black tom might have planned for his son. K'Dash continued to smile and watch the far away scene from some human's eyes.

"Strategy, dear kit. Your father is the first and last piece of my game."

"Toby, you have to stay calm. He's baiting you."

"Oh it's much more than that," K'Dash said.

He wondered if the tom was talking to him, but his eyes didn't refocus on him. Victor closed his eyes and ransacked his memories for anything that might be useful. He needed to get information to his son, make him understand that he needed to find help.

"I have great plans for this world."

A half buried memory floated to the surface. So long as K'Dash was focused on Toby, it might work, provided his partner didn't die first. Victor took a deep breath and emptied his mind of as much emotion as he could, then ordered his thoughts into one mental image he hoped would convey everything.

"Perhaps, but even if you manage to find me before I make the final move, you cannot end the cataclysm I've begun."

Victor opened his eyes and stared into K'Dash's unfocused gaze. It was a long-shot, but it was worth a try. Summoning all his willpower, he flung the image at the black tom and hoped he wasn't just deluding himself that he could project a message through K'Dash when the tom wasn't trying to be receptive.

The tom drew in a shuddering breath, his eyes flashing brown again. Victor wanted to leap with joy, but there wasn't time.

"Just listen. He's kidnapped a master artificer and plans to force him to build some kind of doomsday device. You need to get help." The black tom drew in another breath. The brown was fading from his eyes. "Tell Toby I love him."

K'Dash blinked, his piercing green gaze still unfocused, but returning with his feral smile.

"There's no letting go now. Your friend is mine."

The black tom crouched as if to spring. Victor scrambled to the far end of his cage away from K'Dash and hunkered down into a tight ball, flattening his ears and squeezing his eyes shut. He knew it wouldn't make any difference, but instinct ruled his fearful mind.

A howling wind buffeted his body, building to a scream. He wanted to mewl like a kit, but his voice caught in his throat. A soft brush of fur stroked his mind, calling up an old memory of him with his mate and Toby during a picnic. The young orange kit had batted their leftovers into a patch of marigolds and Adele made him fetch them. Victor chuckled as his son fell over, sneezing again and again.

He could feel the bite of K'Dash's energy as it tried to rip his mind and heart from his body. He held onto the memory as if he were holding a struggling bit of prey, waiting for the hurricane inside the room to cease.

The biting spirit winds died as fast as they had risen, leaving Victor panting and weak. He opened his eyes to slits. The room was in complete darkness. He perked his ears up, listening intently for any sound. There was just his own ragged breathing. He turned toward the other end of the room, expecting nothing but more dark.

Victor blinked. He could see the outline of the other tom, wreathed in sickly gray, the tom's eyes glowing green. Victor's stomach clenched with dread at the cat's satisfied smile.

"Help will not be coming," K'Dash said.

O'dorn wanted to choose the location for their clandestine meeting this time. As much as he enjoyed the tea and scones at the Cat's Tail Pub, he felt too exposed for the information they were about to pass to each other. David had the opposite opinion, saying that being in the open like that would send the signal that nothing was unusual, just two old friends having a meal together and talking about old times. In the end, they had both yielded to Aaron's suggestion to find a location that fit both views. It hadn't been easy, but, after a couple heated debates, they agreed on a place to meet.

The little restaurant was very different from anything Clarence had been to, but Aaron had raved about its cuisine and said they had a type of tea that he would fall in love with. He peered into the small cubicles as the petite woman ushered him toward a room at the back. Clarence's eyes widened at the low tables and cushions, and he wondered if the wildcat had considered what sitting on the floor would do to old bones. Still the atmosphere was pleasant and the cubicles were private, which suited their needs.

The young lady slid a door open to the last cubicle and motioned him in with a smile. Clarence nodded his head and ducked inside. He grinned as he noticed the table and chairs.

"This will be perfect," he said, turning to the young woman. "My friends should be joining me shortly."

"Can I get you drink?" she asked, her far eastern accent light.

Clarence clapped his hands together and rubbed them enthusiastically. "I've heard you have a hot tea that is simply divine. I'll have a pot of that."

The woman's smile widened as she bowed, then slipped out, closing the sliding door behind herself. Clarence chose the chair facing the door and sat. He stared at the two sticks resting on a square piece of polished wood next to the woven place mat, wondering what they were used for.

The door slid open again and the young woman brought in a tray with a small black teapot and two little bowls and set it in the middle of the table. Clarence watched with a quirked eyebrow as she poured an amber liquid into one of the bowls and set it before him. She smiled again, then bowed her way out of the cubicle.

He leaned over the little bowl, letting the the steam drift to his nose. It smelled lovely, like tea, but with an earthier

176

scent. He picked the bowl up and sipped. A satisfied smile crept across his lips as the hot liquid slid across his tongue and down his throat. Aaron had been right. It was love at first taste. When the door slid open again, Clarence looked up to see David ducking in with Aaron padding along behind.

"How's the tea?" asked Aaron, his whiskers splayed.

"Magnificent, just as you said it would be. If the food is as good as the tea, I may have found my new favorite restaurant."

"I hope you don't mind, but I took the liberty of ordering for us. Once you try the spicy chicken, you'll be hooked."

They watched the young woman fill the other small bowl and set it before David. She bowed her way out again, leaving them to their privacy. The man frowned as he stared at it, then sighed and looked up at Aaron.

"Next time can we pick a place that serves normal food and drinks?"

"Would you prefer I took you someplace that served hagas?" his partner asked, chuckling.

David wrinkled his nose and grabbed the bowl of tea, sloshing a little onto the woven mat. He slurped as he drank, then put the empty bowl back on the table and turned to Clarence.

"So what news?"

"I've had some very productive visits with both the original head mistress of the orphanage and with her trustee's assistant. The headmistress has confirmed our suspicions that Adele had a brother and that he died while she was still at the orphanage."

"Do tell," David said, leaning back in his chair.

"Apparently, an official from the King's Men brought them to the orphanage soon after their mother abandoned them."

"Why would a King's Man play guardian to a couple of abandoned kits?" Aaron asked.

"That's one of the interesting details," Clarence said, pouring himself another bowl of tea. "If you remember, in your investigation of Adele's case, you uncovered something about her mother's partner murdering her mate."

"I remember that. The accused never made it to trial 'cause he was killed by a mob on the way there," David said.

"Indeed. Well, it would appear that there's more to it. Adele and her brother were witnesses to the murder."

"The poor bairns. What kind of sot kills a parent in front of his children?"

Clarence rubbed his temples between the fingers and thumb of his right hand, feeling guilty for never pressing his friend for details about her family. If he'd known, perhaps he could have offered her more comfort through her trials while they were at the academy.

"That explains the need for a guardian, but not a King's Man. They're only posted to missions that don't exist."

Aaron nodded. "They're ghosts."

"Except when they're not," David said, raising an eyebrow at Clarence. "Apparently this one wasn't. I don't suppose you got a name."

"No," Clarence said, shaking his head again. "Just a description of a skinny yellow tom."

"Could be anyone."

The door slid open. Two young women carried in several large plates of food and placed them on the table with three empty plates. Their server traded their small teapot for another one shaped like a long serpent with sharp teeth and claws and refilled the two tea bowls.

"Enjoy," she said, then bowed her way out of the cubicle again.

Clarence looked at the array of food and then at the empty plate and sticks before him. He glanced at Aaron in question.

"You're supposed to use the sticks to pick up the food," the wildcat said, twitching his tail to float a lumpy bit of something dripping in thick sauce and dotted with red flakes to his plate. "The long sticks resting on the serving plates are to get the food to your plate. The sticks by your plate are to eat with."

"Oh for cryin' out loud. You mean we're supposed to stab our food with little wooden dowel rods?" David asked.

"Actually," Aaron said, his whiskers quivering, "you use the sticks together to pinch the food and bring it to your mouth."

Clarence hid his smile behind another sip of tea. Sometimes he wondered if Aaron purposely chose places and situations for the sheer pleasure of torturing his partner. *All in the name of exposing him to cultural diversity, of course.* He watched with amusement as David attempted to spear a piece of broccoli with the longer serving sticks. It might have been entertaining to watch his friend continue his attempts at spearing food while it dodged around the plate, but his stomach growled.

"Perhaps our hosts have an alternate means of eating this food," he suggested. "The food smells delicious, by the way."

"It is," Aaron said, he snickered as a large mushroom scooted away from his partner's efforts to stab it. "You could try the utensils stored in the cupboard beside the door."

David jerked his gaze to the wildcat and scowled.

"In the cupboard? You wait until now to tell me there's real silverware in the cupboard?"

"If I had told you there were forks in there when we arrived, would you have tried to eat with the sticks?"

"Of course not," he growled, standing up to retrieve a fork for both him and Clarence.

"I thought as much," Aaron said, nibbling his food.

David rolled his eyes as he handed a fork to Clarence, then sat down to dip food onto his plate with the serving spoon he'd found. After mounding his plate with the rice and vegetables, midst some grumbling about the lack of real meat, he handed the spoon to Clarence.

"Okay, so we know a King's Man took interest in Adele's case. What else did you find out?" he asked, stabbing a piece of broccoli and stuffing it in his mouth.

"Miss Florence said that he came back a few days later to take them to the trial and that they'd seen the partner's demise on the way."

David choked on his food and Aaron looked up, his eyes wide and ears at half mast.

"Good grief. You mean they witnessed two brutal murders within days of each other?" David asked.

Clarence nodded. "That seems to be the case."

"I take it that isn't the end of the story," Aaron said, his whiskers clamping together.

"I wish it were. A few months later, the King's Man came back with a black tom that she said could have been Adele's brother's twin. They talked to her brother for some time, then Adele's brother left with the King's Man and the other black tom for parts unknown."

"Let me guess," David said, "That's when he supposedly died."

180

Clarence nodded. "Miss Florence said Adele was inconsolable for days, then one day came to dinner and announced she was moving on with her life and that was the end of it."

Aaron and David stared at each other for several moments, then looked back at Clarence. David nodded slowly.

"Your lady was one strong cat."

"That I knew already," he said, smiling sadly. "I just never guessed how strong."

The group finished their meal in silence, accented by the clicking of silverware on ceramic dishware and the occasional hushing of the sliding door as the server replaced their tea again. Clarence pushed his plate aside and took another sip of tea, cradling the little bowl in his hands for its comforting warmth.

"Adele didn't just move on. She reached back later and took care of the head mistress."

"How's that?" asked David.

"When I went to see the trustee, I found out she was the one who set up the fund that supports Miss Florence. The odd thing is," he said, placing his tea bowl on the table, "she put the whole thing together to look like a great aunt passed away and left a large inheritance."

"Why would she do that?"

"And where did she get the money?" asked Aaron.

"I don't know. It makes no sense. I know she didn't spend much, but the amount of money she invested would have taken her nine lifetimes to accumulate."

"Unless she was paid for her brother's death," David said.

"What do you mean?"

"When you become a member of the guardians, you can

choose to sign a Petition of Responsibility stating that, should you die in service, your family will receive recompense for a certain length of time," Aaron explained. "I would assume that the King's Men sign something similar."

"If Adele's brother went on some secret mission, he must have signed the petition and made Adele the beneficiary. That makes sense."

"But why would she give it to an old lady at an orphanage she grew up in? Did they have some special connection?"

Clarence stroked his beard and stared at the white paper rectangles in the sliding door. There were so many pieces still missing to this puzzle, but the picture it was making looked dark. Two identical toms in the service of the King's Men. Adele's brother died and left her with a large amount of money, which she gave away. He knew his partner could be generous, but she was also sensible to a fault. It would have been more logical to donate a portion to the orphanage and invest the rest for a rainy day. A dark thought wiggled through his mind and he sat up straighter.

"Giving the money away like that doesn't make sense unless she was afraid and trying to protect someone."

"You think she was protecting Miss Florence. From whom?" asked Aaron.

"Well, we already suspected that the brother didn't die. What if she was protecting the headmistress from him?"

"Is it possible he's behind all this?" asked David.

"You said yourself when you got into your investigation, that it looked like someone was trying to erase Adele's brother's very existence. Who else would want his entire life erased?"

David tapped the table with an index finger. "I've got

another hunch for you. Didn't you say Adele's brother was an identical match to the black tom the King's Man brought to the orphanage?" Clarence nodded. "What if, like you said, her brother didn't die? What if, instead, he somehow got himself partnered with a human willing to do his dirty work?"

"That's a wild accusation," Aaron said, frowning at his partner.

David shook his head and leaned forward, casting a glance between them. "Not when you consider that it would take a lot of pull in some pretty high up places to manage this disappearing act. Add that to what we've learned and you've got a pretty good idea whose making the puppets dance."

"Care to let me in on your discoveries?"

David waved his hand at Aaron, indicating he should fill Clarence in.

"David overheard Councilman Damon giving Guardian Gillespie a dressing down about someone digging into his master's affairs. When we checked it out, we found out that two clerks from the Hall of Records had disappeared with several boxes of old files."

"Any idea who they were?"

"One Alie Workman and her partner Dora, both graduates of the academy's liaison program. Rumor has it they were a couple of bright stars in the program."

"Yet they ended up as clerks?"

"Just one more thing that doesn't make sense unless you connect the invisible dots," said David.

Clarence rummaged through his memories. "I think I remember Toby saying something about some friends he had in the liaison program back when he was an apprentice. You don't suppose those are the same two?"

"It wouldn't surprise me."

"Have you located them"

"We think we tracked them down to a temple in the Outer Reaches. Problem is the one cat we thought they would contact isn't saying anything to us," David said.

"Who is it?"

"Some Brother named Terence."

"I know him, most honest and loyal feline you could ever want as a friend when you're in trouble."

"Think you could talk to him? Find out what he knows?"

"We need to know what's in those files that Councilman Damon's master doesn't want found," Aaron said.

"I can try."

"Good. Let us know what you find out," David said.

"In the meantime," Aaron said, "let's just hope we can stay ahead of this black beast."

Toby stood on his hind legs with his nose half a tail length from Lorn's prone body, watching his friend's chest rise and fall. *Just one more thing to add to my list of failures.* Nadine hadn't been able to tell him if his partner would live or die. All she would say is that he wasn't suffering like last time.

He closed his eyes and sank down to the floor. He'd brought Lorn back to their cell himself even though several Brothers had offered to help carry him. It was his fault his friend was like this. Toby refused to let anyone else take responsibility for his care. The soft sound of paws made him swivel his ears back.

"Any change?" Nadine asked.

"No."

She laid a soft tail over his shoulders. "He's a fighter, like you. Have a little faith."

"I don't know if I can," he said, looking at her from the corner of his eyes. "Are you sure you can't help him?"

Nadine shook her head. "He's locked inside his own mind. Only he can find the door out."

They sat watching Lorn sleep. Nadine turned to look at him. He wondered why she didn't use her gift to soothe away his pain like she had before. Her whiskers widened slightly.

"You're like an open book," she said. "I can see the question on your whiskers as well as if you'd asked it out loud. The truth is that easing your pain now would do you a disservice."

"Why?"

"Feeling the pain keeps you focused on the task at hand. It reminds you of how to be compassionate."

"You don't think I'd help my friend if I weren't feeling so miserable?" Toby asked, eyes widening. *What kind of monster have I become?*

"You're not a monster, Toby. You're mortal. We all need to be reminded from time to time that suffering is a condition we all share."

"Seems all I get are reminders," he mumbled, looking down at his paws. He looked back up at Nadine. "I wish I were strong like my father."

"How do you know you're not?"

"Look at me. I can't even keep my partner safe."

"He volunteered for this. His choices are his own, as are the consequences."

"Doesn't make it right."

"No, it doesn't. But do you honestly think your father never had to do things he regrets?"

Toby looked away, toward the leather bound book on the night stand, then back at his partner. Nadine's tail brushed his side as she stood and walked to the table. He watched her stretch on her hind legs to peer at the book, then turn to look at him.

"Who gave you this?"

"A cranky old tom named Harold."

Her ears twitched and she blinked, then turned to look at the book again.

"You haven't read it yet," she said, lowering herself back to four paws. She faced him and cocked her head to the side. "Why are you afraid?"

"I'm not afraid. I just don't see the point in reading something that's bound to be nothing more than more riddles."

"And yet, you were the one who dug the rat from his hole nearly seven years ago. The Toby I remember would never have shied away from gaining more knowledge, no matter how convoluted it might first appear to be."

"I'm not him any more."

"Or maybe you've just forgotten who you are."

Toby glared at her. Nadine twitched her tail, settling the book in front of him, then padded toward the door. She looked over her shoulder at him.

"You might be surprised at how much you have in common with your parents."

She closed the door behind herself, leaving him alone

with the sound of his best friend's breathing and the silent demands of the unopened book.

The pages crackled as he opened the book. The dusty smell of old paper floated up to tickle his nose. Toby wasn't sure what to expect. Old stories? A mission log? Some long forgotten diary? Whatever it was, the old tom seemed confident that it would help him figure his life out, though Toby doubted it.

He twitched his tail, flipping past the first blank page. The next page was also blank. Toby frowned as he continued to turn blank page after blank page. *What kind of sick joke is this?* He slammed the book closed, glaring at the image embedded in the leather cover, a pair of crescent moons with tips facing each other. The longer he stared at the twin moons, the more they began to coalesce into the eye of a cat.

The cat's eye shimmered. Toby blinked. Did he really see it shimmer? He looked closer, a whisker breadth between his nose and the eye. The pupil dilated, pulling him in. A gray-blue mist floated up from the embossed picture, wreathing his body, and a deep voice sounded in his mind.

*"Dahm tzah'ack Dahm*
*MishKar rah'ah nahkahn*
*Maht'sah shel'kah mah'slool*

## Virginia Ripple

*Hitkahdehm Shyam K'Dash."*

A shiver ran down Toby's spine. The sound of the voice set alarm bells ringing in his head. He couldn't place it, but he knew he'd heard it before. The thought flew from his mind as he was whisked into the midst of a dreamlike scene.

His heart raced and his paws were sweating. It felt as if he were hiding from a faceless evil stalking him with murderous intent, yet nothing seemed out of the ordinary. He prowled alongside a massive black tom in a darkened bedroom. They glanced out the window, seeing the full moon bright in the black sky. The doors to the balcony were open and a cool breeze laced with the scent of lilacs drifted in.

There was the soft scrape of a door. They turned their heads toward the sound, watching with keen cat eyes as, near the floor, a corner of the tapestry shifted. Another large black tom padded out, his eyes reflecting green in the moonlight.

"Have you found it yet?" the other tom asked.

"No, but I know I can get the information if we stay just a little longer," they said in the rumbling voice he'd heard before.

"We're out of time."

"But no one suspects. How can we be out of time?"

"They may not suspect us yet, but they will and soon. Gravin Athenios is due back tomorrow. He knows his partner as well as he knows himself. You won't be able to fake your way past him."

"I can do it. I can use my gift."

"No," the other tom said, shaking his head vehemently. "It's too risky. We're not here to be heroes."

"But think what this information could do. It could mean the difference between living free or dying in slavery."

188

The other tom looked toward the door, then back. His whiskers were clamped tight.

"You have until daybreak."

The black tom left and the room melted away, replaced by a sheer drop less than a paw step away. The ground felt slick beneath his paws. He could see water droplets spattering the cliff face beside him, the deafening roar of the waterfall making him flatten his ears.

"You have to jump," the black tom yelled at them.

"I can't. I don't have any powers."

"You can swim, right?"

They looked down into the churning water far below. Toby's stomach flipped at the thought of being sucked under. They turned back to the green-eyed tom and shook their heads.

"I can't swim in that."

"You can. Believe in yourself."

They stared at the cliff's edge, backing away. "I can't. I don't have any magic."

"You don't have a choice," the other tom said.

Toby felt the impact of the massive black cat against their side. The next instant, they were tumbling head over tail, screeching and clawing the air. They hit the river and sucked in a mouthful of icy water. Toby felt as if some large creature was slurping them along, as he rolled over and over under the current. He wasn't sure which way was up until his head broke the surface for one gasping breath.

They saw the other tom reach the far bank, then they were drawn back under. Toby pulled against the current until his muscles screamed, finally breaking the surface again to see the other tom searching the river.

"Adair," he called. "Adair, where are you?"

They opened their mouths to yowl and swallowed another mouthful of water. The river pulled them under again. When they resurfaced, the other tom was slinking away into the woods. They tried to call out again, but the water tossed them around and under, bashing them against rocks as they were swept further downstream. Toby thought his heart would explode from fear as he paddled with waning strength.

A cat-sized piece of driftwood bobbed up within paw's reach. They stretched toward it, their claws slipping across the wet surface. It spun away and they went under. Despair cascaded over him and their legs stopped moving. They peered through the murky water, seeing the silver disk of the moon wavering over them. They closed their eyes and let the river take them where it would.

With a rush more powerful than the pull of the water, Toby's thoughts were swept back into his mind and the vision ended. He blinked, staring down at the twin crescent moons. With a gasp, he shoved the book away. His heart was still pounding. He could still taste the muddy water in his mouth and smell the putrid stink in his nose.

Toby took a deep breath, forcing his heart to slow. He bent to wash his shoulder, then shook his head until his ears popped. Calmer, he let the memories replay in his mind. There were two big black toms. The one he'd been part of had felt familiar, though frightening as well. He tried to place the voice, but it slipped away.

Failing to identify his phantom partner, he concentrated on the other tom. The green eyes reminded him of the black tom at the cemetery, yet there was a warmth there that the black beast didn't have. The way the cat moved spoke volumes on the amount of physical training he must have gone through, yet Toby could tell he didn't have the finesse as he would have in several years. He searched his memories for any black cat that could fit the description. In a flash, his mind provided an answer.

*Father?*

# Chapter 10

The rainbow colored dragon sitting on Clarence's mantel was no bigger than a teacup. If the sun hadn't been shining through his workroom window, he would have missed the little messenger altogether.

"Good morning, sir," the little dragon said in its bell-like voice. "I bring you a special message from Brother Terence."

The dragon breathed a wreath of smoke in front of it, then reached in with a tiny clawed hand. When it pulled its hand free of the smoke, it held a piece of folded paper as big as itself. Clarence smiled and held his hand out to receive the message.

"Thank you, my friend."

"My pleasure, sir. Have a good day."

With a pop the dragon disappeared. Clarence stared down at the folded parchment in his hand and raised an eyebrow. He unfolded it and stared at the blank sheet of paper. David had said he thought Terence was giving sanctuary to the partners from the Hall of Records. Now it looked as if his friend was correct. Why else would the little patched tabby use a special dragon messenger to send him a blank parchment?

He carried the paper to his small kitchen and set it on the table while he prepared a pot of tea. As the water heated on the stove, he sliced a lemon, then took it to the table. With a quick swipe, he ran a lemon slice over the paper, revealing the hidden message. He smiled as he remembered how Lorn and Toby had used this trick before, a trick Lorn had learned from his Uncle Hecktor when he was a boy. Clarence shook his head and placed his glasses on his nose, peering at the message.

*It is I. Thrice doNe have my Brothers' partNers' looked for you. Thus today should you uNfailing meet thy fate. ArraNged have they to Not have this much valuable aNd uNtoward iNformatioN uNder such speculatioN. It shall eNd aNd be the momeNt of strife. You mustN't meet thy Creator at breakfast, uNless S'Temple be the first of the day to make service. Bide thee two for the weeks aN'it pleasure heNce.*

*B.T.*

Clarence placed the lemon on a saucer beside his hot cup of tea and took it and the odd letter to his workroom. Once there, he shuttered the window and locked his study door, then set a mage light burning above his work table. He sat down on a stool, placing the letter and a blank piece of paper side by side. Grabbing a charcoal nub from thin air, he carefully selected every third word and wrote it on the blank paper. When he'd finished, he read the rewritten note.

*I have partners you should meet. They have valuable information speculation. End the strife. Meet at S'Temple first day service. Two weeks hence.*

*B.T.*

He put the new note down and stared into the cold fireplace. New logs lay ready for the morning's fire. He said a short incantation and flames leaped up from the wood to pop and crack. Clarence looked back at the two notes, the writing on the original one already fading. Where was S'Temple?

He stepped to his bookcase and ran a finger over the spines of several books on the top shelf. Locating the one he wanted, he pulled it from its place and carried it to his worn-out old chair by the fireplace. He opened the book of maps to the index and searched for the name. S'Temple wasn't among the city or town names. He continued his search through the names of prominent temples. Still no luck.

Clarence sat back and closed his eyes, letting his mind wander over everything he could remember about Toby's friend, Terence. The patched tabby was from the Lower Districts. He'd started his magical career as a loner-in-training at the King's Academy of Mages, but chose to leave to become a Brother at the same temple as his mentor, Brother Yannis. As far as Clarence knew, he'd been there ever since. He looked back down at the book of maps.

"So where is S'Temple?" he asked the empty room.

*Perhaps I should figure it out by distance from his temple.* He opened to the page for the Outer Reaches and placed his finger on the little triangle denoting the temple Terence was serving in. *What if he meant it would take them two weeks to reach their destination.*

"R'TRAY d'NES tin ASHUN," he said, circling his finger around the little triangle to include all the points within two weeks coach ride. Several small dots indicating towns fell within the circle, but none named S'Temple.

He wondered if the little tabby had selected a location that would take both them and him to reach within two weeks. Clarence raised an eyebrow at the thought. He said the incantation again and circled the area around his home in the Middle Districts, searching for a place where the two circles intersected. They were two finger widths apart.

He searched between the two circles, thinking maybe there was a small, nearly invisible triangle between them. There was nothing but a stretch of flat plains. Clarence sighed and sat back again. He studied the pieces of paper on his work table. *What am I missing?*

He stood up, setting the book on the edge of the table, and stretched until his spine popped. With a groan, he leaned over the papers again to re-read his copy. He frowned at it. He'd copied the correct words. He was certain of it, but now that he looked at it again, something was missing.

Clarence swiped the lemon slice over Terence's letter again, revealing the words once more. He studied the two side by side.

"Why would he capitalize all the n's?"

He glanced at the open book of maps, then back at the letter and its copy. Standing up, he examined the map, noting all its details, including the legend in the bottom right hand corner. At the top left was the usual illustrated version of a compass with its N E S W printed at each arrow point. A grin spread across his face and he laughed. *Clever little tabby.*

"R'TRAY d'NES tin ASHUN," he said again, tracing a northerly line from the temple and one from his home. When he reached the two week point, the lines intersected at a minuscule triangle called Temple of the Sun. Clarence tapped the spot on the book and nodded. *Let's shine a little light on the subject, shall we?*

"I thought you'd like to know your imprisonment is nearly over," K'Dash said.

Victor looked up from washing the stitches on his leg to see the big black tom grinning, a large velvet wrapped package on the floor beside him. The white tom who cleaned the room sat about a tail length behind.

"Whose your friend?"

"Just a loyal servant. No one to be concerned with."

"Is that what you are, kit? No one?"

The white tom looked away. Victor returned his gaze to K'Dash, pleased to see the tom's fur had risen. *It's the little things.*

"What's in the package?" he asked, jerking his chin at the large velvet rectangle.

"That is the little surprise I told you about, the one that will make all our plans possible."

"Am I supposed to guess what it is?"

"While that might be amusing, it would be a waste of time." K'Dash glanced over his shoulder at the white tom. "Reginald, please show our guest what our amazing prize is. Be sure he gets a good view."

Reginald stared at the package and twitched his tail. The wrapping slid away and a glowing leather-bound book as large as a cat lifted itself from the floor. Its radiance made him narrow his eyes to slits as he watched it drift closer. It floated close enough to the wire mesh that Victor could see the image of two Winged Ones kneeling on either side of its cover. Between them was the raised emblem of the sun, an enigmatic eye within the disk. His eyes widened as he recognized the book.

"I thought this was just a myth. Where did you find it?"

"The Book of Knowledge is certainly not a myth, my friend, as you can see. As for how I came to own this treasure, let's just say I have friends in low places willing to steal anything for a price."

"You can't open this, Adair. It'll mean the end of the world."

"Don't be a fool," K'Dash said, wrinkling his nose. "I have no intentions of opening it. However, I have discovered its power, even closed, is sufficient for remaking certain aspects of this world without unmaking existence."

"What do you mean?"

"Ah, now that is my little secret for now."

K'Dash motioned for Reginald to re-wrap the book. When it was covered again, the black cat nodded toward the door, then followed the younger feline. Victor stared down at his leg as the hair along his spine rose.

Aaron trotted down the hall toward the doors. He

thought maybe he could sweet talk one of the clerks at the Hall of Records into letting him see the old registries for the King's Men. It was a long shot, but better than not trying.

"Hey there, Highlander, where you been?" called a lanky brown tabby she-cat from an adjoining hallway. Several other cats followed behind her. Aaron's whiskers splayed at the motley crew of friends.

"In the thick of it, as always, Kahra," he said.

The she-cat chortled. "We were just headin' to the Cat's Tail for a little celebration, care to join us?"

"Depends. What are we celebrating?"

"Cody was just promoted into the King's Men."

Aaron peered at the gray and black tabby tom who was grinning.

"Nah. It canna be. Why would they promote a mouse-brained pigeon to the King's Men?" Aaron asked, whiskers splaying.

"You're jus' jealous, old timer," the tom said, aiming a mock blow at him.

"Eh?" he asked, scratching his ear. "Wha's that, sonny? My ears aren't what they used to be, so speak up."

"I said, you're an old sot," the younger tom said, laughing.

He looked around at the gathered cats, noting that several of them were even older, their coats growing coarser and whiter with age. Of those, most of them had retired from active duty, though they still kept abreast of current affairs within their respective fields. Then he saw two of the oldest in the group, a tabby she-cat and a gray tom he recognized as being retired King's Men.

"Are you sure you want an upstart like that in your fine regiment?" Aaron asked them.

"Can't be any worse than some of the ones we've worked with," the she-cat said with a drawl indicating she was from one of the Southern Reaches.

"Alright, then," he said, an idea forming in his mind. He turned back to Kahra, "On one condition."

"What's that?"

"We must regale our young celebrant with stories about the old days until he learns to respect his elders."

"No. Let's have a Tell Tale," called another cat.

"Perfect," Aaron said.

"Wait, what's a Tell Tale?" Cody asked.

Kahra laid a tail across the tom's back and led the procession out the door toward the pub.

"A Tell Tale is a story war."

"A story war?"

"That's right," Aaron said. "We each tell a story—"

"Or three," Kahra said, cutting her eyes at Aaron and smiling.

"Or three," he said with a chuckle, "until no one can top the last one told."

"Then we all buy a drink for the one who tells the topper."

"So, let me get this right, if I tell the best story, you all buy me drinks?"

"Yep, but you've got stiff competition. You see those two old long tooths back there?" Aaron said, jerking his head toward the retired King's Men. The tom glanced back and nodded. "They've won just about every Tell Tale they've ever been part of."

The tom looked over his shoulder at the tabby she-cat and gray tom, his eyes narrowing. When he turned back to Aaron his whiskers were splayed in a sly smile.

"I think I can handle myself."

Aaron glanced over his head to Kahra, who smiled wickedly.

"That's what they all say."

The group entered the pub and announced to everyone that there was about to be a Tell Tale. A cheer went up from the small crowd. The servers made quick work of refilling everyone's glasses as the group made their way to the table nearest the small stage.

"Whose going first?" Kahra asked.

One of the older she-cats volunteered and the storytelling commenced. Aaron continued to watch the two retired King's Men while the others regaled them with alternately funny and spine-tingling adventures. He waited until the time between stories lengthened several minutes before he made his move.

"Surely there's a story you're dying to tell," he called to them.

The old she-cat shook her head and waved her tail in dismissal. "This is a game for young cats."

"Nonsense," he said. "With the number of missions you've been on and the various cats you've had to work with, there must be an adventure in there worth a drink or two."

"Perhaps," the old tom said, "but we'd have to kill you afterward."

The group of friends guffawed and encouraged them to tell a story. Finally the old tom relented.

"I don't suppose any of you youngsters have a request, do you?"

"I've heard tell," Aaron said, narrowing his eyes, "that the King's Men have brought in outsiders for certain missions. Any hair raising tales about missions with them that have gone tail under belly?"

"Yes, let's hear a scary one," someone else called.

The old tom's tail twitched and he swiveled his ears back.

"I can only think of one, but it didn't happen to me," he said, turning to look at the tabby. She shrugged and nodded toward the stage.

"You know this story as well as anyone, Kurt. You were his best friend, so perhaps it's best they hear the true version from you rather than some stretched out of shape, unrecognizable version from someone else," the she-cat said.

Kurt nodded and took the stage, leaping to the stool and then looking at each cat and human in the pub until the silence was thick as cream.

"Most of you were no more'n kits when she came into her power. Her mentor liked to say she walked with angels, that she was a cat with powers only the Beloved could understand. The fact is she had the rare ability to heal the broken spirits of both humans and cats, something I hadn't seen before or since. But like all rare and powerful gifts, it came with a price—one that many paid dearly for."

Kurt looked around at each of them, his eyes narrowed and his tail swishing like a pendulum beneath the stool. Aaron had to admire the old tom's storytelling abilities as he glanced around at the others. They were leaning forward, waiting to find out what would happen next. No one suspected that he'd asked for this story in hopes of finding out more about their current foe. He smiled to himself as the the old tom continued.

"Like most of us, this special feline had a human partner. She also had a mate and two kits. It was the love of all four that often carried her through times of exhaustion. My friend said that between them, the man and the tom, she

202

found her purpose. The key to her power was her trust and love of both human and cat. Without them, she was no more than a half-Malkin, able to talk and think, but without the spark that makes the Malkin special.

"Everyone in the kingdom from the trapper in the Outer Reaches to the king himself sought after the healers. As a King's Man, my friend was in charge of the partners' security. It was his job to protect this rare duo and see to their family's safety. They never made it easy because they wouldn't turn a soul away. Unfortunately, as is the case more often than we care to admit, it's in hind sight that we see the true danger. The tragedy didn't begin from some outside source. It grew from within.

"It was the late nights and days without rest that always brought contention between her partner and her mate. The human's passion for healing the masses was as great as hers. A King's Man understands the drive to put your work before anything or anyone else, but outsiders can't. Had he known what was going on, he might have been able to defuse it, but he didn't.

"He could tell you stories of explosive nights between the human and the tom. It was on one of these nights that the end of this group began."

Kurt paused and licked his ruff. Aaron's whiskers twitched as he wondered if now he would find out more about the twin black toms and Adele's brother and how they were connected to the King's Man. When Kurt looked back at the audience, his whiskers were clamped together.

"You've all heard how the human was accused of killing his partner's mate. You've probably all heard stories of how the queen killed her partner in front of her kits and a host of humans and then disappeared. What you haven't heard about is what happened afterward.

"It was my friend's responsibility to take care of the entire family, but that family was now reduced to two terrified kits. What does a single tom dedicated to his career know about raising kits? Nothing," he said, lashing his tail. "He did the one thing he knew to do. He took them to an orphanage. From time to time, he would check in with the head mistress to see how they were doing, but that was the extent of his contact with them."

The tom's ears flattened and his eyes narrowed.

"That was all until the Great Houses planned an uprising led by Gravin Athenios. You all know from your history lessons back at the academy about how Athenios fashioned himself into a would-be tyrant king. The King's Men were told that he had found an ancient weapon and planned to use it to gain the throne. He contracted with the southland, Eros, and they were marching on our kingdom. Caught between the Demon King and the Depths, we were forced to look for a way to infiltrate Athenios's lair. Damian found it.

"He knew that one of the young queen's kits had the same gift she had, though he didn't have any other magical abilities. He believed that we could use that gift to find out where the weapon was located. Of course, getting the kit into the lair was going to be difficult. We already had a cat inside, but switching them out would be problematic unless the kit was willing to undergo a bit of magic that would permanently alter his appearance.

"I don't know what Damian said, but the kit went along with the plan, despite his sister's vehement requests that he stay at the orphanage where it was safe." Kurt shook his head. "It would have been better if he had done as his sister wanted.

However they went through with the plan. The smaller black tom was altered to look like his much larger counter-part and they snuck into Gravin Athenios's inner court.

"We don't know exactly what happened, but the two cats didn't meet up with Damian at the appointed time. The guardians stormed the palace on schedule and when the screaming stopped, the only one left of the two infiltrators was our cat." Kurt's ears flattened and he looked toward the old she-cat. "After that, Damian left the King's Men, a broken feline, to become a Brother Cat, even taking a new name, and we," he said, turning a hard stare on the newly promoted patched tabby, "no longer use untrained kits to do our job."

Aaron watched the old tom drop to the floor and pad back to his table. The bell on the pub door rang in the silence, ushering in a small group of academy partners. Their laughter grated against his ears. A vote was called for the best story and drinks were served to the winner. The awkward moment was broken and the celebrants went back to celebrating.

Aaron watched as Kurt and his friend said their final congratulations to Cody, then padded toward the door. He excused himself from his friends and trotted after the two retired King's Men.

"That was quite a story," he said, catching up to them. "And you say that's true?"

"True as any secondhand story can be," Kurt said.

"So did the kit die?"

"No one knows for sure. He was presumed dead, but we never found a body."

"Why was he presumed dead?"

"Because his partner said he saw him drown in a river."

"Whatever happened to the other cat?"

"He went on to be one of our best loners. I believe he

became the mate to his dead partner's sister, didn't he?" asked the she-cat, looking at her friend.

"That's what I heard. From what I understand, their kit was the one who uncovered the mess we're in now with this terrorist."

The she-cat shook her head. "Seems that family is cursed to be in the middle of bad things."

"Aye to that," Aaron said. He turned to the old tom and smiled. "I bet your friend Damian found being a Brother quite a change from being a King's Man."

"Calls himself Brother Harold now, but other than that I wouldn't know. Never talk to him anymore."

"That's too bad. Took a vow of silence, did he."

Kurt snorted. "That old curmudgeon? Hardly. He gets his kicks from grumbling. I'd wager he wouldn't be happy in the Havens if he didn't have something to complain about. I suppose that's why he went to the temple out near Transformation Mountain."

"Why's that?"

"It's the furthest away from civilization you can get. Lots to complain about out there in the hoodie bushes."

"It may be out in the wilderness, Kurt, but Harold's smart. No better place than Transformation Mountain to keep an eye on things around the kingdom. You can bet your fur he's up to something."

"Up to something?" Aaron asked. "What would he be up to way out there?"

"Harold had some crazy notion that Gravin Athenios had taken in some apprentice, trained him how to use the weapon. Even went so far as to suggest it was the dead kit."

"That sounds odd. What do you think?"

Kurt shook his head and glanced at the she-cat. When

he looked back at Aaron, his ears were at half mast.

"With what we've seen over the last seven years, I'm not sure what to believe anymore."

"Well, it was nice to meet you, young'un," the she-cat interrupted, "but my old bones are for bed."

Aaron smiled and stepped aside. "Pleasant dreams," he said to their retreating backs. He watched them walk away, wondering what more their friend Harold might be able to tell him.

The bolt slipped out of his hand again and landed on the floor, skidding under the machine. Sylvester stared down at the tool in his other hand as it beat a staccato rhythm on the metal. He threw it on the work table and clasped his hand together, trying to massage the tremble out of them.

"I always thought a master artificer would treat his tools like a gentleman treats a lady," said the black beast from behind. "Is there a problem, Master Sylvester?"

Goosebumps prickled along his arms.

"No. I think I just need to eat a little, maybe take a little rest. My hands are getting fumbly."

"By all means, eat, rest," the tom said, pacing around to stare up at the Light Intensifier. "I took the liberty of bringing food with me."

Sylvester turned to see a ragged white tom and two large blue Russian twins sitting beside the work table, a plate of food and a mug of something just settling on its top. The sight of the bread and cheese made his mouth water. He couldn't remember when he'd last eaten. He wobbled over and sat down on a stool.

Grabbing the hunk of bread, he tore it in two. He stuffed a chunk in his mouth, chewed a couple times, then swallowed it, washing it down with the mug of tepid herbal tea.

The black tom was pacing around the machine, alternately looking at it, then at the smaller version on another work table. He turned his piercing gaze on Sylvester, making it hard to swallow the cheese he'd just stuffed into his mouth.

"Is it ready?"

"Not yet," he said, shaking his head.

"What's still to be done?"

"There's that bolt I just dropped—"

"This bolt," the tom asked, sliding it out from under the machine with a paw. Sylvester nodded. "Reginald, come here." The little white tom padded forward, his whiskers drooping and his tail dragging the ground.

"Put this in that slot up there. Be sure to screw it in securely. We wouldn't want any nasty accidents, now would we?" he said, staring at Sylvester with narrowed eyes. "Is that all?"

The master artificer forced another bite of bread down, then pushed the plate away. He lifted his cold hand up from the table, his trembling fingers brushing the rough wood, and clasped them in his lap.

"Th-there's th-the... I-I m-mean...," he stuttered. He swallowed the sickening sweet taste in his mouth and breathed deeply. The tom's piercing green eyes never blinked.

"Was there something else?"

Sylvester shook his head. "It's ready," he whispered.

"That is good news, master artificer," K'Dash said, his whiskers splaying in a wide grin. He turned to the twin toms. "Ready the subjects. I want to test the device." They trotted from the room and the black tom turned toward Reginald. "Place the Book in its holder at the large end of the contraption."

Sylvester watched as the white tom floated a large velvet wrapped package to the metal cage he'd designed to K'Dash's specifications. He unwrapped it and floated the glowing leather book into the cage with a twitch of his ragged tail. Sylvester's breath caught as he recognized the design on its cover. He gawked at the black tom.

"You'll kill us all," he choked out.

K'Dash's tail twitched, but his eyes never left the white tom. The twins trotted back in just as Reginald finished latching the final clasp to hold the book in place.

"All is ready, my lord," said one of the twins, his Ruska Kingdom accent thick.

"Excellent." K'Dash glanced at Sylvester. "Let us see just how good the master is. SHELkah Ahdohn tihlPEHN! KAHM!"

Golden light burst from the book, bounced off the black metal cage and shot through the large crystal lens. Sylvester imagined the beam of light being forced through the progressively smaller crystal lenses within the machine until he saw it burst through the final lens, which was as big around as his fist.

Screams echoed from the next room. The light hit the stone wall, punching a hole through it as if it were made of nothing more durable than parchment. The screams cut short with a deafening boom that left Sylvester's ears ringing. He gaped at the black tom.

"R'pah R'shah," K'Dash said. He turned and grinned at Sylvester. "You truly are a master. Tonight we celebrate," he said, turning to the other cats, "for we are on the brink of a new world."

The black beast led the way out the hole in the wall. Sylvester watched the white tom re-wrap the book and float it to the floor. Reginald looked up at him, fear shone in his eyes. He shook himself from head to tail as if he were trying to dislodge something filthy from his fur, then left through the hole. Sylvester stared at the completed machine for several moments, then closed his eyes and took a shaking breath.

"By the One," he murmured, "what have I done?"

# Chapter 11

Lorn shifting on the cot brought Toby to full attention. He stared at the man, ears perked forward and eyes wide to catch any slight movement. Lorn lifted a hand to his head and moaned.

"Did anyone get the ID on the delivery wagon that hit me?"

Toby leaped to his partner's chest, purring and head bumping his raised elbow. Lorn gave him a thin smile and stroked his back.

"Hey, buddy, nice to see you, too," Lorn said.

"I thought you were dead," said Toby. His whiskers quivered with suppressed emotion.

"So did I." He turned his head and the mage light fell across his pale face, making him wince. "Nope. Head hurts too much to be dead."

Toby twitched his tail to dim the light. "How's that?"

"Better," he said, squinting at the tom. "You wouldn't believe the dreams I had."

Toby glanced at the book on the floor, then back at his partner. "Try me."

"I honestly can't remember a lot. Most of it is mixed up with what I saw through that cat's eyes. I'm not sure what's that and what I dreamed."

"Why don't you just tell me everything you remember

and we'll sort it out together."

"Can I get something to eat first? I'm starving."

Toby's ears flattened to half mast. He nodded and jumped to the floor, shoving his irritation aside. *I should be grateful he's alive, not irritated that he's not as eager to tell me what he knows as I am to hear it.* The frustration grew with each thought until he shook his head, making his ears pop. He trotted out into the hall and stopped the first Brother he saw. Food ordered, he returned to Lorn's cot and smiled at his friend.

"Food's on its way."

"Great. Wanna tell me what happened while I was out?" he asked, covering his eyes with his arm.

Toby swallowed a sigh and twitched his tail to return the book to the night stand. "Not a lot. Mostly just sitting here waiting to see if you were gonna wake up."

"That had to be boring."

"Not entirely," he said, glancing at the book again. Lorn lifted his arm and squinted at him again.

"What aren't you telling me?"

Toby looked down at his paws. "I think—"

"Food's here," announced the cheery voice of a Brother. Toby exhaled in relief and jumped to the floor as Lorn sat up.

"Good to see you're awake," Nadine said, padding in behind the monk. Lorn grinned and reached for the food.

"Can't keep me down for long. Toby was just telling me he was keeping busy while I was out."

"I'm sure he did," she said, cutting her eyes at him and raising her eye whiskers. Toby gave a slight shake of his head, glancing at Lorn from the corner of his eye.

"Who knew taking care of a sleeper was so much work," Toby said with a laugh. "By the way, you still snore louder than a hibernating bear."

"When did you ever listen to a hibernating bear?" Lorn asked, tearing off a chunk of bread and stuffing it in his mouth.

"Just a guess," he said with a shrug.

Lorn smiled around the lump of food in his mouth and went back to eating. Toby shifted from paw to paw, trying not to show his impatience. He glanced at Nadine and wondered how she could seem so calm when locked inside his partner's head were the answers they wanted so badly.

"Can you tell us what you remember?" Nadine asked when Lorn began licking his finger and picking up crumbs with it.

"Like I told Toby, not much. It's all garbled up with dreams I had."

"That's normal. You're lucky they were just dreams and not the Winged Ones come to take you to the Havens."

Lorn grunted.

"Why don't you tell us about both. Between the three of us, we can probably figure out what was a dream and what is a memory."

"Alright," he said, scooting Toby's book over as he placed his plate on the small table. He leaned back against the wall and put his hands behind his head, closing his eyes.

"First thing I know is a memory and not just some kind of dream thing is seeing that black tom in the glowing mesh cage. I'm pretty sure it was your father, Toby."

His heart beat faster. Finally proof that his father was still alive. But he was a prisoner. He wanted to grill Lorn for more details, but clamped his mouth shut on the barrage of questions. His partner continued without noticing.

"After that everything gets fuzzy. There's somebody

yelling about someone named Adair and something he can do. Then there's my dad standing there waving some kind of bar of light. He keeps yelling something about the game pieces being in place, but when I look around all I can see are groups of kids playing a game of tag." He rubbed his temples, then looked at Toby. "I'm sorry, partner. That's all I can remember."

"It's okay. That's more than we had."

"Yeah, but it doesn't feel like enough to be worth worrying you."

"Wait and see, Lorn. You may remember more as time goes by," Nadine said. "Our minds have a funny way of filtering out unimportant information and leaving behind gold."

"I know, but something bothers me about the whole thing."

"What's that?" she asked.

"Well, through the whole dream thing—whatever you want to call it," he said, waving a hand in dismissal, "there was this overwhelming feeling of time running out. It's like there's this big hourglass somewhere and it's almost empty and, when all the sand runs out, somebody's going to flip it. The problem is that, if we don't get to it first, whoever's going to turn it over is going to suck the world into a howling abyss."

Toby's eyes widened and he turned to Nadine. "Is that even possible?"

"I wish I could say no," she said, eyes narrowing, "but my experience tells me otherwise."

## Master Cat

Clarence sat in the small alcove off the main chapel, listening to the Brothers' chant reverberate around the temple walls. The soothing scent of incense hung in the air. He wasn't sure how long he'd been waiting, but he'd lost feeling in his bum. *I just hope I don't have to leave in a hurry. I'm pretty sure even a three-legged cat would be able to catch me if I have to drag a sleeping leg behind.*

He shifted the curtain aside again to peek out at the few congregants gathered in the quiet chapel. He guessed there might be a dozen worshipers present, no more. Still no sign of Terence or his new friends. He slid the curtain closed again and shifted position, trying to ease his leg out so it would regain some feeling.

As he was stretching his back, he heard the shush of the curtain and looked down to see Terence pushing into the alcove. He smiled, leaning down to take the cat's offered paw.

"Good to see you again, Master O'dorn," the patched tabby said. "Any word from Toby or Lorn?"

"I'm afraid not."

"I s'pose that's not surprising."

He glanced over his shoulder at the curtain, then leaned closer. Clarence leaned further down, his back protesting as he did so.

"I wasn't sure you'd understand my message."

Clarence nodded and leaned back, massaging his lower back.

"I must admit it took me awhile. I'm not as adept at

215

reading code as Adele was. Victor taught her how to do that. Something he learned at the academy, I suppose."

"That's one of the first classes Chivato wanted me to take," Terence said. He flicked his ears. "Makes sense now, but at the time I thought it was a dumb idea. That class was tougher than a first year oughta take."

"What do you suppose he had in mind?"

The little tom shrugged. "Not sure. I s'pose he planned to make me into some kinda messenger or sum'thin. Doesn't matter now, so I don' think about it more'n I have to."

"A good plan. And might I add that your coding was very clever."

"Thanks."

"When do I get to meet your new friends?"

"We can go right now, if you're ready."

Clarence smiled and tapped his leg. "Certainly, so long as you'll go slow. My leg fell asleep."

"Those benches'll do that to ya," Terence said with a chuckle.

Clarence levered himself up and pulled the curtain aside. He limped along behind the little patched tabby as quietly as he could, trying not to disturb the silent worshipers. Terence led him behind the pews to a small door with the sun carved in bas relief, an enigmatic eye weighing him from its center. He ducked inside behind the tom, glancing back as he closed the door behind himself. His hand sparked against the door handle as he let go.

"Ouch," Clarence said, raising his fingers to inspect them. They tingled a bit, but nothing looked damaged.

Terence glanced over his shoulder. "This way is protected against anyone — and anything — that opposes the Followers of the One. It's just checking to make sure you're welcome here."

"May I assume I passed the test?"

"If you didn't, you'd never know it."

"How do you mean?"

"Let's jus' say you'd be givin' your accounting with the saints 'bout now."

Clarence stared with widened eyes at the door. Paw steps drew his attention back to the hall ahead of him. The little tom trotted down the lantern lit hallway to another small door. He scratched a rhythm on it, then waited. From the other side came another scratched rhythm. Terence answered it with a haunting yowl and one long scratch down the door's wood.

The door opened onto a well-lit garden that reminded him of his herb garden and reflecting pond. He blinked in the sudden sunlit brightness. As his eyes became accustomed to the daylight, he looked around to see several varieties of flowering plants, including lilacs, roses and three butterfly bushes that came up to his shoulder height.

"Impressive," he said.

"Not mine," the patched tabby said, "though I'd love to get my paws on a few of these unusual hybrid roses."

Clarence shook his head. Terence might be a Brother Cat, but he'd never forgotten his dream to become the world's first garden growing feline. He followed the little tom down a wood chip path to a group of dragon willow trees, their slender blue leaves belying the feeling of spring in the garden.

"I see the dragon willows know what season it is outside."

"Yep. One of their odd magical properties, apparently." Terence glanced at him as the little tabby nodded toward a group of dragon willows. "Our friends are just inside this grove."

Clarence waved his hand toward the trees, indicating the tom should lead them in. He parted the willow branches and smiled at the small group sitting on benches around a low table. A dark haired woman sat on the furthest side, her horn-rimmed glasses giving her a slightly owlish look. On her left sat a dainty little tortie she-cat and on her right was an odd looking she-cat. It was as if this strange feline was somehow two separate cats vying for the same body, a black cat with enchanting green eyes and a mottled orange cat with eyes the color of a summer sky. He felt himself being drawn into the green eye, as if he were being pulled into a deep green whirlpool. Clarence blinked and the sensation ceased.

Terence hopped onto the closest bench, leaving room for Clarence to join him. They were all silent for several moments. Terence watched the oddly colored she-cat as he shifted from paw to paw. When she nodded, he exhaled and turned to the partners.

"Alie, Dora, this is Master O'dorn. He's the one who made the cure for the plague."

"Actually, I must give credit to Toby and Lorn for much of it. Without their efforts uncovering Chivato's scheme, I wouldn't have had a clue how to create the cure."

"A pleasure to meet you, sir," said the little tortie she-cat. "I wish it were under better circumstances."

"As do I. I understand you have some important information you wanted to discuss."

"We all do," said the other she-cat.

Clarence raised an eyebrow and looked at her expectantly.

"I am Chaeli, leader of the Protectors. My people and I guard the secrets of the One."

"Might I inquire what secrets those are?"

"You may ask, but I cannot tell you more than that what we keep hidden is for the good of all creation. I'm afraid this young woman and her partner have stumbled into something much bigger than they bargained for and it seems your young friends have become enmeshed in it as well."

"If you're referring to the war between the cats and humans, we are well aware of it."

The she-cat shook her head. "It began as a simple war, but our enemy has taken a keen interest in your foe and has provided him with a weapon so powerful it could undo existence."

"Surely you exaggerate."

"I wish I were. Somehow, in the process of moving this artifact to a new, safe location, our enemy was able to steal it away. We've been keeping an eye on your current conflict and have come to the conclusion that the Book of Knowledge is now in the possession of the black tom who has been orchestrating this war."

"The Book of Knowledge?" Terence's eyes widened. "You mean it's real?"

"Quite. And even more powerful than our ancient stories tell us."

Clarence looked from one cat to the other.

"May I assume that the stories are at least accurate in that life will be undone should someone open the Book?"

"Yes. The promise in the stories is that the one who reads from the Book will be able to remake the world in whatever way he or she chooses. It's a seductive promise."

"Indeed. However, I believe there is a caveat that whosoever seeks to unmake the world will also be unmade. Am I correct?"

"Yes," Chaeli said, nodding. Clarence's eyes narrowed as he stroked his gray beard.

"From what I've learned about our foe, he isn't crazy enough to open the Book if it means loosing his hold on this life."

"How can you be sure?"

"Simple deduction. He was enlisted by the King's Men for a mission and supposedly died. Now, from what we've uncovered thus far, it would seem that, while he wanted the rest of us to believe he is dead, he may have let his sister know that he was still alive."

"You know this for certain?"

"No," Clarence said, shaking his head. "As I said, it is a guess on our part. All we have are clues such as a witness relating that my partner's brother went with a King's Man and the story about what happened with her parents before that. Then there's the evidence that she set up a fund to keep her former head mistress at the orphanage safe and well cared for. Beyond that, all we have are suspicions of who this beast is, nothing solid."

"We might be able to help with that," said Alie.

She reached behind her and mimed putting something large on the table. Dora stared at the empty space, then twitched her ears. A box appeared with a pop.

"We've been copying documents for some time now," Alie said, "storing them in these invisible boxes. We were going to give them to Toby because most of them have to do with his uncle and mom, but then he disappeared."

"After that, we weren't sure what to do with them, but by then we'd uncovered so much relating to Adair and this war he started against humans we didn't dare throw it all away," continued Dora.

"Adair?"

"That's Toby's uncle's name."

"At least that's the name he was born with. After he was listed as dead, he re-appeared using the name K'Dash Shyam," Alie said.

Chaeli hissed. "That is blasphemy."

"Is there something significant about that name?" asked Clarence.

"It means New Life," Terence answered. "It's a term of endearment the Followers of the One reserve for the Beloved."

"If he's taken the name for himself, he may be even more dangerous than we thought," the she-cat said. "It is imperative that we find where he is hiding the Book and what his plans are."

"You have our word that we will help you in any way we can, but right now we have no clue where he might be."

"Neither do I. We have an operative searching as we speak, but we haven't heard from her in over a month."

Clarence looked down at Terence. The little patched tabby's whiskers were clamped tight and his ears were flattened to half mast.

"How long has it been since you heard from Toby or Lorn?" asked Clarence.

"About two months."

Clarence nodded and turned back to the rest of the group. "I think what Terence is inferring is that our friends have met up with your operative. If that's true, they might be close enough to our enemy that they can't call for help."

"If that is true, may the One be merciful. Everything now depends on them."

*Virginia Ripple*

He could hear Lorn's soft snoring from the cot across the room. Toby twitched his tail and floated his book down to his nest, watching and listening for any changes in the man's breathing. He wasn't sure why he felt guilty for wanting to see the book again, but he did. Being a part of the vision had felt like voyeurism, yet, if he wasn't supposed to use the book, why would Harold have given it to him.

A shiver ran down his body as he touched a paw to the soft leather. Would he see the same vision again or would another nightmare await him? *No time like the present.*

He moved to within a whisker breadth of the twin moon symbol on the book's cover, wondering once more at how much it looked like a cat's eye. The pupil dilated, pulling him in again and the gray-blue mist floated up to encase his body. The deep voice sounded in his mind.

*"Dahm tzah'ack Dahm*
*MishKar rah'ah nahkahn*
*Maht'sah shel'kah mah'slool*
*Hitkahdehm Shyam K'Dash."*

A shiver ran down Toby's spine. The alarm bells rang in his head once more. For an instant he considered that this might be the reason he wanted to hide what he was doing from his partner. If his instinct was screaming something was terribly wrong, then he knew he should listen, but he wanted

222

to know more. The voice sounded so familiar. He yearned to know who it was. Maybe this time he'd find out.

The thought flew from his mind as he was whisked into the midst of another dreamlike scene. Toby stalked along next to a small black kit, feeling the heat of rage burning from the little tom. Another tiny kit, a she-cat, paced along beside them. He wanted to turn and see who she was, but couldn't. He was forced to look and feel whatever his unknown companion saw and felt.

In front of them was a skinny yellow tom that reminded him of a younger version of Brother Harold. Toby could feel anger and jealousy washing over him when they looked at the tom's backside. Voices drew their attention away from their guide. A wave of chaotic emotions crashed against them as they neared the crowd. Toby felt disoriented, buffeted like a twig on a rushing river, from the various feelings and thoughts entering his mind. Rage boiled up under him and lifted him away from the chaos.

"We'll have to go around," the yellow tom said, looking back at them. "There's a back door. Give me just a moment to flag down another King's Man and then we'll get you inside and into the courtroom."

As soon as the tom disappeared into the crowd, leaving the kits sitting under a bush by a side wall, the black tom turned to the she-cat. The little kit's yellow eyes were wide as she stared at the crowd of humans and cats.

"This will be our only chance. Don't roll on your back now," he whispered.

"I don't think I can. Please don't make me, Adair."

"We talked about this. It's the only way to get justice for father. You know those humans won't convict one of their own. And forget about giving him the death penalty."

223

"But what if Damian's right? What if mother just lost control of her gift? She was so tired and—"

"And nothing. Look, Adele, you're going to help me do this or I'll make you regret it," the tom hissed, raising an armored paw.

The she-cat sunk lower under the bush. Adair sighed and lowered his paw. He put a soft tail over his sister's shoulder.

"I know this isn't how you want to use your magic, but sometimes you have to shoot the fox yourself if you want to make sure the chickens are safe."

"But John isn't a fox. He's a human and he was mother's partner."

"All the more reason we need to take care of this now. It's not just about what's happened to us. What about all the others out there he's supposedly helped? How do we know he wasn't pretending to help while all the time he siphoned off mother's power? You know it's possible."

Adele shook her head. "But he seemed so sincere about wanting to help all those poor souls."

"Con men are always sincere. That's how they get what they want. Father could see through his scam. That's why John killed him."

"Do you really think so?"

"You know I do."

They could feel the she-cat's resolve wavering. A bubble of satisfaction rose beneath Toby. She stared at the crowd, watching the jailer's coach pull to the curb. As two guardians helped the man out of the box-like structure, a wave of despair crashed over them. Toby knew it came from the man in irons, but didn't know how he knew. They leaned closer to Adair's sister.

"Look at how he holds his head high. He knows he's going to get away with this," he lied.

"What is he feeling?" she asked.

Another bubble of satisfaction rose beneath Toby as the tom said, "Are you sure you want to know that?"

Adele nodded. "Please, Adair, tell me. I need to know."

Another rush of piercing sorrow rained over them. Toby realized his companion was like Nadine. He could feel what others felt. *But can he project like her?*

"Happy," he whispered.

Toby had thought he knew what his mother's anger felt like from the many fur-stripping tongue-lashings he'd received as a kit, but this was nothing like those. The air was crushed from his dream body as the searing heat cocooned him. Her ears flattened and she bared her teeth at the man being ushered through the crowd.

"Do it," she said.

A shard of ice he recognized as Adair slid past his mind, snagging a strand of Adele's heated rage. The tom focused his deadly thoughts toward the crowd. At the apex of the shard's trajectory, it shattered, pulling strands of Adele's anger apart until it wove an intricate net. The net engulfed the crowd and Toby felt Adair pull it closed, twisting it until everyone inside was choking on rage. Terror gripped him as he realized what was about to happen to the man.

The sound of tearing cloth gave way to screams and wetter sounds that made bile rise in Toby's throat. The anger the little she-cat had been feeling suddenly turned to horror.

"Stop!" she yowled.

Toby felt her fear push against them, making Adair's hold on the crowd waver. He thought for a moment that the net would collapse, but the black tom reached deeper into his sister's energy, pulling out everything he could grasp.

"No," she moaned.

A moment later she collapsed against them and the sounds ended. The next instant the sound of running foot steps was competing with the sounds of retching. Toby wished he could shut his eyes and flatten his ears, but he was forced to see and hear everything Adair did. Finally, the black tom turned to look at his sister, lying on her side and gasping for breath. Panic seized them.

"Adele," he said, washing between her ears. "Speak to me. Please."

The she-cat opened her eyes, the pupils dilated and unfocused.

"You lied to me."

Adair bent to groom her ears again. Adele shifted backward, the hard glint Toby had become so familiar with as a kit surfaced in her eyes. The black tom held his breath as golden eyes in a charcoal gray face flashed through his thoughts.

"No. I didn't."

"You said he was happy. I felt his sorrow through you. I felt his terror when they ripped him apart."

They looked toward the crowd, watching as city guards ushered humans and cats toward a makeshift corral down the street. The creeping horror Toby had encountered in the first vision edged closer to him as Adair turned their gaze back to the she-cat.

"He deserved to die."

"That was for the courts to decide. You made us judge, jury and executioners."

"I did what had to be done," he said with a shrug.

Adele's eyes narrowed and her ears flattened. Her gaze

flicked behind them, then back.

"As long as I live, I will never allow you to do that again," she hissed.

Paw steps behind them drew the tom's attention and he swiveled his ears back.

"Are you two okay?" asked the skinny yellow tom.

"My sister's shaken up, but otherwise we're fine. What happened?"

"Not sure," the tom said, shaking his head. "There'll be an investigation, but, for now, let's get you two back home."

"Yes," Adair said, cutting his eyes at Adele. "Let's go home, dear sister, and put this... tragedy behind us."

Toby caught the look of fear in his mother's eyes just before he was dropped back into his body by whatever forces had been locked into the book. He blinked several times, registering Lorn's continued snores as background noise. He flattened his ears against the wet ripping sounds and screams, but they continued on unfiltered through his mind. As he stared at the door to their room, his mother's expression of fear haunted his thoughts. Now he understood why she refused to help him find the monster who had captured his father so long ago.

Victor looked up when he heard the scrape of the door. The ragged white tom peeked around the door, his eyes searching the room before he stepped inside. Victor raised

his eye whiskers and strained his ears. The little tom had
never acted so skittish before now. He paced toward the cage,
looking back over his shoulder as if he expected someone to
appear out of thin air.

"Could you hear them down here?" he asked, his eyes
wide. A glimpse of the tom's fluffed tail as it momentarily
lashed into sight spoke volumes for his fear.

"Hear who?"

"Doesn't matter," he said, shaking his head. He peered
over his shoulder again, then edged closer to the cage.

"If you were free, could you stop him?" the white cat
whispered.

"It's Reginald, right?" The white tom nodded.
"Reginald, I don't know if I can stop him, but I'm willing to
do everything in my power to try."

"I guess that's as good as it gets."

Reginald peered over his shoulder again. Victor looked,
too. When he turned his attention back, he lowered himself to
the young tom's eye level.

"When can you get me out?"

"Not right now. It'll have to be after the move."

"What move? Can you give me any details about
what's going on?"

Reginald shook his head. "I don't have a lot of
information. All I know is that we're moving a contraption,
you and a master artificer to Transformation Mountain so
Master Shyam can complete his plans."

"Do you know when that's going to happen?"

"No, but it won't be too long from now."

"What about the contraption? Any idea what it does?"

The white tom's ragged fur fluffed and his eyes grew
wider.

"I don't know what it does except that it focuses the energy from the Book of Knowledge toward whatever target its aimed at." A shiver ran across his fur. "Thank the One that I wasn't in the room with the test subjects. I could hear them screaming through the wall."

His gaze darted to the right where the torches hung. "They weren't as thick as these. I would give anything to have been here cleaning your dirt pile instead of there, listening to them die."

"Listen to me, Reginald," Victor said, putting as much fatherly command into his voice as he could. "You couldn't help them then, but you can keep it from happening to anyone else. Do you understand me?"

The white tom turned his frightened gaze back to Victor and nodded. He held the young cat's gaze until his fur began to lay flat again.

"Good. Now, I need to know as much as you can tell me about the test subjects. How were they chosen? Was there anything about them that might have made them more susceptible to the device?"

"They were all kids from that school Toby and Lorn took down a couple months ago. Orphans, all of them."

"Are you sure they were all orphans?"

"Yes, sir. Master Shyam chose them himself and brought them here."

Victor paced his cage, trying to piece together the puzzle from the little hints Adair had given him over the years. First he'd taken over a school and used his abilities to alter the thoughts of the first students and mold them into suitable subjects. Then there was the disease he'd had his alchemist release, starting in the Lower Districts. After that, Adair had tweaked the school's programs, conducting new experiments. Now he'd said his plans were almost complete. All that remained was taking this mysterious contraption to Transformation Mountain, along with himself and a master artificer.

He glanced at Reginald. The young cat was alternately watching him and the door. Victor went back to pacing. *Orphans? The Lower District? What do they have in common?*

A soft brush of fur caressed his thoughts, making him stop. *K'Dash Shyam. New Life. Of course!*

"Reginald," he said, spinning around. The tom jumped, his ears swiveling backward as he hunkered down. Victor trotted over to him and smiled.

"I think I understand what Adair's plan is. I'm going to need you to make sure you come along when we're moved to the mountain. Think you can do that?"

Reginald cocked his head to the side, then nodded. "I think I know a way."

"Good. When the time comes, you'll need to be ready to do exactly what I tell you. Think you can follow my orders?"

"Absolutely," he said, straightening to attention. His tail tip vibrated with excitement.

"Alright, then. You need to get back to whatever you're supposed to be doing. We don't need Adair getting suspicious."

"Yes, sir."

The white tom gave a crisp nod, then trotted out the door. Victor sat down to give his ragged fur a good washing while he pondered his new insight into his enemy's plans. *Adair was an orphan once and now he's styled himself as a born again savior. What better way to begin the re-creation of the world than from the lowest level of society just like the Beloved. Unlike the Beloved, though, this savior isn't in it for the ones he wants to*

230

*save. Good thing not everyone's been sucked into his delusions of grandeur.* Victor looked up at the door with narrowed eyes. Adair's playing piece had just given away his strategy. The next move was his. Victor smiled. *Time to topple a would-be king.*

# Chapter 12

C'mon, Toby. You know this isn't a good idea. I mean, just look at me," Lorn said, holding out a trembling hand. "And that's with me concentrating on holding it steady."

"I agree with your partner. Leaving now could spell disaster," Nadine added.

Toby closed his eyes, instantly regretting it as a vision of the murderous crowd popped into view. His eyes flew open. He licked his ruff to hide his discomfiture, then looked back up at his partner.

"I'm not asking you to go. And," he continued, turning to Nadine, "if we wait until Lorn's back to full health, that monster could trigger the Apocalypse before we have a chance to stop him."

"I'm usually the one wanting to rush into things. What gives?" asked Lorn.

Toby shifted from paw to paw, forcing himself not to look toward the book on the table. Lorn leaned back against the wall and stroked his shaggy brown beard.

"It's your father, isn't it? I saw him there, alive, and you're itching to rescue him."

"Yeah. That's it," Toby said, catching the excuse with figurative claws and hanging on. "I need to rescue my father before he can be tortured anymore."

Nadine cleared her throat, catching their attention.

Toby's heart sank at the frown on her whiskers.

"There is more at stake than rescuing your father," she said. "I believe you understand that better than anyone else."

She didn't look at the book. She didn't have to. He knew she suspected he'd found something disturbing in there, but at least she seemed willing to keep it to herself. Though for how long, Toby couldn't guess. Lorn shifted on the cot.

"Alright, fine. If you think we need to go, then we'll go," he said, "but I'm warning you now that I have no intention of letting you do all the work on the way."

"That makes two of us," Nadine said.

The partners looked at her with stunned expressions.

"Whoa. Wait a minute. I thought you couldn't get involved," Toby said.

"I can't," she said. "Not in the way you want. I have my own mission to see to and it happens to go along with what you're trying to do. Besides," she continued, giving each of them a hard stare that reminded Toby of his mother, "if you two are determined to run straight to the Demon King's lair, you'll need someone who can lead you back out in one piece. Now, if you don't mind, I think I'll get some sleep. The morning will come early, so I suggest you do the same," she said. She scowled at them a moment longer, then left.

"Is she serious?" Lorn asked.

"Seems so."

Lorn shook his head. "That's one crazy feline."

"No more than we are," Toby said.

He stared at the closed door a while longer, listening to the sounds of his partner settling in for the night. He wanted to be angry with Lorn and Nadine for insisting on traveling with him, but he couldn't. As he turned to knead his nest into a more comfortable shape, his gaze fell across the book. His skin twitched.

He laid down, resting his head on an outstretched paw. Watching Lorn out of the corner of his eye, his thoughts turned back to what he'd seen in the last vision. His tail fluffed. *If even part of what I saw was true, then maybe being crazy is the only way to survive this thing.*

Clarence tucked himself against the wall at the table, watching the sports fans at the bar and nearby tables with interest. The owner must have known his investment in the sports bar and grill would pay off well because he had purchased the services of a master mage and Master Sylvester to create a large box hanging from the wall above the bar. Inside the box was a moving picture, made possible through both the master artificer's gadgetry and the mage's magic. A cheer went up from the crowd as the man in the picture kicked the black and white ball past another man and into a large net. Money was exchanged between several patrons and others downed tiny glasses of amber liquid. The waitresses bustled between tables, refilling glasses and replacing baskets of marinated chicken wings.

Clarence chuckled. He knew very little about the game, but apparently it was cause for some interesting side games and gambling. The bell above the door jingled, almost lost in the voices around him. He looked up to see David and Aaron stride through the door. When they turned his direction, he waved to them and they made their way over.

"Whose winning?" David asked, nodding to the moving picture.

"If I had to guess, I'd say the ones in the blue and white are ahead, though not by much."

"They show the score yet?"

"If they did, I didn't notice. I've been too busy watching the games going on here to pay any attention."

"What games?" Aaron asked, looking around the crowd.

At that moment another man in red and black jumped on the screen, letting the ball bounce off his chest. His team mate danced down the field, the ball jiggling between his feet. He kicked it into the air toward another of his teammates. The man flipped himself into the air and kicked the ball past a player in blue and white and into the net. The crowd moaned and more money was exchanged. Clarence nodded toward a nearby table as the customers downed another round of shots.

"Those games."

"Just some friendly wagers," David said and chuckled. He waved to a passing waitress. "Two ales and a basket of wings."

"Any milk today?" she asked, smiling at Aaron.

"Don't suppose you have any spiced milk, do you?"

"I believe so, would you like me to check?"

"Sure. If ya don' then just stick your bonny finger in it. That'll spice it up, jus' fine," the wildcat said with a wink.

David rolled his eyes and Clarence hid his smile behind his hand. The waitress grinned and left.

"Stick her finger in it? Where do you come up with that shtick?"

Aaron shrugged. "In case you haven't noticed, that

shtick gets us the best service here. Without that we'd probably have to fetch our food from the kitchen ourselves," he said. Just then another goal was made and the crowd cheered.

"Just look over there at that table," Aaron said, nodding toward a group at the far side of the room. Clarence wondered if the woman's hand might fly from her arm the way she was waving it at the waitresses bustling around the sports fans. "I rest my case."

David humphed and turned back to them.

"At any rate, we didn't come here to get great service," he said, turning toward Clarence. "Did you speak with Terence yet?"

"Indeed I have and I must say he has gained some very interesting friends."

"Interesting how?"

"It seems we are not the only party interested in halting the terrorist's plot. Besides Alie and Dora, there was a she-cat at our meeting—an odd looking feline named Chaeli."

"Did you say Chaeli?" Aaron asked.

The bell above the door jingled in the relative silence. The next moment the crowd erupted again in cheers. Clarence glanced up, frowning at the noise, then leaned closer to the wild cat.

"Yes. Do you know her?" he asked, raising his voice.

"I've read some reports on her activities. Apparently she has a special ability to create bubbles in time. It's even been reported that she can time travel."

"That's impossible," David said.

Aaron's ears twitched. "It's not traveling through time like you're thinking. What she can do is pull herself and anyone or thing she wants into a space between now and a future moment. Then she stays there until the time she's been waiting for arrives outside the time bubble and exits into that moment."

"Time travel," said Clarence, nodding in understanding.

"It'd be a good way to hide an army," David growled.

"That's one of the reasons the King's Men have been looking for her. They say she has an army of her own, loyal only to her and her vision."

"Guerrillas. I suppose they're planning to overthrow the king."

"I don't think so. I'll admit it's odd," Aaron said, cocking his head, "but everything I've heard seems to indicate she doesn't have much interest in politics at all."

"That's the feeling I got when we met. Her plans seem to run toward some deeper, more spiritual path. I almost mistook her for a Sister Cat."

"Great. A religious nut. Just what we need on our side. Don't suppose she had anything helpful to add to our investigation," David said.

"She didn't tell me a lot that would help us piece together our puzzle, but she did give me a warning to pass along. It seems our foe has acquired the Book of Knowledge and intends on using it."

"Wait. First you tell me you spoke to a time traveling she-cat, then you expect me to believe there's a book from a fairytale out there about to be used as some kind of weapon?"

"Strange, to be sure, but I saw no reason to doubt her."

The waitress arrived with their ales and hot wings and placed them on the table between the men. She set Aaron's spiced milk in front of him with a wink, then left. The hum of the crowd's voices swallowed the sound of her footsteps. David leaned back in his chair, frowning at Clarence.

"Okay, let's just say that what she said is true. It doesn't get us any closer to stopping this maniac. Did the two clerks have anything helpful?"

"You could say that. They gave us a name for our elusive fiend, Adair, and they gave me something else that I think will prove quite useful," Clarence said, patting the air beside him. David raised an eyebrow and Clarence leaned closer, pretending to carefully choose a hot wing. "It's the files."

David and Aaron looked at each other, then back at Clarence as he sat back, taking a bite of the tangy, spicy chicken wing. Aaron placed a paw on the table and searched the crowd, his ears swiveling back and forth.

"Gillespie's here."

"Fantastic. How are we supposed to get those out of here with him watching us?"

"We don't," Aaron said.

"You saying we should leave 'em here?"

"Short term storage. No one would think to look for them at a sports bar."

"And how do you presume we hide them?" asked David, glaring at his partner.

"In plain sight," Aaron said, grinning as he bent to lap some spiced milk.

David shook his head and reached for a wing. "Like the tapestry I suppose."

"Something like that."

The wildcat twitched his tail and Clarence felt a slight breeze as the invisible boxes floated past to whatever hiding place Aaron had thought of. He took a sip of ale and grimaced, placing the mug back on the table.

"I dare say that I much prefer my tea to this." He plucked another wing from the basket, looking at David over the rim of his glasses. "I'll leave that to you two. Did either of you find out anything new while I was away?"

"A colleague of mine was promoted to King's Man."

"Not that little scrap of fur?" David asked.

"Aye."

"Any chance he can help us?" Clarence asked.

"Nah. He wouldn't have access to what we want. But," he said, narrowing his eyes and grinning, "I did happen to tag along on a Tell Tale that was very, shall we say, enlightening."

"Spit it out furball," David said.

"Well, the King's Man who drafted Adair on that mission became a Brother Cat not long after. Rumor has it that he believes Adair was the apprentice of Gravin Athenios and that he learned to use the gravin's super weapon. Brother Harold moved out to a temple near Transformation Mountain."

"Isn't that the cat Toby befriended at the New Life Temple School?" asked David, quirking an eyebrow.

"I believe so. According to our reports, it was a Brother Harold that called the situation in to the OKG."

"That's quite a ways away from his temple. I wonder what he was doing there."

"Perhaps one of you should ask him," suggested Clarence.

"Do we know where he is now?" David asked.

"As far as we know, he returned to his temple. I'll see if I can contact him," Aaron said.

"Good," David said, turning his gaze toward the crowd. "I'll follow Gillespie. 'Bout time that rat turd found a new hobby."

Clarence raised his glass in a mock toast and said, "I don't envy him your persuasion."

## Master Cat

Gillespie focused on the portrait of his wife on the wall. The picture hardly looked like her now. The woman's round face and pink lips looked nothing like the hollowed cheeks and pale, dry lips of the wraith he'd left sleeping at home. He ran his hand through his thinning hair and tried to remember what it was like to hold a woman in his arms instead of a skeleton.

A knock at his office door made him turn. Bile rose in his throat as he considered what he was about to do. It was nothing new, but it always made his stomach sour. He patted his robe down, grimacing at the way it hung loosely on him now. The knock came again, more insistent. Gillespie took a deep breath, held it for a count of ten, then released it, hoping the stress would leave with the exhalation.

"Enter," he said.

Councilman Damon pushed the door open and lumbered to the chair in front of his desk. Gillespie felt his jaw tighten and swallowed back the sour taste in his mouth. At least he wouldn't have to deal with the black beast this time.

"Well, what news do you have for us?" the councilman asked, lowering his doughy body into the chair.

"They've made contact with the clerks."

"Did they say where the boxes are hidden?"

Gillespie shook his head. Damon glared at him, patting sweat from his forehead with an embroidered handkerchief.

"What good does that do us? If we don't know where the boxes are, then we can't retrieve them. Your master will

241

be very displeased to hear you have failed," he said, a smirk creeping across his lips, "yet again."

"How am I supposed to find out where they've hidden them? I can't very well just go ask," Gillespie said, throwing his hands in the air. He would have liked to tell Damon and his black beast to go to the Pits, but he kept it behind his teeth.

"No, I suppose you can't do that. However, you have a job to do and if you can't, then there will be consequences."

Damon glanced at the portrait and smiled thinly. "By the way, how is your lovely wife?"

"You know how she's doing," Gillespie growled.

"Ah, yes. One wonders how such a lady of virtue could have ever contracted the wasting sickness. Such a terrible way to die."

"She's not dead yet."

"True. Though it may not be much longer without proper remedies. The apothecary will surely call for payment on your debts soon. How long did you say it's been since you were able to pay him?"

Gillespie clenched his fists, lowering them below the desktop.

"It's too bad that someone can't help take some of the burden from you," Damon said. "Of course, with the amount of aid you would need, I'm certain you would feel obligated to work out some form of compensation. Only the Brothers work for free, am I right?"

"I can't give you what I don't have," he said, imagining his hands sinking into the folds around the councilman's neck.

"That is too bad. I shall let your master know that you no longer require his assistance."

Damon placed his beefy hands on the arms of the chair to lever himself up. Gillespie's heart jumped. He searched his memory for anything that might be of value to the black beast and his puppet.

"O'dorn mentioned something about a cat who could travel through time," he blurted.

"Don't be preposterous. No one can do that. If you can do nothing but make up tales, then we have nothing more to discuss."

Damon heaved himself up and waddled toward the door. Gillespie shot from his chair.

"What about the King's Man named Harold. Aaron plans to interview him soon. They're going to ask about the first mission."

The councilman stopped, turning a narrow eyed gaze on him.

"What do you know about that?"

"Nothing more than the stories that float around here, but Aaron has a way with people. If he gets the truth out of that cat, then they'll be able to put everything together."

The two men stared at each other for several moments. Gillespie's heart beat hard in his chest.

"When?"

"They didn't say for sure, but I'd wager it'll be soon. Maybe even within the next day or two."

Damon grunted, then fished in his vest pocket, drawing out a small vial of clear liquid.

"I am well aware of Guardian Aaron's ability to charm." He handed Gillespie the vial and turned to go.

"Wait a minute," he said, thrusting the vial in front of the councilman's face. "There should be two of these."

Damon glared at him until he let his hand drop, then smiled.

"The worker is only worth what he brings in," he said.

His smile faded. "Consider this your final warning."

The door shutting echoed in his mind as he contemplated the vile of remedy. He turned his gaze to the portrait of his wife, the image blurred from tears he refused to shed.

Toby padded through the ferns, gritting his teeth and lashing his tail. He knew what was supposed to happen next. Racing down the packed dirt path, he vowed that this time would be different.

He burst through a wall of ferns into a small clearing. There she sat next to a pool of clear water. He gazed at the pool, knowing it was out of his reach. Anger burned its way through his mind and he turned to glare at his mother.

"You lead me here every time, yet you never let me drink. All you give me are riddles, just like everyone else. Why can't you just tell me the truth?"

She smiled at him.

"All is well, my son. He knows you are thirsty. Drink and be filled."

"You know I can't. Why won't you help me? Why didn't you tell me about your brother?"

Adele blinked and sighed. "I didn't think you would ever need to know the truth."

It was Toby's turn to blink and stare. He'd had this dream countless times before, but she had never answered him so directly.

"This isn't a dream, is it?"

"Not exactly. You're asleep and I'm not here with you physically, but the One has allowed me to be a part of your life ever since I died."

"Why?"

"Apparently, it's part of the Plan," she said with a shrug.

"What plan? You mean Adair's plan to take over the world?"

She shook her head. "No. It's the Grand Design, the Great Plan of the One."

"So you're a Winged One?"

"Really, Toby, do I look like I have wings?" she asked, narrowing her eyes.

"Then what are you?"

"Does it matter?"

"I guess not," he said with a shrug. He studied the regal black queen. "So when you say you've been with me ever since you died, what does that mean?"

She cocked her head. "You remember those times when you were investigating the temple school and you didn't know what to do?"

"Yeah."

"Do you remember having a spark of inspiration hit just when you needed it most?"

"That was you?"

"Those were the One's ideas, I just helped you see them."

He stared at her a long moment. She might be beyond the veil, but she was still teaching him apparently. His whiskers widened into a smile.

"I think I prefer that method of teaching to the way you used to do it."

Adele looked down at her paws. "I'm sorry for that, Toby. You always did your best to please me and I never saw it until it was too late. Can you forgive me?" she asked, looking up at him.

"There's nothing to forgive, mother. You wanted the best for me and you did what you had to to get it out."

Her whiskers splayed and she nodded. As if it were some kind of signal, his mouth and throat suddenly felt parched. He looked at the cool water, wondering if this time he'd be able to drink from it.

"What's happening? Why am I thirsty again?" he asked, turning back to his mother.

"There is one more lesson I must teach you, but it is one you must discover the answer to on your own."

"I can't do it."

"You must."

The young cat stretched his neck carefully toward the water's edge. Would the bubble be there? When his nose encountered the barrier, disappointment weighed down his fur. He looked back at his mother. She nodded encouragingly at him. He turned back to the water, this time reaching a paw toward it and encountering the same invisible wall. He glanced back at the sleek black queen. She hadn't moved, nor had her expression changed.

"How am I supposed to drink if there's a mage bubble over the water?"

"There is no bubble. There is only you."

Toby lashed his tail, staring at the water and feeling the tug of magic around it.

"I can feel the magic. I thought you were done lying to

me."

"It's the truth, Toby. There is only you between what you think you need and what you truly seek."

His thirst drove his attention back to the pool. His fur fluffed as he turned to unleash his rage upon the barrier. He came nose to nose with the black queen and jumped back. He stared into her piercing yellow eyes.

"You cannot obtain that which you desire most until you gain that which is strongest within you."

"What does that mean?" he growled.

Adele shook her head. "I can't tell you. You must figure it out on your own. All I can say is that it has been the driving force behind your relationship with your partner from the beginning and it's the thing that makes you so much like your father."

The orange tom blinked, his ears twitching. He peered past his mother at the water, his mouth feeling like it was stuffed with cotton. Adele's tail fell gently across his shoulders.

"You've already taken the first step here, but what you must do later will require all your strength."

"What step? What will happen later?"

A faint sound in the distance made him turn to look behind, but he saw nothing except the ferns moving in the still air. A shiver snaked its way from his shoulders to his tail. He could feel something moving beyond those innocent seeming fronds. When nothing else moved, he turned his attention back to his mother, who had returned to her original position further away to his right.

"You must find the strength, Toby. You must—"

Something large and black leaped from the ferns behind Adele. She disappeared in a puff of gray smoke as the beast landed where she stood. Piercing green eyes stared at him above a feral grin. Claws the size of a man's finger dug trenches in the soil as it stalked him. The beast lunged.

Toby turned to run. The black apparition landed on him, flattening his body beneath its massive weight and driving the breath from him. A paw the size of an older child's fist pushed down hard against his throat, its claws piercing his skin. Toby gaped at the beast as it bent closer. As darkness closed in around him, all he could see were the menacing green eyes. The cat's deep voice rumbled through his mind.

"There's no escape. You are mine."

# Chapter 13

Victor lay against the floor of the transport cage as it was floated onto a wagon. The number of cats moving around reminded him of a wasp nest he saw once as a kit. He patted his nose involuntarily as he remembered the sting he'd received when he'd gotten too curious for their pleasure. As he stared at Adair's army, he knew they were even more dangerous.

"Impressive, aren't they?" Adair asked, leaping into the wagon beside him.

"Not the words I'd use," he said.

"And just think, you're guest of honor here. Without you, this would be impossible."

Victor tore his eyes from the seething mass to stare at the black tom.

"How exactly did I make this possible? I never helped you do any of it."

"Don't be modest, my friend. You were the inspiration, the catalyst as it were. If you and I didn't resemble each other so much, I never would have been introduced to Master Athenios. Nor would I have been able to conceive such a grand scheme. I would have been stuck doing penny ante bits of reconstruction rather than masterminding the complete overhaul of creation."

"You're mad."

Adair chuckled. "Perhaps. Mad or not, you must admit that what I have done defies everything we thought possible for one cat to do."

They watched as the light focusing weapon was loaded onto another wagon. Adair grinned and nodded toward it.

"Beautiful, isn't it?" he asked. Victor clamped his teeth around the hiss that wanted to escape. The black tom continued without noticing. "Thanks to Master Sylvester, all my planning is about to come to completion. The game is nearly won."

"Only if the defender is out of moves."

Adair turned narrowed eyes on him. "I have taken all the pieces that matter. There is simply victory from here."

One of the blue Russian twins padded up to them, bowing to Adair. "We are ready," he said.

"Excellent," Adair said. "Send word to our operatives. The pieces must be in place by the time we reach Transformation Mountain."

The brawny tom bowed again and trotted away as Reginald came up to the wagon.

"I've stowed the Book in your wagon, master. Is there anything else you need before I join the rest of your army?"

"That will be all," Adair said. The white tom turned to leave when Adair leaped down beside him. He placed his fluffy black tail across the young cat's shoulders, making Victor's fur bristle. "You seem out of sorts, little one. Surely your heart leaps at the thought of being free from cleaning up this one's filth."

"Of course, master," Reginald said, glancing back at Victor. "I'm just thinking of the long trip to the mountain."

"Take heart. Once this is all over, you will be a king amongst the rabble humans and cats such as that one will trouble you no more."

The young tom's whiskers widened and his tail vibrated. "I can hardly wait," he said.

Victor watched them trot toward the lead wagon and began working on a new plan of escape.

Aaron gaped at the piles of books packed into Brother Harold's tiny office and wondered what kind of cat Brother Harold must be. Every speck of horizontal space from the floor to the desk and two straight-backed chairs were crowded with well-worn books and rolled up parchments. A massive bookshelf crammed with more books teetered in the corner. He'd been told that this temple boasted a library that rivaled the High Temple, but Aaron wondered if Brother Harold had borrowed them all and stuffed them into his tiny office. He heard the click of the door opening and turned to peer around a pile of books.

"Good day," he said, nodding to the skinny yellow tom who entered. "Brother Harold, I presume?"

"I'd like to know who else uses this office," the yellow tom said, his tail jerking.

Aaron shifted, knocking some books off the pile next to him. "From the looks of it, every would-be scholar in the Reaches," he said.

Harold grunted and sat, wrapping his rail-thin tail around his paws. "I see there's no loss for jesters in the OKG. Too bad. We might have saved ourselves a war if you kits spent more time studying your enemy rather than learning new ways to trade a jibe."

"Touche," Aaron said and smiled. He began to wonder if he'd met the canary he couldn't charm from the branches. Gathering his thoughts, he continued, "Actually, that's why I'm here. My partner and I have been on the trail of the cat we believe is behind all the terrorism in the kingdom. It's our understanding that you might have some important background information."

Harold grunted again. He stood and turned to leap onto the book-piled desk chair. Aaron held his breath, expecting an avalanche, as the old tom leaped to the top of the pile with a grace that belied his age.

"So they finally believe me," he said, stepping onto the desk and threading his way through more piles. "Took them long enough."

Aaron sighed silently. Harold might be warming up to the discussion, but Aaron wasn't sure what he was about to say would keep the conversation going in the right direction. Taking a deep breath, he stalked ahead.

"I'm afraid there are few who believe it, just my partner and I and a master mage named Clarence O'dorn. We were fortunate enough that two young partners were able to ferret out some old documents from the Hall of Records that back up our story, but without something to connect the dots in a way that any Outer Reaches bumpkin can see it, I'm afraid we'll never get a conviction."

"And so you've come here, hoping I could give you the last piece of the puzzle to help you nail the mangefur. That about right?" Harold asked peering over a stack of rolled parchments.

"That's our hope, yes."

"Whatever happened to that youngster who brought down Father Hanif?"

"Lorn?" Aaron asked, blinking in confusion.

"No, no. Not his partner. The orange tom. Where's he?"

"Toby?"

"That's the one."

"He left the OKG to search for his father."

"Well, I know that. I was there when he made the decision," Harold said. He scowled as he continued, "Don't tell me the mighty OKG didn't keep tabs on their most promising kit."

"We're not sure where he is at the moment."

"Fools and dunderheads," the old tom said with a snort. He disappeared behind the stack again. Aaron heard the rustle of paper as Harold muttered to himself. "Ah. Here it is." The yellow tom reappeared around a pile of books and flowed from the desk to the overflowing chair, then onto the floor, a book floating behind him.

"I'm going out on a limb here and assuming you know about the raid on Gravin Athenios' compound several years ago," Harold said.

Aaron nodded. "Master Kurt told the story at the last Tell Tale."

"That old furball still around? I thought he'd kicked up his heels by now," Harold said. Aaron's whiskers widened. He was beginning to like the old curmudgeon.

"Well, anyway," Harold continued, twitching his tail to settle the book between them. "After we secured the gravin's compound, we searched it. Rumor was that he was building some kind of doomsday device."

"I'm guessing you didn't find it."

Harold narrowed his eyes at the Highland cat. "If we did, would we be having this conversation?"

"Point taken."

"Problem was, we didn't find the device and our inside informant was missing, presumed dead. We went round and round with Athenios' men, but either they were better trained than we expected or the gravin never let them in on what he was up to."

"What about Athenios himself?"

Harold shook his head. "Never caught him."

"So you don't have anything to back up your claims?"

"I didn't say that," the old tom growled. "We confiscated everything that wasn't nailed down, and a few that were. Went through it all and came away with nothing but religious drivel."

"Except it wasn't, am I right?"

"Now you're catching on," Harold said, nodding. He put his paw on the book between them. "This is a lifetime of searching through riddles and religious mumbo-jumbo. Athenios was good and his apprentice is better."

"So you know who the apprentice is?"

Harold closed his eyes, his head dipping toward his chest. Aaron held himself still, perking his ears as the old tom took a deep breath and opened his eyes. A knock at the door interrupted them. Aaron cursed whoever it was in his thoughts and turned to watch the door.

"Enter," Harold called, his rusty voice seeming even rougher.

"Your tea, sir," said a young boy.

"Thank you, Eustice. Just set it on the floor."

"Would you like me to pour?" the boy asked.

"If you wouldn't mind. You know my old tail isn't

what it used to be," Harold said. The ancient tom smiled, compassion and humor twinkling in his eyes.

"Of course, Brother Harold," the boy said with a grin. Aaron studied the lad, noting how the novice's robe hung loosely on his young frame. He wished he could see the boy's arms to see if he'd been one of the children moved elsewhere after the New Life School went up in flames. His attempts to solve the question frustrated, he turned his attention back to his host.

The old tom turned his attention back to Aaron. "To answer your question, yes, I do know who the apprentice is, though he's the master now."

"What do you mean by that?" Aaron asked, glancing at the serving boy from the corner of his eye. He turned back to Harold as the old tom continued.

"Besides the fact that this upstart is carrying out a plan similar to his mentor, we found Athenios' body about a year after the raid. At the time we had no idea how he'd died, but now I'm pretty sure he was the first in a string of experiments."

"So the apprentice became the master. Poetic justice, I'd say."

The earthy aroma of tea drifted to Aaron's nose as the young boy began filling the bowls. Aaron turned to sniff the heady steam, catching an underlying floral scent. He watched as the lad tipped the teapot back without spilling a drop, then hovered the spout over the second bowl.

"No poetry to it," Harold said. "It was single-minded murder and it wasn't the kit's first time."

"You mean the mob," Aaron said, looking back at Harold.

"Ah, so you figured that out already."

"Any idea how he did it?"

"He has the same gift his mother has, though the accident stripped him of all other magical abilities."

"Wait. If we're talking about the same cat, I know he's been seen using magic before. How is that possible?"

"He uses blood magic to transfer power to himself from his victims. Takes a lot of work, and the stomach for torture," Harold said, his whiskers clamped together, "but it can be done."

"Based on what we've seen so far, I don't doubt he has what it takes. Any ideas how we can cage this monster?"

Harold opened his mouth to respond just as hot amber liquid splashed over Aaron's paws. He danced backward, crashing into a pile of books, then turned to stare at the serving boy. The lad's mouth was forming voiceless words, his eyes unfocused and staring into space. Aaron slammed a shield over him and closed his eyes, not wanting to watch yet another child explode while he stood helpless.

"R'pah R'shah," shouted Harold.

Aaron felt a thump against the interior of the shield and opened his eyes a slit. His eyes widened when he saw the lad slumped against the invisible barrier. He turned to stare at the old yellow tom.

"How did you know what to do?"

"A little incantation I discovered back at the New Life School. Seems the cats doing all the experiments made sure there was a universal kill switch for every experiment in case of failure."

"I suppose it would have been inconvenient to blow up the school," Aaron said. "Obviously one of us was the target."

Harold stretched his neck over the bowls of tea, his nose working. When he looked back at Aaron, his eyes narrowed and ears flattened.

*Master Cat*

"From the smell of that brew, I'd say it wasn't just one of us. If we'd managed to keep from setting Eustice off, then we'd be just as dead when we drank the tea," he said, nodding toward the bowls. "That's laced with something made from blood magic."

"How do you know?"

"Let's just say I don't drink floral scented teas anymore thanks to an old friend's allergy."

"Toby's father. So you think the new master sent us a gift of the plague?"

"Or some derivative."

Aaron stared at the child and shook his head. "Word will get back to his master that the deed failed."

"Only if we let it," Harold said.

Aaron whipped his gaze to the old tom, raising his eye whiskers. Harold shrugged.

"I've been expecting something like this for some time."

"You have a plan."

Harold snorted. "Wouldn't have been much of a King's Man if I didn't know how to outflank my enemy, now would I?"

"So what do we do?"

"First we hide the boy and disseminate a little rumor. Then we get you back to your partner with your missing piece of the puzzle," Harold said, flicking his tail toward the book he'd shoved away from the spilled tea. The old tom gave him a penetrating look. "How strong's your stomach?"

"As strong as any cat's, I suppose," Aaron said, cocking his head to the side. "Why do you ask?"

"'Cause you're going to need it. Come on," Harold said, standing and twitching his tail toward the door. "I have

257

a friend I'd like you to meet."

Gillespie stepped out the OKG door into the frosty air. He could see the stables across the alley, but not much else beyond, thanks to the fog. He patted his breast pocket again, watching his breath fog around him as he sighed. The beast had given him a bonus. A celebration gift, Damon had said, for helping them take out the last obstacle to the grand plan. Gillespie patted his pocket again. The single vial would have to be enough to keep her going until he could figure out a way to get more.

He minced his way past the frost covered bushes toward the stable to borrow one of the guardian horses, trying not to think about how degrading it was to need to borrow one. It didn't matter. His wife was more important than any horse. He just wished the money had gone further. As he stood looking into the dim stalls, he ran his hand over his balding head and listened for the restive stamping of a horse. The stable was quiet.

His shoulders slumped as he considered the one alternative he had to getting home. Riding in a city coach was even more degrading than borrowing a horse from work. He turned to leave, when a sound at the far end of the stable caught his attention. He smiled, thinking the One must be looking kindly on him for once as he mince-stepped toward the last stall. He turned the corner and looked in. It was empty. He peered over the top of the half-door, thinking maybe the beast was lying down. Nothing there except a layer of hay. Gillespie sighed and turned around to make his way back to the coach stop at the end of the alley. The last thing he saw was a fist headed for his face.

He heard the voices first, low and indistinct. As his mind cleared the pain in his face reminded him of what happened. He concentrated on keeping his breathing slow and even as he tried to determine who the voices belonged to.

"What does it matter that I popped him one? I got him here didn't I?"

"True, but slamming your fist into his face wasn't necessary."

"Maybe not, but it sure as fire felt good."

"Well at least we've got a back up plan if this doesn't work. How's he coming on deciphering the book?"

"It's coming. Would have helped if you'd brought back a cipher with it. Better yet, would have been a whole lot simpler if the old boy had written it out in plain speech."

"And what if it had fallen into enemy hands?"

The other voice snorted. "At least we're doing something now that'll get us closer to our goal."

"Assuming your fist didn't joggle his brain too much."

Gillespie ran the voices through the short list of who would want to capture him. That Highland accent could only be from one individual, he was sure. That meant the other voice had to belong to the wildcat's partner.

"You're going to be in serious trouble for this," he said, hissing as his jaw sent a dull ache through his head. He opened his eyes to see the partners standing in front of a closed door, David's arms crossed over his chest as he leaned against it. The room was empty, save the chair he was tied to, and the dull blue paint was peeling from the walls. It had to be a storage room, but where?

"See, didn't even knock any more screws loose," David said, glaring at his partner.

The wildcat sighed and turned to Gillespie.

"We need information and you're the sole person we can get it from. Now, as you can tell, my partner has his own ideas of how we should get it from you, but I disagree. I think you can be reasonable and I'm hoping you'll prove me right."

"What information do you think I have?"

"We know you've been working with a cat by the name of K'Dash Shyam."

"You mean Councilman Damon's cat? I've seen him around, but that's about it. What do you want with him?"

"We have reason to believe this cat is responsible for the terrorist activities."

"You can't be serious," Gillespie lied.

He could feel the sweat trickling down his sides. They knew he was a traitor. Not that it mattered. What mattered was, did *he* know they were on to him?

"Come on, Gillespie, I've seen Damon corner you in the hall like a whipped dog and we know it was you who tipped them off that Aaron was going to the temple. Spill it or I'll march you into the prison myself."

"I can't," he groaned, dropping his head to his chest.

"You spineless little weasel," David said, stepping toward him. "I should—"

"Wait a minute," Aaron interrupted. He paced forward, staring up at him. "You were a prison guard when they brought in Chivato and Gravin Arturo, weren't you?"

He nodded. The memory of finding Gravin Arturo dead in his cell, poisoned by an agressive form of Chivato's plague, floated through his mind. The vacant eyes and foamy blood pooling under the dead man's head still haunted him. He'd seen plenty of dead men during his time as a prison guard, but he still woke up in a cold sweat from those nightmares.

"If that's the case, then why not help us catch the fleabag?" asked Aaron. "You know what will happen if we take you to prison."

"I'm dead either way, but—."

He shook his head. He might be a dead man, but perhaps his wife still had a chance. If they believed he hadn't told them anything, maybe the black beast could find it in his twisted heart to cure her. Perhaps he could make him think it was a way to torture him past the grave. He could feel the sting of tears he refused to shed. Aaron placed hard paws on Gillespie's knees and stretched his nose toward him. He shuddered at the touch, leaning back as far as the chair would allow.

"You don't care about dying. You're protecting someone, aren't you?" he asked.

Gillespie looked away, staring at the flecking paint on the wall. He heard the shuffle of feet near the door as David moved closer.

"If you're protecting that black hearted beast, you should know that he plans on enslaving all humans and the ones who can't or won't serve him he's going to kill. And from what I've heard, whatever weapon he plans on using is going to make the plague look like a First Day picnic," David said.

He continued to stare at the wall. The guardian made a sound of disgust and returned to leaning on the door. Gillespie glanced at Aaron out of the corner of his eye. The wildcat was watching him, his head cocked to the side, as if he were a sparrow hopping along just within reach. It made his skin crawl.

"How's your wife?" Aaron asked.

"Don't you dare mention her," he spat, jerking his gaze to the large feline and glaring.

"They have her, don't they?"

"Leave her out of this."

He leaned forward, struggling to launch himself at the wildcat. He succeeded in upending himself onto the floor. The small vial slid out of his vest pocket and rolled across the floor until it came to rest in front of the cat's paws. Aaron studied the container, then turned to his partner.

"What would you wager that this is just enough medicine to keep Gillespie's wife alive, but not enough to cure her?"

"Makes sense," David said, picking up the vial.

"No. You can't. She needs that," Gillespie sputtered. The partners stared down at him. "Please," he begged.

David looked down at the vial in his hand, then back at him. Gillespie could feel his heart hammering in his chest. The guardian pocketed it with a frown and crossed his arms. Gillespie closed his eyes and let his head sink to the floor. He should have known. *Bad guys deserve no mercy.*

"We'll help you save your wife on one condition," David said.

He raised his head and stared at the man in disbelief. After everything, they were willing to help him? Memories of his wife singing as she sewed floated through his mind. His arms ached to hold her again, to crush her warm body next to his in a bear hug like he used to and to hear her sweet laugh as he rubbed his whiskers over her cheek. A tear slipped out of the corner of his eye and traced a wet path to his ear.

"Name it."

# Chapter 14

Toby gazed up at the plateau. Snaking along the steep path toward the top was the black beast's army in an unbroken chain of wagons, cats and human slaves. Toby felt like he'd stepped into ice water and his paws had frozen solid, but it had nothing to do with the sleet hissing against the sagebrush. The hair along the ridge of his back rose as his eyes widened, trying to take it all in.

"There's no way the three of us can stop them alone," Lorn said on his right.

"I agree," said Nadine on his left.

Toby wondered if anyone could stop them. *And father's in that mess.* He took a deep breath and backed away into the sage brush surrounding the lower rise. His companions followed him.

"We can't turn back now."

"I'm not saying we should, but it'll take more than just us to take them down," Lorn said. "We need to get help."

"That'll take too long," Toby said.

"We don't have a choice."

Toby lashed his tail. It had taken them over a week to make it here. He stared through the undergrowth toward the walled temple Nadine had said was on the adjacent plateau. It would be at least a day's walk to get there to call for help. That was assuming a mirror call wouldn't be intercepted.

This close to the enemy, he couldn't even be sure a dragon messenger would make it through.

"There's got to be something we can do," he growled.

"I think you're both right," Nadine said.

He stared at her, ears flattening. "What is that supposed to mean?"

"As Lorn said, we can't stop an entire army by ourselves."

"I think we've already established that."

"Let me finish."

Toby rolled his eyes.

"Go on," Lorn said.

"We can't stop them, but maybe we can stall them until help can get here."

"First, how are we supposed to call for help? And second, how do you propose we stall them? It took us over a week to get here," Toby said.

"I know a way to contact my mentor that is untraceable. With her help, I know we can get your people here in time."

Toby and Lorn looked at each other, then back at the she-cat.

"Do it," they said together.

Nadine closed her eyes. As they watched her, Toby felt a familiar tug on his mind. When he closed his eyes, he was brought into Nadine's spirit world. The she-cat's smokey blue form looked the same as before. Curious, he turned to look at Lorn standing next to them. The man's form shifted and eddied in alternating yellows and grays like a murky pool being refilled with clean water. Toby glanced at Nadine, wondering if she knew why.

*The link. Lorn is working to bury it once again, she said into his thoughts. Given time the darkness will be locked away again, as it is in all of us.*

A ripple of unease coursed through him. Time wasn't something they had. A gasp from his partner caught his attention.

"This is spectacular," Lorn said. He looked down at Toby. "So you think it's always so colorful?"

"Only when everything is in harmony with the One. Take a look at the plateau," Nadine said.

They turned to see the monolith called Transformation Mountain bathed in a gray mist that rolled down its sides like fog.

"Whatever he's doing up there goes against the Will of the One. It's not just human lives he's messing with. He's messing with all things spiritual as well."

Toby turned narrowed eyes toward the she-cat.

"I think I know why. Better contact your mentor quick. We need to get our people here as fast as possible."

"I'm already here," said an oddly colored she-cat.

The she-cat's face looked as if two cats were vying for supremacy over it. She stared at him out of two different color eyes, a blue one on the orange side and a green one on the black side. The green eye pulled him in, making him feel like a fur-less kit set adrift in a placid lake. Toby blinked.

"I brought your friend with me," she said, nodding to her right. Terence padded closer on spirit paws and nosed his cheek.

"Good to see you again," the patched tabby said.

"Are we glad to see you," said Lorn.

"There will be time for getting re-acquainted later," the she-cat said as she turned toward Nadine. "What have you found?"

"You were right, mistress, the one calling himself

New Life has the Book of Knowledge. He plans to use it on Transformation Mountain."

"My father's up there, too," Toby said.

"You found him?" asked Terence.

"Lorn did."

"How?"

"It's a long story," Toby said, shaking his head. "I'll tell you about it if we get through this."

"You mean when," the patched tabby said, giving him a stern look. Toby smiled and nodded. Despite the overwhelming odds and his own gnawing fear, he wanted to believe his friend's optimism.

"We must get the Book away from him," said Nadine's mentor.

"There's a problem with that. There's an army between us and that Book of yours," Lorn said.

"If we don't retrieve the Book of Knowledge before he uses it, then everything will be plunged into chaos."

"Listen, lady, it's not that we don't want to get that book, it's that we can't do it by ourselves and anyone that can help is weeks away by horse. Nadine said you can help with that."

The she-cat narrowed her eyes at him. "I can get your people here within the day, but they must be willing to make the journey," she said, then turned to look at her student. "They will not trust an outsider, I think."

"But what about the Book?" Nadine asked.

"It has waited this long, I think it can wait a bit longer while we gather reinforcements."

"But you just said—" Lorn began. The she-cat turned her odd gaze on him.

"I know what I said, young man. Wisdom is in knowing

when to move and when to stay still. That is how the prey is caught and the family fed."

"What about my father?"

The she-cat stared at the plateau for several moments without speaking.

"There is one who will help you already in the enemy's camp. He works to free your father as we speak."

Toby looked at Lorn. The man shrugged.

"We must go now," the she-cat said. "The Brotherhood must prepare for the spiritual battle to come. We are depending on you, Brother Terence, to alert them and help them to readiness."

"It's my duty and my honor, Time Keeper." He turned to Toby, his grim expression calling up memories of the patched tabby as they prepared to dig into Chivato's plot. At least this time the little tom would be somewhere safe. Toby glanced toward the plateau once more, watching the sickly gray fog drift down its steep sides, and swallowed the lump that clogged his throat. *If we can't stop that, no one will be safe.* He turned back to his little friend.

"Pray for me," he said.

"Always do, buddy," said the little tabby, flicking his tail. "See ya when it's all over."

Toby nodded and closed his eyes again. When he opened them he and Lorn were sitting alone in the brush.

"Okay, so that takes care of calling someone. What about stalling? Any ideas how we should do that?" Toby asked.

"Nope. Not a clue."

The sleet hissed around them, sounding like thousands of angry felines. As they stared at the plateau together, noting that the end of the black cat's army was just coming into sight on the trail, a shiver ran down Toby's back. He glanced down at his paws. His orange fur would stick out like dog pee on new snow. *How are we going to sneak in there?*

David crossed his arms and leaned against a building, ignoring the slush trying to seep into his boots as he scowled at the house bathed in sunlight across the street. The sole thing he liked about this plan was that he'd be able to keep an eye on Gillespie. Although the man had agreed to give them all the information he had on the black beast's plans, David wasn't sure they could trust him. For all they knew, Gillespie could be setting them up.

At least O'dorn was working his way through Brother Harold's book. *Too bad the old furball refused to come back with Aaron. Could've used his help—or at least a blasted cipher.* The old tom had told Aaron he would be more help prepping the Brotherhood for spiritual battle than chasing the bad guys around a One-forsaken hunk of rock. David snorted. The only battle about to be fought would be in this street if Gillespie was leading them into a trap. *If...*

There were so many possible variables. They could get caught while trying to free the man's wife, which would land them in prison, assuming Gillespie was telling the truth about the guards. Or they could succeed, use whatever bogus information Gillespie gave them and walk right into K'Dash's paws. Either way, working with Gillespie would be like using a scorpion to inject poison into someone—chances were you'd get stung in the process.

David's breath fogged around him as he watched the street. A bum lounged outside a local pub three buildings down where the residential area became businesses. He tipped up his bottle to swig away the contents, then let his arm drop, the pottery thunking into the cold ground beside him.

A woman in a heavy cloak decorated with garish red and green brocade walked her cat-sized dog past his hiding spot. David chuckled as she crossed the street before getting to the bum. He glanced back the way she had come. A wiry cream-colored feline sat under an evergreen bush that served as a fence along the neighbor's yard.

David shook his head as he returned his gaze to Gillespie's house. He had to admit. They were pretty clever. Unless you were looking for unusual things, you wouldn't notice the signs that none of them belonged there. The bum's clothes were dirty, but in good repair. The woman's cloak was obviously a leftover from Solstice, something no self-respecting woman in this neighborhood would wear after the holiday. As for the cat? The only well-fed felines lounging around under bushes in this post-plague world were usually there for a reason, and not a good one.

The curtain in the downstairs window shifted as Gillespie pulled it aside. David held his breath, watching carefully. The signal was right side first if they were alone, left side first if they had company. When they'd first come up with the idea of using the curtains to signal, Aaron had questioned whether their watchers would get suspicious. Gillespie had said that opening the curtains was a routine his wife had begun when they were first married, one he'd continued for her after she got sick.

Alone. That was good. Now all he needed to do was sneak in the back way and lead them to the tunnels under the city. No problem so long as no one looked out their window. Of course, Aaron had a plan for that. David glanced up into the neighbor's evergreen. Although he couldn't see his partner, he was certain the wildcat had made it up into the fir bows. At least he hoped so, otherwise their plan was blown.

He pulled his hood up and darted behind the building, making his way around to the back of Gillespie's house by a circuitous route. As he stepped through the backyard gate, he felt the tingle of magic over his skin that told him Aaron had done his job. If anyone looked back there now, their eyes would just slide over him as if he were a bit of snow glare, too bright to look at. It worked better when the ground was entirely covered in snow, but they were hoping there was enough snow left between the puddles of meltoff to convince a casual observer. David tapped lightly on the back door, then darted in.

"I told her what we're doing. She's ready to go," Gillespie said, reaching his hand down to a bundle of blankets on the chair beside the door.

Skeletal fingers reached back from under the blankets, making David catch his breath. He'd almost convinced himself that Gillespie had been lying, that this was all some kind of ruse to trap them. But staring down into the hollow brown eyes of the man's wife put all doubt from his mind.

"Let's go," he said, bending to pick the frail woman up.

Gillespie stepped in front of him. "I'll carry her," he said.

David nodded, turning to peer out the door into the frozen backyard. It was empty. He glanced back to the couple and jerked his head to indicate they should follow. Just as the group readied themselves to dart outside, there was a knock at the front door. Gillespie's face drained of color. He glanced at his wife, then at David.

"Get her to safety. I'll join you as soon as I can."    .

David took the bundle from his arms, his mind hardly comprehending the feather weight, and nodded. The man turned and left them. David didn't dare look in the woman's eyes. He knew they would beg him to stay and help her husband, but he'd made a promise he intended to keep. He crept outside with the bundle in his arms and re-traced his steps through the yard.

The back door banged open and someone shouted. David ran. Something sizzled past his head as more shouting rang out behind him. Two steps further and he felt the tingle of magic on his skin again. He was in full view now.

More magic was thrown at him. From the corner of his eye he saw the glowing mesh of a magic net headed his direction. He threw up a shield and directed it away from them, toward the net, making the glowing mesh ball bounce off and ensnare its maker.

David's lungs were starting to burn with the effort of running with the bundled up woman. *Guess the furball's right. I need to go for a run more often.* Hadn't seemed important at the time, since he was never given a field assignment anymore. He clenched his teeth as he kept running toward the corner just ahead. If he could make it that far, they'd be able to disappear in the tunnels. He just needed to get there with enough space between him and his pursuers to slip through the hidden door without being seen. *Sure could use a distraction right about now.* He never considered himself a praying man, but at the moment he was willing to cover all his options.

There was an explosion behind him. He stumbled, but held tight to the frail woman in his arms, forcing his legs to stay under him. Crowds of people streamed out of their houses and businesses to find out what had happened. Either Aaron was on his game or the One had finally heard one of his prayers. Either way it didn't matter. David smiled as he slipped around the corner and through the hidden door.

Victor shook himself, dislodging as much of the sleet from his fur as he could. The cold seeping into his skin from the freezing rain was nothing compared to the chill creeping through his thoughts. He'd overheard one of the Russian twins tell Adair that all the pieces were in place. That had to mean that he would use the contraption soon.

He watched through slitted eyes as the black tom gave orders from his throne-like chair on a makeshift raised dais. The sleet ran off his heated shield in rivulets, congealing at the bottom and turning the whole thing into something resembling a giant's snowglobe. It would have been touching, except Victor knew the tom was anything but a harmless fluff ball.

A streak of dirty white caught his attention from the corner of his eye. He glanced over to see Reginald shivering, wide-eyed behind a stack of crates. Victor shook himself again and settled down as if he were going to take a nap in the sun. He purred as loud as he could, hoping it would help calm the young tom. Reginald bellied closer.

"I'm here. Now what?"

"I need you to find the ends of the spell on this cage."

Reginald glanced toward the mass of cats moving about following Adair's orders. "Won't he know?" he whispered.

"Don't touch them, just look at the web with your mage sight. So long as you don't touch anything, he'll never know what you're doing." When he continued to lay belly to ground, Victor added, "Imagine the spell is someone's dirt and you have to figure out how to remove it without getting it on your paws."

The white tom nodded and took a deep breath. Victor kept his slitted gaze on the activity beyond them. He could feel the young cat's eyes on him, as if staring at a pile of cat dirt. He would have smiled if it wouldn't have given Reginald away. If they survived this, he would appeal the young cat's case to the academy personally.

"Found them. How do I show them to you without touching the field?"

"Just tell me where they are. I should be able to see them myself."

"How? From what I can see, they won't show up on your side."

"It's like being inside a pillowcase," he said. When Reginald didn't say anything more, he glanced at him to see the young cat with his ears swiveled back and his head cocked to the side.

"I'll see the pucker," Victor explained.

Reginald's eyes widened and his whiskers began to splay.

"Don't smile, just tell me where to look."

He heard the tom suck in a breath and he mentally

shook himself for his harsh tone. It had been a long time since he'd had to deal with a kit, even one as old as Reginald. This tom might be out of his kitten fluff, but it was apparent he'd had little loving guidance over the last few years.

"It's okay," he said, trying to calm the young cat. "No one's looking this way. I just want you to be careful, is all. Now, where do I need to look?"

"Lower left corner behind you."

Victor arched his back in a spine-popping stretch and yawned, then sat down to wash his back leg, surreptitiously studying the spot Reginald had indicated. The pucker was the size of the tip of a sparrow quill. *No wonder I couldn't find it.* He had to marvel at the skill of Adair's mages. While it was possible Adair had done this work himself, Victor doubted he would have left such an important structure to his limited magical abilities. More likely, he'd employed the talents of a master. It made his fur twitch that so many master level cats would be willing to work for him. Were they doing this of their own free will, or had he manipulated them just as he had the crowd that tore his mother's partner to pieces? He glanced at Reginald again and nodded.

"You did good."

"What else can I do?"

Victor thought for a moment. There had to be a way to delay Adair's plans. If he knew more about the contraption, he could tell Reginald how to disable it. A brush of fur crossed his thoughts and he purred.

"Go find the master artificer."

"What do you want me to tell him?"

Victor splayed his whiskers in a feral grin. "Time to create a little havoc."

## Master Cat

"Psst."

The sleet hissed againsted the open air tent. Sylvester let his chin sag onto his chest, his mind going over different ways to sabotage the black beast's plans.

"Psst."

Sylvester blinked. That wasn't sleet. Someone was trying to get his attention. He squinted at the crates stacked on the other side of the tent.

"Don't look over here."

He turned his gaze back on the preparations going on near the machine, watching with some amusement as cats hesitated before leaving the heated boundary into the cold sleet.

"Who are you?" he whispered.

"A friend. I'm here with a message from Master Victor. He says we need to create a distraction."

Master Victor? It had to be the black tom in the cage. He'd seen them loading the cat up just before they'd left for the mountain. A shudder that had nothing to do with the cold wet air ran down his back as he considered why that might be.

"Can't help you. I'm a bit tied up at the moment," he said, lifting his bound hands from the small of his back. The voice chuckled.

"Kit's play. I'll have you free in a moment."

Sylvester waited quietly, expecting to feel a tingle at his wrists. Nothing happened.

"Well?"

"Mage locked. I can chew you free, but I might bite you in the process."

"Do it."

He felt the tug of his restraints in reply. Sylvester gritted his teeth as his ally alternately tugged and clawed at the rope, sometimes raking his arms or hands with needle-like claws or nipping his flesh with tiny fangs. He let his gaze roll over the area beyond the tent, watching for any sign of discovery as the enemy cats cautiously padded over the sleet covered plateau. When he felt the bonds loosen, he pulled and twisted his wrists, using the blood as lubricant to slip free.

"What's the plan?" he asked.

"I don't suppose you could whip up some contraption that could take that machine apart without us having to get too close."

"If I had my tools, maybe, but—"

"Stay here. I'll be right back." Paw steps scurried away. Sylvester glanced toward the sound, catching sight of a ragged white tail disappearing behind a stack of crates. There was a muffled whump, then several moments of silence. Sylvester began to wonder if the little white tom had been discovered.

"Looks like they brought several of your gadgets here, but I don't know what's useful."

"Describe them."

"There's a little machine that looks like a box with a tail and a couple flat sticks on top, some little metal things that look like spiders and a leather strap setup with large glass disks attached. Anything useful there?"

Sylvester forced his mouth into a frown, denying the giddiness he felt. "The leather straps contraption, does it look like it could fit on a cat or a human?"

"A cat."

"Good. Now find the small box with the levers and bring it to me."

"I didn't see that in there."

"Check again. It should be packed with the whirligig — the box with a tail."

The cat disappeared for another couple moments, then reappeared, gently batting the box between his paws. He peered around a crate, then swatted the box across the opening between them. Sylvester snatched it up, tucking his hands behind his back again.

"Do you need the whirligig, too?"

"No, just get it clear of the crate."

"What about the other stuff?"

"Get the spiders out and head them toward the beast's machine, then put on the closer up eyes. You can use them to see where the spiders are and move 'em where you want 'em."

"How?"

"Ya got magic, don't ya?"

"Of course I do."

"Then just give 'em a nudge in the right direction. They'll do the rest."

"But they'll be seen."

Sylvester grinned. "Nope. Our friends'll have other things to think about. Just let me know when you're ready."

The tom disappeared again. There wouldn't be much time to create some chaos, either the sleet would get too heavy on the miniature wings or one of the cats would discover a way to bring the whirligig down. Sylvester studied the cats milling around the icy plateau, judging where he could cause the most confusion as far away from the machine as possible.

"I don't know if I can use these closer up eyes," the tom whispered. "I thought I was going to trip over every pebble on the way over here."

"You'll get used to them. All set?"

"Ready."

"Send in the spiders."

The tom's paw steps scurried away and Sylvester focused his attention on his target. He pushed the up lever on the little box and the whirligig lifted into the sky. The reaction from the first cat he dive bombed was priceless. Although the she-cat was half-way across the plateau, he could hear her screech from where he sat. Before she recovered, he grazed the ears of another cat and followed that up with shaving the tail of yet another. In moments the entire plateau was alive with swarming, screeching felines trying to catch the whirligig without getting a tail docked or fur ripped out. Sylvester couldn't help but laugh.

"Over there," shouted a cat. "He has the controller."

A wave of felines careened toward him. He wished his ally good luck as he levered himself up and hobbled in the opposite direction. The chase would be short, he knew, but maybe it would buy his new friend enough time to hide. It was the best he could do.

Sylvester grabbed a tent pole as he stepped out of the lean-to and turned to face the oncoming mass. He swung at the first to arrive, knocking the cat away like a child's stuffed toy. The others slid to a halt, their fur bristling and fangs bared. He lashed out again, receiving hisses and growls in return. A she-cat hunkered down and wriggled her hindquarters.

"Just try it," he said, brandishing the pole.

As one, the felines sat. Sylvester narrowed his eyes, shifting his glance from left to right then on past the front row. Every cat on the plateau was sitting still, watching him. Gooseflesh crawled down his arms as they silently parted for the black beast.

"My plans cannot be stopped by a childish prank, master artificer. You should know that."

"Man's gotta try."

"I suppose you're correct. Of course, in trying one must either overcome obstacles to success or deal with the consequences of failure."

"I'm willing to sacrifice myself for this. Are you?"

The black beast's eyes narrowed and his whiskers widened. "Absolutely."

The tom's eyes drew him in as the cats around him seemed to grow as large as family cottages, their feral grins mocking and bloodthirsty. The hissing sleet sounded like a horde of demon fiends calling for his innards. Sylvester's heart hammered in his chest. He took a wobbly step backward and swung his pole. The swing overbalanced him, forcing him to take another step backward. His foot slipped on a patch of ice. He circled his arms, trying to regain his balance. As the ground fell away, he wondered if someone would ever build a flying machine.

# Chapter 15

Clarence studied the blue tapestry in David's office, its golden images creating a disturbing picture. For every clue, there seemed to be five more unanswered questions. The biggest of them being precisely what K'Dash had planned and where he would put it into action. Clarence glanced at his friend when he sighed.

"Even with all the documents backing up our claims, it's not enough. Any luck on transcribing that old tom's journal?"

"I'm slowly wading through, but it's taking a lot of time."

"Time you need for Gillespie's wife, am I right?"

Clarence nodded, gazing into his glass of liquor as he swirled it. David nudged him toward a chair across from his desk.

"How's she doing?" he asked as they took their seats.

"Too soon to say. She seems to have an altered version of what Adele had. I've given her the remedy that worked before, but until I have the full analysis done on what was in the vial, I can't be sure."

"How long will that take?"

"Hopefully by the end of the week." He took a small sip and frowned. "What about Gillespie? Did he make it out of there?"

"Won't know that until Aaron gets back with us. He'll contact us as soon as he's clear of Shyam's henchmen."

"Too bad. I was hoping to be able to give his wife some good news."

"May not be any good news. Better prepare her for that, too. If we can't finish deciphering that mangefur's notes, then we're still nowhere near ending this whole mess. We need to know where that beast is going to strike so we can be there," David said, placing his glass of amber liquor on his desk. "And Harold's journal is the one lead we have to that."

"It would be the final nail in the coffin," Clarence agreed. "Do we have enough to have Councilman Damon arrested?"

"Arrested, yes. Enough to send him to prison for the rest of his life?" David shook his head, bringing his glass to his lips and downing the contents. He reached for the decanter and poured himself another. "Even if we arrest him, chances are Shyam will lay waste to the entire country before that dung beetle says anything."

Clarence nodded as he continued to watch the amber liquid make loopy waves in his glass. "Are you sure Aaron wasn't captured?"

"The day that furball gets himself caught will be the day we retire," David said with a lopsided smile.

It made Clarence recall the times he and Adele had been so certain of the other's whereabouts and safety. His chest tightened with the thought. David set his glass on his desk, drawing Clarence's attention back to him.

"This is different. Aaron knows there's someone out to kill him. He may get his tail docked, but he'll come out of it alive," he said.

"I suppose you're right," Clarence said, smiling sadly.

"You two have been in worse scrapes than this, I'm sure."

"Absolutely," he said with a lopsided grin. "In fact, have I ever told you about when—"

David's eyes widened, his gaze focused on something behind Clarence's chair. He turned to see what his friend was staring at. A purple globe the size of a wagon wheel hovered a hand span above the floor. As he watched, it grew another foot larger, thinning until it was translucent with three smaller shapes inside. He heard David murmuring behind him. Something about the shapes made him hold up his hand to stall the guardian before he could unleash whatever spell he was preparing.

An instant later, the globe disappeared with a pop and tinkle as if a glass ornament fell to the floor and three cats dropped to the carpet. Clarence recognized the unusual colored one as the she-cat, Chaeli, he'd met at the Temple of the Sun. The black and white she-cat looked familiar, too, but he couldn't place her. On Chaeli's other side stood Terence, his expression grim.

"Master O'dorn," the Protector's leader said, bowing her head slightly. "May I present the Huntress, Nadine. And I believe you know Terence."

"Good t'see you again, Master O'dorn," the patched tabby said, curling his tail around his paws.

"I take it something has happened since our last meeting."

Chaeli nodded. "Nadine has important information regarding the cat you seek and your late partner's son."

"It's a pleasure to meet Toby's first mentor and friend," the she-cat said with a small bow and a smile.

"Clarence, do you know these cats?"

He glanced over his shoulder. David's hand was bent

in a claw at waist level, barely concealing the spell glowing around his fingertips. Clarence raised an eyebrow and gave a minuscule nod, hoping his friend understood the signal to hold until they knew why the cats had appeared, then turned back toward the three felines.

"May I introduce you to Chaeli, the leader of the Protectors. She is the Time Keeper we spoke of before. And I believe Huntress Nadine is the operative we hoped had made contact with Toby and Lorn," he said, nodding to each. He turned his attention to the black and white she-cat. "May I ask how you came to know Toby?"

"We were partnered during orientation spell casting at the King's Academy of Mages," Nadine said.

"I see. He told me it was a rather intriguing spell the two of you had to perform. What was it again?"

"An invisibility spell," Nadine answered, her tail twitching irritably despite her otherwise calm demeanor. "It was Toby who corrected the incantation for the potion and made it possible for us to pass the test."

Clarence smiled, then turned and nodded at David. The guardian clenched his fist, extinguishing the spell and sat down behind his desk. He motioned toward the other empty chair.

"What news do you bring us from our friend?"

"I wish it were good news," she said, hopping onto the proffered seat. Clarence held his breath and said a quick prayer. "As you know, the black beast you've been investigating, the one calling himself K'Dash Shyam, has obtained the Book of Knowledge. According to Toby and his partner, he plans to use it in a contraption to detonate all the human bombs at once."

"And how will he do that?"

"Dung beetles," David said, slamming his fist on his desk. "I think I know how." He ran his hand through his hair. Pointing a finger toward his office door, he continued, "I told him that machine of his was a bad idea."

"You know about the machine?" Chaeli asked.

"Yes, I just didn't think they'd be able to modify it, but then that's why they needed Sylvester. It all makes sense now." He looked at Clarence, frowning. "You know how Sylvester is always tinkering around in his workshop. Well, he made this contraption that could focus light into a single beam that could burn through stone."

"By the One," Clarence exclaimed. David nodded, then looked at the cats.

"But I didn't think the Book gave off any light."

"It doesn't," Chaeli said. "It gives off energy. We thought it could only be used as a weapon if it were opened, though it would destroy the one who opened it as well as the rest of creation. However, it seems your adversary has discovered another way of using it."

"He's going to use the machine to focus the energy. But how would he get all the bombs to explode at once?"

"By using Toby's father as the catalyst," Nadine said. "Lorn was able to see Victor when I helped him reconnect his psychic link to the beast."

"Wait, you did what?" asked Clarence.

"It wasn't my desire, but they were adamant that it was the fastest way to get the information we needed."

Clarence sighed and slumped in his chair. "That sounds like those two. Always going after their goal by the most dangerous route."

"We believe the beast thinks Lorn is dead," Nadine said. "We're hoping to use that to our advantage."

"How?"

"By coming here and telling you everything we know in the hopes of convincing your people to engage the beast in battle."

"Toby and Lorn plan to stall them as long as they can, but—" Terence began.

"What can two journeyman do?" David finished, giving Clarence a knowing look.

"Even those two," Clarence added, closing his eyes and nodding. He drew a deep breath and opened his eyes. "Where is this battle supposed to take place?"

"The top of Transformation Mountain," Terence said.

David nodded. "Brother Harold said something about that being the reason he chose to serve at his temple. Would've been helpful if he'd come back with Aaron instead of sending us a book of riddles."

"Brother Harold has other matters to attend to," Chaeli said.

Clarence held his breath as David opened his mouth to protest. He had no idea what the Time Keeper was capable of, but given the way her tail twitched, he doubted if she were one to defy.

"Regardless," Nadine interrupted, "we are here to ask your help in bringing our mutual enemy to justice."

Clarence let out the breath his was holding as his friend threw up his hands.

"Even if we could convince Captain Gage, there'd be no way to get there in time."

"I could get you there," Chaeli said.

"How?" asked David.

"The same way I brought Aaron to you so quickly. The same way we came, through the space between time."

David grimaced. "Do I want to know what's going to happen when we go between time?"

"Probably not," Clarence said, shaking his head. He turned back to Terence. "I know you've had some limited battle training as an apprentice, but as Brother Cat, are you up to this?"

Terence shook his head, narrowing his eyes and widening his whiskers, "I'll be tail deep in the other side of this battle."

"The other side?" David asked.

Clarence held up a hand. "Nothing you want to think about right now, my friend. Best keep this simple for the time being." He turned back to Chaeli and Nadine. "Would you be willing to speak with Captain Gage?"

"Certainly, though I am sure she may not trust me since I am an unknown outsider to your government."

"Then it's time we make your acquaintance," Clarence said. He smiled at David who grinned in return.

"Let's go end ourselves a war."

If he hadn't been working on his focus through meditation and magic battle practice for the last week, Lorn never would have attempted climbing the smooth slopes of Transformation Mountain. The very idea would have been ludicrous, especially since they didn't bring climbing gear with them. However, Toby had convinced him they could inch their way up the columnar sides of the mountain using the flotation spell to keep them from falling as they climbed. Lorn glanced over his shoulder at the sheer drop below and swallowed. He leaned his forhead against the wall he clung to and closed his eyes, hugging the slippery rock.

"Why do I let you talk me into these things?" he said to his sleet-covered orange-furred friend. The tom sat just above him on an outcropping just big enough for a cat.

"We're getting close. The top is just a couple more man heights above us. I'm putting a sound dampening field around us now, just in case someone's patrolling above."

Toby shook himself, sending a shower of ice pelting down. Lorn clutched the igneous rock and focused on steadying his breathing. He glanced over his shoulder one more time and swallowed. He stared at the gray and brown rock under his fingers. *Just a few more feet to solid ground.*

"Remember how I said I'd start taking our job seriously when humans learned to fly?" he asked, reaching up to grab the outcropping Toby sat on.

"Yeah."

"Well I'm rethinking that now."

He felt the brush of fur against his fingers as Toby moved. Lorn cringed and waited. The cat's voice came from higher up.

"Almost there."

"Easy for you to say," he grumbled under his breath as he pulled himself upward, thankful that the levitation spell made his body weigh half as much as normal.

"Look out," Toby called. A metal pole sliced the air a hand span from his head as it plummeted past, flipping end over end.

"What in the Pits was that?" he asked, looking at Toby.

The tom didn't answer, his head tilted back to see the cliff edge above them. Lorn tilted his head further back, straining the muscles in his neck to see what had silenced his friend. Time slowed as he recognized the large shape looming over them. Master Sylvester toppled over the cliff side in slow motion. Lorn's eyes widened as he sucked in a breath. He reached toward the man as he dropped past.

"Levah TAH teh," he shouted.

The spell caught the man, terminating his descent. Lorn's muscles screamed as his energy shifted to holding the master artificer in the air instead of keeping his own body lighter. He squinted at Toby through watery eyes.

"Help me."

Toby stared at him without blinking for several moments, then looked toward the cliff top. Lorn could hardly believe his eyes as the tom leaped to the next outcropping and continued on until he reached one just below the top. The tom hesitated a moment, his fur shifting to gray as he peered over the ledge, then leaped out of sight.

Lorn continued to stare up, hoping to see his partner's friendly gray face. When Toby didn't reappear, he dropped his gaze to the stone wall he clung to. Memories of the school fire, of Toby lashing out with unsheathed claws as Lorn reached toward him in comfort, flashed through his mind. Toby had left after that without so much as a goodbye. Lorn had thought they'd made up again at the temple, but Toby tried to leave him behind to come here. He squeezed his eyes shut as realization dawned. *How many times does he have to leave you behind before you get the hint? He even said he might not make the same choice again. By the One, I'm a fool.*

His fingers slipped a hair's breadth on the outcropping as Master Sylvester's weight continued to pull downward.

Lorn grit his teeth and gripped the slippery rock as tightly as he could. He didn't have the strength to pull them both up. Could he lower Sylvester to a larger outcrop?

He took a deep breath and peered below. The closest one looked the size of a wine barrel. *Too far.* A lump formed in his throat as he considered what he could do. He stared out at the gray, sleet covered landscape, wishing he believed in miracles. Closing his eyes, he steadied his breathing, readying himself to accept the consequences of his decision.

Suddenly the strain lessened. His eyes flew open and he stared down at the slowly swinging body of the master artificer. Lorn could still feel the connection to the spell holding the man aloft, but the drain on his energy was no more than a trickle now.

"Hurry up," Toby shouted from above him. "I can't hold him like this forever."

Lorn twisted his wrist, locking the spell onto himself, and reached up to finish the short climb to the top. He swung his leg onto the plateau and helped his partner pull their unconscious cargo up. Once the man was safe, Lorn rolled onto his back, shielding his eyes from the sleet with an arm.

"I thought you'd left."

"I considered it," Toby said, drawing a rasping tongue over his fur, "but then who'd watch my tail when the magic starts flying?"

Lorn glanced at his friend and smiled. "So why aren't we being hauled away yet?"

"I moved some crates over here to hide us and set up a thought slide shield. No reason one of Shyam's cats should come over unless there's something in one of these boxes they need."

"Good thinking."

"We still got one problem," he said nodding toward the master artificer. The man groaned, but otherwise didn't show signs of waking. Lorn sat up and looked around them.

"Can we hide him here?"

"Not a good idea. The shield could fail at any time."

"We can't just carry him across the plateau in plain sight of hundreds of blood thirsty cats."

Toby stared at him. The sleet hissed as it hit the ground, muting the low murmurs of the black beast's army beyond their hiding spot. Lorn knew that look. His cloak grew too warm as frustration flowed through his body.

"No way. I'm not staying here to watch over him while you go face down Shyam."

"You just said we can't carry him out in the open."

"Yeah and you said we can't hide him here because the shield could fail."

"It won't fail if you're here feeding it energy."

"Why don't you stay and feed it energy?"

Toby stared at him again, cocking his head to the side.

"Alright. Fine. Just stay low. I'll see if I can't figure out someway to sabotage that contraption in the mean time."

Toby nodded and slunk away, leaving Lorn wondering if he'd ever see his friend again.

Toby watched from behind a wagon wheel as Shyam's army went about their preparations for world domination. As far as he could tell, they paid no attention to each other. There didn't seem to be any guards on anything. It was as if they knew they were safe from prying eyes. *So much the better for me.* He ducked his head to lick his ruff as a tabby tom trotted by, thankful he'd learned how to create a nearly undetectable illusion to change his bright orange fur to a charcoal gray color. He'd stick out like a bonfire in a cave if he tried to walk through this camp without it.

He stared across the wide plateau, trying to gage the most likely place they'd hold his father. At first, he considered the wagons. Some of them still had supplies loaded under tarps, so it wouldn't be a stretch of the imagination that Victor could be under one of them if K'Dash considered him no more than another means to an end. However, the more he thought about it, the more he thought the black beast would keep his father close by. He'd kept Victor captive since Toby was a kit, so it made sense that he would treat his father like a prize he didn't want out of his sight.

Toby studied the lean-tos and tents further on. *If I were K'dash, which one would I choose?* Near the middle a canvas covered tent pole stabbed toward the sky, far above the rest. Toby grinned and narrowed his eyes. *I'd take the biggest, of course.* He trotted toward the back of the tents, skirting the narrow cliff ledge, until he reached the largest tent. He darted into the shadows of a tent flap and raised his nose to sniff the air. A familiar smell tickled his senses, bringing with it the feel of home and kittenhood. *Father?* He opened his mouth and took a deeper breath, letting the smells around him slide over his scent glands.

A powerful sneeze rocked him onto his haunches as the smell of bloody marigolds overwhelmed him. He gasped, trying to see through watery eyes if he'd alerted anyone to his presence. The more air he dragged in, the more he retched and gagged on the smell of blood magic. He flopped into the open, blindly clawing his way away from the tent. His lungs screamed for fresh air. The pain shred his concentration and he felt the inflow of energy as his gray fur disguise melted away.

"Son?" A rough tongue brushed its way over his ears. "What is it? Speak to me."

"Can't breathe," Toby gasped. "Blood magic."

"Hold your breath," the voice ordered. Toby did as he was told, despite the searing pain in his chest. "When you can't hold it any longer, take several shallow breaths and one long exhale."

The pressure on his chest continued to increase and blue shadows roamed across his eyes until at last he couldn't bear it any longer. His eyes flew open and he drew in three short breaths, then reveled in the long exhale.

"Thank you," he said, turning to stare into a pair of green eyes in a black furred face. His heart jumped.

"Better?" the tom asked, his eyes wide and warm.

Toby blinked, then flipped onto his paws, staring in awe at the massive tom. It couldn't be the same black beast he'd been stalking. This tom's entire body radiated warmth and caring from the quirk in his tail to the slight splay of whiskers. There could only be one other giant black tom on this One-forsaken plateau.

"Father? Is that really you?"

"I see you inherited my allergies."

A rumbling purr burst from Toby's chest as he stared at his father. Victor looked him up and down, whiskers widening.

"I take it that was a disguise," he said. Toby nodded.

"You did a good job. I almost didn't recognize you. In fact, I was just about to claw your ears off when you sneezed."

Toby blinked, realizing his father wasn't in a cage.

"Where were you going?" he asked.

"I was on my way to help Reginald with—"

"Reginald?" Toby's fur began to rise. Memories of the white tom standing over the punch bowl at the academy's Spring Festival sprang to mind. If anyone had drunk it after the traitor had released Chivato's plague into it, they would have died, suffocating on their own bloody vomit.

"Yes. He said he knew you from the academy. Do you remember him? A white tom."

Toby backed away. "I knew him. He's a traitor."

"Toby? What's wrong?"

"Well, well, well. What do we have here?" K'Dash said, pacing out from behind a tent. "Is this a family reunion? How sweet."

K'Dash smiled, padding toward Toby.

"Stay away from him," Victor growled, leaping in front of the black beast.

Toby stared from one black tom to the other, eyes widening. They could have been twins. Memories from the book zipped across his mind: the two toms planning in the dark room, Victor plowing into them and forcing them over the cliff, drowning in the river as the other black tom ran away.

"It's true," he whispered, staring at his father with wide eyes. "You left him to die."

Victor jumped as if someone had poked him with a firebrand. "What do you mean?"

"And you—" Toby said, turning his wide-eyed gaze on the other tom, "you made them kill him. You turned those people into—into—. They ripped him apart."

"How could you know that?" Victor asked, backing away from them both. He looked from K'Dash to Toby. "He has your curse."

K'Dash shook his head. "I could wish for a thousand years, but it wouldn't be true."

He smiled at Toby. For a moment his piercing green eyes melted into a pair of stern yellow eyes, a match to Adele's regal gaze, then it was gone. Toby's fur twitched.

"You read the book, didn't you?" K'Dash asked. Toby stared at him.

"What book?" asked Victor.

"My book," K'Dash said, turning a hate-filled gaze on his almost twin. "The book where I unmask everyone of their lies and betrayal. The book of truth."

K'Dash turned his piercing gaze back on Toby, taking a step in his direction, despite Victor's fierce growl.

"Don't deny you saw what he did," he said, nodding toward Toby's father. "The mighty Victor took an untrained kit on a dangerous mission. Told him it was a simple information gathering expedition. And when it went bad, he turned tail and ran. Left me to die in a One-forsaken river."

"I came back for you," Victor hissed.

"Too little. Too late," K'Dash said, sitting and curling his tail around his paws. He continued to stare at Toby, drawing him into his piercing green gaze. "You felt the fear, the betrayal."

Toby's heart hammered against his chest as a wave of fear crashed over him. Anger burned across his mind as the black tom's memories of Victor running into the forest, away from the river, leaped to view. He turned his heat-filled gaze on his father.

"Why did you run away? He was still alive."

Victor turned, startled. "I didn't know that. It was dark. The river was churning so hard. I didn't see him."

"He didn't look, Toby," K'Dash said. "It was in his plan."

Rage seared through his body as he stared at his father. Victor's gaze swung from Toby to K'Dash and back. Toby's fur spiked along his spine.

"Just like it's his plan now," K'Dash said. Toby lashed his tail. "Why else would he be out of his cage, heading for your archenemy?"

"Traitor," Toby yowled.

He leaped toward his father, claws extended. Victor rolled aside. Toby landed where the black tom had been, spun around and ran toward him again. Victor scooted backward, ears flat against his head. Toby gathered himself and launched. Victor rolled onto his back, using his hind legs to propel Toby over his head. Toby landed with an "Oof," righting himself with a side roll.

"He's altering your emotions," Victor shouted. "Think. Use your head."

Toby faced his father. The tom's eyes seemed to shift from the warmth he remembered from kittenhood to icy hatred, almost as if Victor's entire personality was changing from moment to moment. Toby shook his head. *That's not possible.* Another crushing wave of anger surged over him. *Being toyed with.* The alien thought echoed through his mind even as his body rushed low to the ground to knock Victor off his feet.

Victor leaped over him. Toby skid to a halt, turning to rush his father again. Victor rolled to the side as Toby's momentum carried him past the tents and into plain view of K'Dash's army. He turned, planning to rush him again.

Victor crashed into Toby's shoulder, sending him flying a full cat's length away. Toby righted himself and stared at Victor. He hunched himself down, teeth bared and growling, as he watched for an opening.

Lorn stared at the master artificer for several moments. He didn't know the man very well, but he hoped he was the kind who wouldn't build something without putting in a fail safe. Shaking his head, he turned on his knees to peer through an opening between the crates. He searched the area around the contraption, looking for anything he could use to cause it to self destruct or otherwise not work. Short of throwing rocks, he was out of ideas. As he sat staring at it, one of the rocks underneath shifted by itself.

"What the—?"

He leaned forward, placing his hands on the crates beside him and trying to get a better look through the narrow gap. A lid slid open a finger width. He jerked his gaze to the open box, leaning back to read the label. He smiled as he realized it was loaded with stuff from Sylvester's workshop. Lorn peered around the pile of boxes, making sure no one was looking his direction, then pushed the lid open wide enough to shove his hand into it.

He rummaged around until his hand touched a leather strap. Walking his fingers down the strap, he discovered it was attached to something smooth like glass, flat on one side and rounded on the other. Lorn drew it out of the box and turned it over in his hands. The leather straps were shaped like some kind of head gear. It reminded him of the contraptions Father Hanif's cats had used to help them brainwash the children. Except, instead of ending in claws, this one was connected to round pieces of glass.

Lorn searched his memory for any mention of what this thing was, coming up with a vague recollection of them being some kind of visual aid. He frowned and glanced toward the space between the stack of crates. With a shrug, he put the straps over his head and adjusted it until the glass pieces covered his eyes. The wood grain in the nearest crate jumped into focus in minute detail. Lorn shoved the contraption up and took another look at the box. It looked normal. He slid the glass pieces over his eyes again and grinned as the grain came back into focus.

He felt his way to the space between the crates and tried to find the rock that had moved. The ground zoomed by, making his stomach lurch. He closed his eyes for a moment, then tried again. He found the rock this time and was amazed to see that it wasn't a rock at all. The little metal spider trudged toward Shyam's giant contraption. It started to turn left, away from the device, when an invisible force nudged it back on course.

"An ally?"

He flipped the glass pieces up and stared across the plateau. Magic worked best when there was line of sight, so where was his new friend hiding? He scanned the area. On the opposite side stood the wagon train with horses on a picket line further on. Most of the wagons were empty, but a couple still had tarps over what Lorn guessed were more crates. He slipped the contraption back over his eyes and searched the tarp-covered wagons for any sign of the ally. Light glinted off something shiny in a wagon for an instant, then was gone. Lorn smiled. He turned his attention back to the little spider making its way to the enormous contraption. It was almost there.

A yowl sounded from the direction Toby had gone, drawing the attention of the army of cats. Lorn swung his magnified gaze toward the disturbance. His chest tightened. The fur along his partner's back stood straighter than he'd ever seen it and his tail lashed. Facing him stood a massive black tom, back arched and fangs bared in a fierce snarl. As he continued to watch, another gigantic black tom stalked out of the shadows. Lorn's hands trembled and his breathing quickened. He would know that loathsome creature anywhere.

"Start the countdown," the black beast shouted.

Lorn mentally shook himself. He looked back at the device, seeing a dozen cats moving toward it. *The spiders. They'll see them.* He checked the little saboteurs progress. Still another three feet to go before they could climb the device and get to work. Another invisible nudge sent one of the spiders onto its back. Lorn grabbed the first idea that struck. Wrapping Toby's thought sliding spell around a ball of his own energy, he flung it toward the spiders and hoped his unseen ally would feel the change.

The spiders paused in their hurried scuttle toward the device. The cats following Shyam's orders ran past, never glancing down at the oddly shaped rocks. Lorn let out the breath he'd been holding. They hadn't been discovered, but now they had a problem. He glanced at the wagon, wishing he could talk to his ally face-to-face. A flash of light shone from a knot in a side board, giving him an idea.

*Why can't we talk face-to-face?*

Lorn touched one of the glass pieces and murmured the mirror spell, twisting it just a bit so that the image would be projected in front of him a few inches rather than onto the glass itself. He felt the familiar tug of magic as the spell sought the echo of its companion glass and the snap as it found it. The next instant he was staring at a straggly white cat wearing a miniature version of the head gear Lorn had on.

"Reginald?"

"Looks like you're finally getting control of your magic, Ribaldy. Nice idea, tweaking the mirror call."

"What in the Pits are you doing here?"

"Later. We don't have much time. The artificer told me the spiders can dismantle the internal workings of that thing, but we have to get them there first. Any ideas?"

Lorn clamped his lips over the snide remark that flashed through his mind as he glanced toward the doomsday device. Reginald was right. The cats were finished setting the countdown sequence. He could see the numbers rolling upward on the dial. It looked like they might have two minutes. Shyam's guards stood between their spiders and the device, and they still needed to get past the mage bubble protecting it.

Memories from the academy floated past. They'd shielded their quarters to keep bullies like Reginald from getting in to cause mischief, yet Master Natsumi had been able to move Lorn's magic ingredients around inside the shield without ever entering the room. And Toby had said Terence could move things from one place to another inside a shield as well. He focused on Reginald again.

"Move them into the shield like Natsumi did when she made the bomb in our room at the academy."

"On it."

Lorn watched as the little spiders leaped into the air, curled their metal legs under themselves, and disappeared. An eye blink later, they reappeared under the contraption. They scuttled up its braces and into the device. Lorn stared at the contraption, willing the spiders to work faster as the numbers continued to roll backward.

# Chapter 16

"Begin the count down."

Somewhere he heard someone speak. The voice seemed to come from miles away and inside his head at the same time. He knew the words should mean something to him, but he couldn't think what that might be.

"Remember the mob," Victor said. "He's doing the same thing to you. Fight it, Toby."

*Deserved it...* Toby shook his head, his eyes blurring as he tried to focus on the beast in front of him. *Not a beast. Father.* His own thoughts felt like they were wrapped in canvas and floating in molasses.

"He left you, too. Just a kit and he put his job before your well being," K'Dash said.

The memory of Victor leaping into the black coach unfolded in his mind. It was fall. The warm sun soaked his fluffy kitten fur and made him purr as the sunflowers in the neighbors yard danced in the breeze. He looked up into his mother's eyes. There was a glint of sadness and then it was gone. She knew. The queen smiled down at him and brushed his head with her rough tongue, then sat back, still smiling.

"Yes, I knew he might not come home," she said.

Toby blinked, growing to his adult height in an instant. Everything around him disappeared except the black queen.

"Mother?"

"I'm here, son."

"Mother, I don't understand. What's happening?"

"I'm giving you time. It's the only gift I can give you now."

"Time for what?"

"To decide."

Toby's ears twitched. Riddles. It was like his entire life was made up of riddles and questions. In a flash, the scene changed. He stared around himself at the little cottage. On one side of the room was a simple kitchen. On the other was the sitting area with two small chairs, barely large enough for a human, and several cushions. At the far wall stood a low table, a portrait above it of two adult cats, a solid black tom and a charcoal gray queen with a bright white patch on her ruff, and two kittens, black as their father.

"Where are we?"

"Home," Adele said, her voice both happy and sad at the same time.

Toby opened his mouth to say it didn't look anything like he remembered, when the two kittens raced by. The little tom leaped onto the rug, grasping it with his claws, and slid across the room, outdistancing his sister.

"Cheater," she cried.

"It's not cheating. It's strategy," the tom called back as he leaped free and tumbled behind a cushion.

The little she-cat squealed and pounced on the bright red pillow. Toby looked back at his mother, her smile sad as she watched the kits play. Angry voices came from the door behind them. Toby's ears swiveled backward, trying to hear what was being said. The door banged open. He turned to see a charcoal gray queen stalk out of the room, a large black tom pacing behind.

"You don't see it," he said. "He's pushing you too hard. You don't have enough energy when you come home to do anything but sleep. The kits need you more than those others do."

"More than *those others* do?" she snapped, turning and baring her fangs at the tom. "So now it's us vs them? What kind of message does that send to our kits?"

"You know what I mean. I just think you need to slow down."

"Why? So I can be the docile house kitty like your mother was?"

"Don't bring my mother into this."

"Why not? She's always here anyway, even now that she's dead."

The tom growled. "You wouldn't be saying that if you weren't so tired and you know it."

"You're right. I'm tired," she snarled. "I'm tired of being treated like a criminal every time I come home. I'm tired of you picking fights just because I'm not like your mother. I'm tired of you judging my partner and treating our mission like it was just another job, something anyone could do."

The queen turned and sat, her tail thumping a staccato on the wood floor. The tom sighed. He padded closer and placed his tail across her shoulders.

"Don't touch me," she yowled.

Wind screamed through the little cottage. Toby flattened his ears and narrowed his eyes, glancing at his mother. She sat perfectly still, her whiskers drooping, not a single hair moving though the hurricane swirled around them. Toby stared around the room, expecting a piece of furniture to fly past, but nothing moved. Still the howling continued.

He whipped his gaze toward the cats. The queen's eyes

were scrunched closed, her fur standing on end. She looked like a person holding onto a pole during a tornado. The tom's ears were flattened to his head, his body poised as if he were walking into a gale force wind. He slid a paw length backward. His eyes flew open and he flattened himself to the floor.

The outer door banged open and a human stumbled in, his hands raised as if to cast a spell. The tom glanced toward the door, then back at the queen. Before Toby could blink, the tom was thrown backward, smashing into the wall behind them and crashing down onto the little table. The wind died just as suddenly. Silence descended like a wave.

The human darted over to the fallen tom. He bent down to feel for life, then looked at the queen and shook his head. Her eyes widened. She shook her head. Her gaze darted toward the red cushion next to the smashed table. Toby turned to see what she was looking at. Two little black heads hovered over the pillow, their eyes wide and scared.

The queen gave a keening wail and fled the cottage. The scene faded away as Toby watched her tail disappear into the night. He turned to his mother. She was still staring into the distance where the kittens had been. When she turned her attention back to him, her eyes were glassy with unshed tears.

"This was the nightmare we were born into," she said.

"Why show me this?"

"You must know it all if you are to make your decision."

"What decision?"

Adele purred and nuzzled his ears. When she bent down to look him in the eye, he felt the fierce heat of her love for him searing its way through his body.

"They know not what they do," she whispered.

The crash of mage bolts deafened him as he blinked the world back into view. The next instant his vision was blocked by a mass of flying black fur. They tumbled backward, sliding into a tent opening.

"Are you hurt?" Victor asked.

Toby shook his head until his ears popped, then licked his ruff. The sounds of battle raged outside the tent. He focused on his father, realizing the overwhelming feelings of anger and betrayal had disappeared.

"What happened?" he asked.

"I'm not sure. One moment you were under Adair's control, the next you just blanked out."

Toby stared at his father, the sounds of battle outside the tent walls pounding in his ears. His thoughts twisted in his mind like dead leaves in a fall breeze. What had happened? He continued to stare at his father, trying to grasp meaning with his paws, when something large blundered into the tent, causing it to collapse. Toby slithered out from under the canvas behind Victor. The gray sky was lit with reds and blues as fireballs and mage bolts sizzled through the falling sleet. Masses of cats and humans converged, pushing against shields, engaging in hand-to-paw combat. Toby spotted Lorn near the wagons on the other side of the plateau fending off K'Dash's personal guard, the Russian blue twins.

"This way," he said, glancing at Victor before racing away toward his partner.

Toby wove his way past combatants, leaping over

tangles of cats and dodging around human legs until he was a few yards from Lorn. He put on a burst of speed, barreling into the nearest twin and knocking him from his feet. With a battle screech, he tore into the tom's hide, yanking out hunks of fur with his claws. Pain seared through his ear as claws ripped through it. He rolled onto his back and pummeled the blue tom, raking his hind claws down the soft belly. The tom twisted away and ran. Toby leaped to his feet to see the cat's brother limping behind.

He turned, looking for his next opponent. The battle had shifted away, leaving them a moment to catch their breath. Toby looked up at his partner. The man bent over double, his breath wheezing in and out, but he spared a smile at him.

"'Bout time you got here," Lorn said. "Out flower picking?"

"Love those daisies," Toby said, whiskers splaying. "Where's Master Sylvester?"

Lorn jerked a thumb over his shoulder at the wagon. "In there with Reggie."

"Don't call me Reggie," the tom said, poking his scraggly white head out. "The artificer is resting in here. Though not sure you could call it resting. He keeps mumbling something about reset and fail safe."

Toby's ears perked up. He looked back at his partner. "The contraption. Did you turn it off?"

Lorn nodded. "We used the spiders just like Sylvester told Reginald to do. Stopped the countdown."

"Are you sure?"

Lorn's eyes widened. "You don't think—"

"Come on. We gotta stop it."

"I'm coming with you," Victor said.

"No. Someone needs to stay here and protect Sylvester."

"Reginald can do that."

"I can?"

Victor gave the young tom a hard stare, reminding Toby for a moment of the times his father had tutored him before he disappeared.

"I mean, I can," Reginald said.

Toby clamped his whiskers together, hiding his smile as his father turned his attention back to them.

"Adair slipped away as soon as the battle started. Where do you think he went?"

Toby's eyes narrowed and he nodded. Without a backward glance, he hurled himself toward the shielded contraption near the middle of the battlefield. Toby dodged over and around screeching felines, pounded between human legs, as he rushed head long toward Sylvester's device. The booming sound of mage bolts and crackling fire balls assaulted his ears as debris from exploding crates and wagons pelted his fur. With a quick prayer, Toby squeezed his eyes to narrow slits and twitched his tail to transport himself into the shield.

He breathed a sigh of relief and shook himself from head to tail, marveling at the sudden quiet. He could hear the muted sounds of the battle beyond the hiss of sleet on the shield. Inside was the click and whir of the timer on Sylvester's contraption and the panting of his partner. Toby cast a quick glance around, glad to see his father a tail length away. He turned to ask Lorn if he had any ideas of how to disable the device.

"Right on time," K'Dash purred, padding around from the opposite side of the the contraption. Toby whirled to stand shoulder to shoulder with his father.

"It ends here, Adair," Victor said.

"Indeed it will. I'm just glad you made it to the

festivities. It just wouldn't be the same without the guest of honor."

"What's he talking about?" Toby asked, keeping his gaze on the black beast.

"He didn't tell you?" K'Dash asked, widening his eyes. "Why, your father volunteered to be the catalyst."

"What's that supposed to mean?" asked Lorn.

"It means, human," K'Dash said, lifting his lip as if he smelled something foul, "that when the counter reaches zero, the energy from the Book of Knowledge will be focused through this contraption into the device my surgeon placed in Victor's back leg." The black tom calmly licked his ruff. When he looked back at them, he smiled.

"Would you like to know what happens then?" he asked.

A chill spread over Toby's skin as the beast turned his piercing gaze on him, his smile turning feral. The timer clicked again, the whirring of its gears quiet against the hiss of sleet and muted explosions outside the shield.

"Boom," the tom whispered. "The world in flames. Chaos unimaginable."

"And you become the new emperor, am I right?" Toby asked.

K'Dash shrugged. "Perhaps. If the Malkin decide to rise up and name me their leader, who am I to object. But, really, I am nothing more than a humble freedom fighter."

"Freedom from what?" Lorn scoffed.

"From you," K'Dash growled. "From your kind and their suffocating ways. You humans brainwash our kind from the time we're kits, offering us partnership with one hand and beating us with a rod in the other."

Toby's thoughts whirled, trying to remember

everything he could about Sylvester's other devices. He needed more time to figure out how to disable it.

"What about your partner?" asked Toby.

"Damon? He's an idiot," K'Dash said with a wave of his tail. "A simple push here and there and he's convinced he'll be the next king. He honestly believes I've done all this for him."

The device clicked again. He was running out of time and he still had no idea how to turn the thing off. *Information. I need information.*

"With your experience with humans, it's no wonder you don't trust them. I bet you even made sure no human could touch the Book, either," Toby said, glancing at Lorn. He paced away from his partner toward the outer edge of the shield. K'Dash narrowed his eyes, watching him with keen interest.

"No one can touch the Book of Knowledge without being struck by lightning. Even you should know those stories."

"Lightning from the One?"

"Of course not," the black tom said, rolling his eyes. "Any kit with a rudimentary knowledge of power knows the Book is no more than a device as simple as a saltwater barrel. The priests deified it to keep the rest of us from ever trying to squirm out of their iron grip."

"So there is no reason to fear it being lifted by a mere human."

"What are you driving at?"

"The contraption the master artificer designed, I assume it's human proof as well?" Toby asked, sitting across from K'Dash and curling his tail around his paws.

"No human has enough magic in them to blast through

the secondary shields I've put around it," K'Dash said. He glanced at Lorn and Victor, lifting his chin. "And no cat can tear through its shields either."

"That's why you brought Sylvester with you, then," Toby said, recapturing the black tom's attention. "Because he has no magic. He couldn't damage the contraption, so long as he was tied up on the other side of the plateau. Yet, in case something went wrong, he would be available to fix it. Clever."

Toby continued to stare at the green-eyed tom, hoping his partner was following his line of thought. There were plenty of rocks he could use, but it wouldn't work unless he'd figured out what Toby was getting at. From the corner of his eye he saw Victor moving soundlessly behind K'Dash, lowering himself into position. A mage bolt exploded just outside, causing rock shards to rain down on the shield. The blast rumbled through his body. Toby ignored the sensation, willing the black beast's full attention on him.

"You know what the problem is with all of that, don't you?" Toby asked.

"What might that be?"

"Humans have hands," he said with a feral smile.

Toby launched himself onto K'Dash's back as Victor knocked the black tom's paws out from under. Together the three cats rolled in a screaming mass of fur. Pain shot down Toby's flank as he sought to dig his fangs into the beast's neck. From behind his closed lids, he saw a brilliant flash of light. A clap of thunder deafened him.

The hunk of fur struggling beneath him went limp. The smell of Father Hanif's singed fur as he dragged his dying body from the burning building burst into his thoughts. Toby tightened his grip and pulled blindly backward. *Not this time.*

312

*Master Cat*

He tugged until his neck muscles burned with effort. Dropping the beast, he opened his eyes and gasped for breath. His ears perked forward, listening to the silence, as he stared at the fallen bodies around him. Toby shook his head, turning in a circle. Nothing moved. The only sound was the hiss of sleet on canvas and stone. He gaped at the charred ruins of Sylvester's contraption. A wagon's length beyond Toby saw his partner's body, laid out like a child's carelessly dropped rag doll. He pulled his gaze away, tracing a path back to his own paws. His father's limp form a cat length away caught his attention. Loss slid like a dagger through his chest.

He tore his gaze away and stared down at the massive black tom he'd dragged with him. The beast's chest moved up and down. Toby felt heat build inside, flowing over his mind and blurring his vision. *All dead because of him.* His claws slipped from their sheaths as he raised his paw and growled at the motionless beast.

A pop behind him made him jump. The sound was followed by the tinkle of broken glass. He watched as Nadine and her mentor strode forward, Master O'dorn and Guardian David behind them. Several more pops sounded around the plateau. Toby looked around to see battle weary guardians, both human and cat, stepping into the gray daylight. He turned toward Nadine.

"How?"

"I was keeping tabs on you as soon as we arrived. I felt your plan in your thoughts. As soon as Lorn snatched the rock from the ground, Chaeli placed the allies into time bubbles."

Toby's tail jerked. He glanced toward his father and Lorn. The leader of the Protectors stepped in front of him. As she shook her head, she said, "I'm sorry. You and your friends were out of my reach under the mage bubble."

313

Toby stared past her toward the wreckage, eyes blurring as his throat closed. He felt Master O'dorn's hand touch his shoulder and looked up into the man's sad eyes.

"We must go."

He glanced once more at his fallen friends, then leaped onto Master O'dorn's shoulders, burrowing his head in the curve of the man's neck and letting himself be carried away.

Toby stared through the stems of Resurrection lilies at the solid wood doors standing between him and the cat he'd hunted for most of his life. Winter was finally giving way to spring, but a chill had settled in Toby that had nothing to do with the season. The doors looked the same as the vision from K'Dash's book, though the crowd wasn't there this time. A fortified wall separated the courtyard and the city streets now. Guardians stood at the single gate. There'd be no escaping for K'Dash—*Uncle Adair*—through mob death or subterfuge. That's what he'd been told. He was here to make certain of it.

The doors opened wide enough for a gray and white patched tabby with a shorn head to slip through. The tom glanced around the courtyard, blinking in the sudden brightness. Spotting Toby, he trotted toward him.

"They're wrapping it up," Terence said.

"About time. Hard to believe it would take this long to make a conviction," Toby said, the tip of his tail jerking.

"He's been pretty slippery up 'til now. They want to

make sure it all sticks."

Toby continued to stare at the doors.

"You should have seen the look on the judges faces when Brother Harold's journal was read. You know he had it all figured out? I can't understand why no one believed him."

"Why would they?"

"Yeah. I guess you're right. It sounds crazy. Who would've believed a young tom would fake his death and tie in with the mad man he was sent to spy on? Add in the myth about the Book of Knowledge and a strange contraption that can focus it through the kind of rock only found on Transformation Mountain to make a whole lot of things explode at the same time and you've got a real fairytale on your hands."

Toby's ears twitched. It wasn't the story that he'd been talking about. His mind drifted back to the hooding ceremony he'd endured nearly two weeks ago. As he'd padded down the aisle toward the king's raised dais, he'd glanced between the legs of the guardians on either side. The audience chamber was packed with High Council members. It had taken all his willpower to keep from snarling at their smug expressions, as if they had known all along that the terrorist was in their midst. As the master's hood was placed upon his head, applause rebounded from the high ceilings and echoed off the marble walls. He could still feel the hollowness in his chest. He blinked, becoming aware again of his friend's chatter.

"It's a good thing Alie and Dora were able to save all those documents. I think seein' Shyam's plans all laid out and backed up by official papers sealed the deal."

"I'm sure the testimonies didn't hurt."

"Absolutely. I bet there'll be an entirely new program at the academy dealing with mind medicine because of all

Master Shyam's meddlin' with peoples heads. Anyone with a headache will be under suspicion until someone figures out how to tell a real pain in the head from a psychic link."

Toby grimaced as he thought back to the number of times Lorn had dismissed his headaches after his brief encounter with K'Dash and his paw picked felines at the New Life Temple and School. He wondered how much of what had happened could have been avoided if they'd known then that the pain he was having was a symptom of the psychic link the black beast had implanted.

"I think it was your testimony that put it over."

A shiver ran down the length of Toby's body as he remembered watching those hate-filled green eyes. He'd forced himself to stare down his foe while answering the prosecutor's questions. Despite Nadine and the Time Keeper sitting guard over the black beast, Toby couldn't stop the fear that somehow the tom would find a way to escape. That was why he was sitting beneath this bush and peering out through the stems of the Resurrection lilies.

After his testimony, he'd hurried out here to wait. He watched as the line of witnesses that had snaked around the front of the courthouse slowly disappeared through the side door. He'd watched intently as they were ushered in the side and released out the front. At first, he'd scanned the line, looking for the special witnesses, until he realized they were in a secure room inside the building. He'd considered going back in and joining the King's Men guarding the room, but decided against it. He wasn't ready to face them yet.

Gillespie and his wife exited the front doors. Toby was surprised to see his overbearing superior gently aid his wife into a city coach. He'd never imagined the man could care about anyone but himself.

"I wish this was the end of it all," Terence said and sighed.

Toby glanced at him, then returned his attention to the doors. "Isn't it? As soon as Chaeli puts that monster in one of her bubbles, he'll be there until he rots."

"He's just a pawn in the war, Toby. We've won this battle, but there are legions more out there playin' their strategies and choosin' their victims with care."

Toby looked at Terence with narrowed eyes. "You sound like Nadine."

"Part of the job of being a Brother Cat. I work in both realms, just like she does."

"I think I'll stick to this one," he said, shaking his head.

"Not a bad idea," Terence said with a chuckle. "It's simpler."

The creak of the doors opening made Toby turn back to the courthouse. Victor and Lorn came out the door and were led away by guardians into protective custody as if they were nobility—*or criminals.* He saw Lorn look for him when he came out the door. Toby didn't move, guilt stabbing his chest. If it hadn't been for him, Lorn would never been so close to dying so many times. He was a good man. He deserved a better partner.

"Same as always," Terence said. Toby glanced at him from the corner of his eye to see the tabby tom shaking his head.

"What?"

"You're a book, you know that?"

"Is that so?" Toby said, returning his gaze through the Resurrection lilies to the doors.

"Do you even know why you're sitting here?"

"To make sure that fleabag doesn't escape."

"They got enough guardians here to make sure a beetle don't get away. That's not why you're here."

"I suppose you're going to tell me."

Terence licked his fur, then shook himself head to tail before resettling into a comfortable sitting position. The silence grew until Toby sighed and looked at his friend.

"Well?"

"Well what?" the patched tabby asked.

"Well aren't you going to tell me why I'm here? Give me some kind of wisdom from the Book of the One?"

Terence shook his head. "Nope."

"That's a first," Toby said with a snort.

Terence smiled. They went back to watching the door. Toby's thoughts meandered to the moments before Nadine and her mentor had shown up with the entire Office of Kingdom Guardianship. If Adele hadn't heisted Adair's nightmare, would he have killed his own father? His skin shivered.

"Wanna tell me about it?" Terence asked.

Toby glanced at the Brother Cat, then turned back to the door.

"While I was under Adair's influence back on the mountain, mother came to me."

He glanced at his friend, trying to gage his reaction. Terence continued to stare at the door as if Toby were talking about the weather. He took a deep breath to continue on.

"She showed me how their mother used her gift to kill their father. She and Adair were just kits. They saw the whole thing."

"That had to be scary. Did she say anything about it?"

"She said she wanted me to know about the nightmare they were born into and then something about not knowing what they do."

"Any idea who she was talking about?"

"No," Toby said, shaking his head.

"You sure?" Terence pressed.

Toby looked to see him cocking his head. For a moment the patched tabby looked like his mentor, Brother Yannis, when the old tom had given him advice about giving his anger over to the One. He felt a brush of fur against his mind and the memory of reading in the New Life School library unrolled. The Beloved's last words before the mob hanged him rose to the surface.

"Forgive them, for they know not what they do," Toby whispered.

Terence continued to watch him, nodding. Toby closed his eyes, letting all his memories of the last few years play across the stage. He heard again his own voice accusing Adele of not believing in his abilities. He watched as he judged Lorn when they had been newly partnered as the boy set the hedges on fire while trying to locate their new living quarters. His side ached as he remembered the fight they'd had the night they tried to reassemble the fragments of ash that had been crucial documents from Master Ribaldy during their investigation of Chivato.

Moment by moment, pain upon pain, Toby relived his past failures until they morphed into memories that were not his own. He relived the scenes from Adele and Adair's lives, felt their sorrow and betrayal.

"*Understand*," whispered Adele's soft voice in his mind.

Toby blinked his eyes open. Terence was still watching him. He had opened his mouth to explain what he'd learned when he heard the thump of the court doors opening wide. He turned to watch as the caged black tom was carried out into the open. Toby glanced at his friend.

"Go," he said.

Toby raced across the courtyard. "Wait," he called.

"Halt," said a guardian, his spear crossing the point of his compatriot's, shielding the beast's glowing cage.

"I need to speak to him."

"No one speaks with the prisoner," the guardian said.

"Please," he said, staring at the tom's piercing green eyes.

"Let the lad have his say," a large wildcat said, limping from behind the group. "He's endured enough from this beast. Let him have some closure."

The guardian stood for a moment longer, then lifted his spear. Toby turned to thank the wildcat.

"Nah, laddie, don't thank me. You deserve to have your say. Just make it quick."

Toby nodded and stared into the black tom's hard gaze.

"I understand now. I forgive you," he said, the words feeling thick in his mouth.

"I don't need your forgiveness," Adair said, lifting his lip as if he smelled rotten eggs.

"No," Toby replied, his fur stiffening into a ridge along his spine. There were so many things he wanted to say, seething retorts he would love to hiss between his clenched teeth. As he stared into the hate-filled green eyes, a whisper of fur caressed his mind, reminding him of his own failures and of the tragedy the tom before him had endured. "You don't need me to forgive you. But I do."

Toby turned away. The shuffle of boots and rattle of chains told him they were loading the cage into the black box that served as a prison coach. The door slammed and the lock clicked with finality. Toby let the boiling anger dissolve away like overheated broth in a tipped over kettle. The soft touch of a tail over his shoulders reminded him that Terence was still beside him. Toby looked at his friend and smiled sadly. It was time to move on.

*Sign up for* Virginia's newsletter *(*virginiaripple.com*) to be the first to know about new releases and receive sneak peeks and fabulous freebies.*

# Author Bio

Throughout Virginia's school years she concentrated on her English courses, going on to earn a Bachelor of Arts in English. She was hired as a part-time Christian Education Director after graduating from Northwest Missouri State University and went on to become a seminary student at Brite Divinity, an Associate Minister and a church elder. Virginia re-discovered her passion for writing while in graduate school and with it a new direction for her life. Since then she has balanced her time between her career as an independent author and being a loving wife and mother.

For more information, visit Virginia's web site at virginiaripple.wordpress.com or scan the QR code below to sign up for sneak peeks and special offers in Virginia's monthly newsletter.